Commander Jack Crusher asked, "And where can we find this man?"

Languidly, keeping his eyes on the bartender's face, he again shook out the three slips of latinum—this time, into his palm. He ran his thumb over the shiny metal and waited for the alien to speak.

"There is a klaapish-klaapish'na house not far from here," said the bartender, his dark popeyes glued to the latinum. "The name of the place is The House of Comfort."

Jack kept his expression as neutral as possible. He wasn't sure what a klaapish-klaapish'na house was, but with the name The House of Comfort, he could make a pretty good guess.

Already, he was formulating his next message to Beverly: Hi, honey. Hope you and Wes are well. My most recent assignment took me undercover to an alien brothel. Hope you understand the sacrifices an officer has to make in the line of duty . . .

STAR TREK
THE NEXT GENERATION®

DOUBLE HELIX

BOOK SIX OF SIX

THE
FIRST VIRTUE

MICHAEL JAN FRIEDMAN
&
CHRISTIE GOLDEN

Double Helix Concept by John J. Ordover and Michael Jan Friedman

POCKET BOOKS
New York   London   Toronto   Sydney   Tokyo   Singapore

This book is a work of fiction. Names, characters, places and incidents are products of the author's imagination or are used fictitiously. Any resemblance to actual events or locales or persons, living or dead, is entirely coincidental.

An *Original* Publication of POCKET BOOKS

POCKET BOOKS, a division of Simon & Schuster Inc.
1230 Avenue of the Americas, New York, NY 10020

ISBN: 0-671-03258-5

First Pocket Books printing August 1999

10 9 8 7 6 5 4 3 2 1

THE FIRST VIRTUE

Prologue

As Governor Gerrid Thul walked through the heavy wooden doors and entered the throne room of his emperor, Tae Cwan, he reflected on how different the place looked.

After all, the three prior occasions on which Thul had visited were all elaborate state gatherings of nobles and high-ranking officials in the empire. He was only a small part of them, though his standing had grown surely and steadily over the years from a respected general to the governorship of an outpost.

But this, the governor told himself, looking around at the cavernous, high-ceilinged hall and the splendid furnishings . . . this was different. He frowned. He was all alone now, without a crowd to hide him.

1

And at the end of the rich, blue carpet that bisected the chamber's white stone floor, the illustrious Tae Cwan himself waited for Thul. The blue-robed emperor sat between two armed guards on a chair of carved nightwood that had given his forebears comfort for more than a thousand years.

It was daunting. Or it would have been, if the governor were one who allowed himself to be daunted. But he hadn't risen to a rank of esteem and power by being timid.

Lifting his chin, Thul set foot on the carpet and approached Tae Cwan's presence. The chamber magnified every sound—the flutter of his cape, the padding of his feet on the blue path, even the drawing of his breath—as if the room weren't filled with simple air at all, but something infinitely more sensitive and unstable.

Finally, the governor reached the end of the carpet and stopped. His emperor gazed down at him from the height of his chair, his features long and perfect, his expression a tranquil one.

Thul inclined his head out of respect—or at least that was the nature of the gesture. Then he smiled his best smile. "I believe you know why I have come," he told Tae Cwan, his voice echoing in the chamber like stormwaves on a rocky beach.

"I believe I do," the emperor replied without inflection, though his voice echoed just as loudly.

Abruptly, he gestured—and a door opened behind him. A couple of attractive handmaidens came through, followed by someone else in the deep blue color that could be worn only by imperial blood. It was Tae Cwan's younger sister, Mella.

The resemblance was difficult to ignore. However, as often happens in a family, the clarity of feature that made the brother a handsome man made the sister look plain and austere.

Nonetheless, the governor turned his smile of smiles on Mella Cwan, and the woman's eyes lit up in response. Dark and vulnerable, her eyes were by far her best attribute.

"Proceed," said the emperor.

Thul inclined his head again. "As you wish, Honored One." He paused, as if gathering himself. "I have come to profess my love and admiration for your sister, the Lady Mella."

A demure smile pulled at the corners of the woman's mouth. Unfortunately, it didn't make her any more pleasant to look at.

"I ask you for permission to make her my wife," Thul continued.

Tae Cwan considered the governor for a moment. He had to know that nothing would make his sister happier than the prospect of marriage to Thul. And yet, the governor noted, the emperor hesitated.

It was not a good sign, Thul knew. Not a good sign at all.

"I withhold the permission you seek," said Tae Cwan, his expression stark and empty of emotion.

To the governor, it was more than a disappointment. It was like a blow across his face, with all the pain and shame such a blow would have awakened in him.

The Lady Mella, too, seemed shocked by her brother's reply. She stared at him open-mouthed, her face several shades paler than before.

Still stinging from Tae Cwan's words, Thul asked, "Is it possible you will change your mind in this matter, Emperor? Or perhaps reconsider my request at a later date?"

Tae Cwan shook his head from side to side, slowly and decisively. "It is *not* possible," he responded flatly.

Thul felt a hot spurt of anger, but managed to stifle it. After all, it was forbidden to show excessive emotion in the presence of a Cwan.

"I see," he said as calmly as he could. "And am I permitted to inquire as to the emperor's thinking in this matter?"

"You need not inquire," Tae Cwan informed him. "I will give you the insight you want."

The emperor leaned forward on his throne, his features severe and impassive. But his eyes, as dark as his sister's, flickered with what seemed like indignation.

"I do not wish you to be part of the royal family," he told Thul. "Certainly, you have been a dedicated and efficient servant who has made considerable contributions to the Empire. However, there is also something dangerous about you—something I do not entirely trust."

The governor's teeth ground together, but he said nothing. After all, it was he who had requested Tae Cwan's response.

"Beyond that," said the emperor, "you are well inferior to my sister in station . . . a former military man, unworthy of the royal family. No doubt, she would be willing to overlook this difference now. But in time, she would come to see it as a problem, as I do."

Mella averted her eyes, her brow creased with disappointment. But like Thul, she was forced to keep her emotions in check.

"These are my reasons for disallowing your request," Tae Cwan finished. "I assume I have made my decision clear."

"Eminently," said the governor, though he felt something twist inside him as he said it. "And though I have not been granted my request, I remain grateful for the audience, as befits a loyal servant of the Empire. May you continue to reign in splendor, Emperor."

Tae Cwan inclined his head, his eyes sharp and alert, though the rest of his features were in repose. "Go in peace, Gerrid Thul."

The governor cast a last, wistful glance at the Lady Mella. But with her brother's pronouncement still hanging in the air, she didn't dare return it.

Thul cursed inwardly. As his wife, the woman would have brought him immeasurable power and prestige—more than enough for him to overlook his lack of attraction to her. But with a few words, the emperor had taken away that dream of power and prestige.

Enduring his loss—one that was no less painful for

his never having had the thing to begin with—the governor inclined his head a third time. Then he turned and followed the length of blue carpet to the doors and made his exit.

But as soon as the doors closed behind him and he was left alone in the hallway outside, Gerrid Thul turned and glowered in the direction of Tae Cwan. Emperor though he might be, the governor reflected bitterly, he had gone too far this time.

He had humiliated one of his most determined servants—one who had risked much and accomplished much on behalf of the Empire both as a soldier and as a politician. He had told Thul in no uncertain terms that he would never be more than what he was—the administrator of a farflung outpost.

The governor swore again. Maybe he couldn't ascend to power by marrying the Lady Mella, but he was still no beast of burden to wallow in self-pity. He was intelligent. He was resourceful. And he was every bit as Thallonian as the feared Tae Cwan.

For some time now, Thul had toyed with an alternative to marrying the Lady Mella—one that would allow him to enjoy the prominence he craved without the need to seek the emperor's blessing. With his first option closed to him, the second came to the fore in his mind.

And the more he thought about it—the more he considered how badly he had been treated by Tae Cwan—the more inclined he was to pursue it.

Chapter One

THUL ENTERED THE REGGANA CITY tavern by one of its several revolving doors, his Thallonian commoner's clothes and attached hood uncomfortably rough against his skin.

The place was loud with jangling music and crowded with a surprising number of aliens. Squinting to see through the dim lighting and the acch'ta smoke, he took a look around.

At first, he couldn't find the one he was looking for. Then he heard a familiar laugh and traced it to its owner—a tall, lean Thallonian youth with an antic sparkle in his eyes and a mouth that seemed ready to break into a grin at any moment. He had clearly had too much to drink.

His companion was an Indarrhi of about the same

7

age. Like most every member of his species, the fellow was slender and as dark as carbon, with deepset silver eyes, a fleecy mop of silver-white hair, and three thick fingers on either hand.

The Indarrhi also had rudimentary empathic powers. Or so it was said of them in the empire.

Spotting an unoccupied table, the governor pulled out a chair and sat down. Then he sat back and watched the Thallonian and the Indarrhi.

"Drink?" asked a gruff but feminine voice.

Thul turned and looked up at a triangular face with a single bifocal eye in the middle of its leathery forehead. A Banyanan, he mused. And this one had even fewer manners than most.

He considered the question that had been posed to him. "Thallonian ale," he decided. "Room temperature."

The waitress grunted. "Room temperature." She sneered, as if it were not very likely his request would be met. Then she turned her angular body sideways and made her way back through the crowd.

Halfway to the bar, she passed the young Thallonian. Winking at the Indarrhi, he grabbed the Banyanan around the waist and drew her to him. But the waitress was stronger than she looked. With a push, she freed herself and continued on her way.

It didn't anger the youth in the least. In fact, it might have been a game he had played with the female before. Laughing out loud, he clapped his companion on the back and lifted a mug to his lips.

The contents, a frothy liquid as dark and scarlet as

blood, dripped down the youth's chin and spattered the table below. Wiping himself with the back of his hand, he swung his arm around the Indarrhi's shoulders and whispered something into his friend's rounded ear.

Yes, Thul thought disapprovingly. The Thallonian had *definitely* had too much to drink.

Suddenly, the youth thrust the Indarrhi away and laughed even more loudly. His companion smiled, appearing to enjoy the joke—but not with the fervor of the Thallonian. The governor frowned.

The youth was a misfit—an embarrassment to his species. Whoever had raised him had done a stunningly bad job of imparting Thallonian manners to him. Were it not for his ruddy skin and his size, one might have wondered if he was Thallonian at all.

"Thallonian ale," said a by-now familiar voice.

Thul glanced at the serving woman as she put his drink in front of him. Then he reached into his pocket and produced an imperial disc. "This should be enough," he said.

The Banyanan eyed it, then plucked it from the governor's hand. "It should at that," she responded. Then, with her overly generous payment in hand, she disappeared again.

With the waitress gone, Thul returned his attention to the youth. He was just in time to see the fellow thrust his leg out in the path of a green-skinned Orion trader.

The Orion, who had a mug in his hand, never saw the danger. With a curse, he tripped on the Thallonian's foot and went flying. So did his drink—into the lap of another Thallonian, a brawny specimen with a scar across the bridge of his nose.

Outraged, the victim rose from his seat and seized the Orion's shirtfront in his fists. With a surge of his powerful muscles, he lifted the trader off the floor.

"Orion scum," he spat.

Releasing the trader with one hand, the Thallonian drew it back and struck the Orion in the face. Thul heard a resounding crack as the trader's head snapped back. A moment later, it lolled on the Orion's shoulder, and the Thallonian let him drop to the floor.

When the trader woke, the governor mused, he would have a headache. A rather *considerable* headache.

"Damn you!" bellowed the youth, leaping to his feet. "That was my friend you hit!"

The Thallonian with the scar glanced at him warily. "The fool spilled his drink in my lap!"

"Only because you tripped him with your big, clumsy feet!" the youth roared at him.

It was anything but the truth, Thul noted inwardly. But, of course, the fellow with the scar had no way of knowing that, and neither did anyone else in the establishment.

"Who are you calling clumsy?" the man with the scar snarled.

"You!" the youth snarled back. "Why? What are you going to do about it, you bulging sack of excrement?"

The older man's eyes popped and his hand went to

his hip. "Sack of excrement, is it?" With a flash of metal, he slid a blade out of its scabbard. "How would you like me to cut your tongue out and shove it down your scrawny throat?"

The youth grinned as he whipped his own sword free. "I would like to see you *try!*" he shot back.

Seeing what was about to take place, the other patrons cleared a space for the two antagonists. The Orion, who was allegedly the cause of the youth's indignation, was the only one who remained in the vicinity—and that was only because he was still unconscious.

The governor sighed. The youth's behavior was worse than embarrassing. It was despicable. He had actually gone out of his way to pick a fight with an innocent man.

Still, Thul didn't do anything to stop the impending combat. He just sat there like everyone else in the tavern, drinking his ale and wondering who the victor would be.

"Serpent!" boomed the Thallonian with the scar.

"Rodent!" came the youth's reply.

Suddenly, they were at each other, their swords clashing in a blurry web of bright metal. The scarred one thrust and the youth parried it. The youth countered and the scarred man knocked his sword away.

Back and forth they went, knocking tables and chairs aside, slashing away at each other with wild abandon. The scarred one was stronger and steadier, but the youth seemed more skilled. In time, the governor mused, skill was likelier to win out.

His theory was borne out a few moments later. The scarred man saw an opening and brought his sword down at his adversary's head, but what seemed to be an opening turned out to be a trap. The youth side-stepped the blow, then swung his blade at his opponent's shoulder.

The metal cut deeply, eliciting a spray of blood and a cry of pain from the scarred one. Then his enemy struck again, battering the sword from the scarred one's nerveless fingers.

The older man stood there, waiting for the death-stroke that did not come. Instead, the youth smiled and knelt beside the Orion, who had been all but forgotten in the melee.

Some of those present might have expected the youth to drag the trader to his feet, since he had claimed the fellow as his friend. But he didn't do that at all. He merely used the Orion's tunic to wipe his blade clean.

Finally, he stood up again and addressed the scarred one. "Next time," he said grimly, "be careful whose wine you catch in your lap." Then he tossed his head back and howled with laughter until the rafters rang with it.

The scarred man, who was clutching his wounded shoulder, just glared at his adversary. He glanced at the sword he had left lying on the floor, no doubt wondering if he might have a chance at revenge if he moved quickly enough. But in the end, he thought better of it and slunk away.

Remarkable, Thul reflected sourly. The youth had made an art form of arrogance and braggadocio.

Downing the remainder of his ale, the governor got to his feet and crossed the room. When he was halfway to the swordsman, the Indarrhi took note of him and said something.

The youth turned to cast a glance at the governor over his shoulder, his eyes intense in the hollows of their sockets. At the same time, his hand wandered to the hilt of his weapon.

Thul stopped in front of him. For a moment, the youth seemed ready to gut the older man where he stood. Then the governor tossed his hood back, revealing his identity.

Slowly, the fire in the swordsman's eyes dimmed. His features softened and his hand left his hilt. "Father," he said, humor and surprise mingled in his voice—along with something like distrust.

Thul gazed at him. "Strong drink does not agree with you. You have looked better, Mendan."

The youth grunted scornfully and cast a sidelong glance at his companion. "Have I really?"

"And you have exhibited better manners," the governor went on, unperturbed. "Was it really necessary to create a scene? To wound an innocent man? And all to prove your valor for the hundredth time?"

His son sneered at him. "Among Thallonians, is the first virtue not courage? And are you not the one who taught me that, before I was old enough to eat with a fork?"

Thul nodded. "I did," he conceded. "But one truly confident of his courage does not pick fights to demonstrate it. He knows life will give him plenty of opportunities to show how brave he is."

The youth shot a conspiratorial look at his companion, the Indarrhi. "You see how it is, Wyl? The man is a font of wisdom." Then he turned back to the governor. "I will try my best to remember what you've taught me, Father. I have *always* tried to remember what you taught me . . . even if I *am* only your bastard."

Thul shook his head, knowing Mendan had no intention of remembering anything. "You are my son . . . the son of a high-ranking Thallonian official. It would be a pleasant surprise if you acted accordingly."

Mendan eyed him. "Why have you come slumming, Father? Do you know how far you are from anything resembling the imperial court?"

Thul's hands clenched into fists at the thought of what had happened at court. With an effort, he unclenched them. "I have come," he said, "because I have a mission for you—one that cries out for a man who can navigate the underside of society."

The youth's eyes opened wide. "So, naturally, you thought of me. Mendan Abbis, the benighted product of a drunken revel twenty-two years ago. And you dare lecture *me* about making merry!"

"If you perform this mission," the governor continued evenly, "you will be rewarded beyond your wildest dreams."

That seemed to get his son's attention. "My dreams may be wilder than you think," he said warily.

"I doubt it," Thul said with the utmost confidence. He leaned closer, grasping the back of his son's chair. "If all goes well, Mendan, you will become the crown prince of a brand-new empire."

The bastard looked at him. "You're joking."

The governor shook his head. "I'm not."

Mendan considered the answer for a moment. Then he said, "Let's talk," and pulled over an empty chair.

"Outside," Thul insisted.

The youth gestured for the Indarrhi to come along. Then he got up and led the way out of the tavern.

The alley outside was cold and wet, but it had the very important virtue of being private. Thul pulled up his hood against the weather and watched wisps of white steam emerge from his son's mouth.

"Well?" Mendan asked, his eyes alive with curiosity. "How do you intend to make me heir to an empire? And why would that pompous windbag Tae Cwan allow such a thing to take place?"

The governor glanced at the Indarrhi. "He can be trusted?"

The boy nodded. "With our lives. Now answer my question."

Thul's jaw clenched at his son's audacity. Clearly, Mendan had a lot to learn. "Why would Tae Cwan tolerate the formation of an empire that would rival his own?" the governor asked. He didn't wait for an answer. "He wouldn't—if he knew about it."

The bastard's mouth pulled up at the corners. "I see."

"I won't lie to you," said the governor. "It won't be

easy to keep this from the emperor. And there are a number of other problems as well . . . which may not loom quite so large if you are successful at your task."

"My . . . task?" Mendan echoed.

Thul shrugged. "Did you think it would all be placed in your lap?"

His son shook his head. "I suppose not."

The governor imparted the most basic details of his plan. It didn't take him long—only a few minutes. When he was finished, he eyed Mendan and waited for his reaction.

The bastard seemed hesitant. "Why should I trust you?" he asked his father. "You've never spoken to me this way before, like an equal instead of an inferior."

"An oversight for which I apologize," Thul told him. "Before, I was blinded by ambition. Now, my eyesight is a little sharper—and I see more clearly who is important to me and who is not."

Mendan's eyes narrowed as he considered the proposition. Finally, he nodded. "All right. What do you want me to do?"

The governor told him.

Captain Jean-Luc Picard of the *U.S.S. Stargazer* was looking forward to a most rewarding day.

His vessel was about to become the first to conduct an in-depth study of the long-vanished civilization of Zebros IV, in the Archaidae sector. Briefly charted about six years before and ignored ever since, the planet was reported at the time to have little to offer in terms of either strategic importance or natural resources.

The only entry, made by one Captain Philip Terrance, was a brief, almost disparaging comment. "The ruins on this world," it said, "are testament to the fact that this was once a thriving society."

But nothing more . . . nothing to whet the appetite of the Federation Council. That was why it had waited such a ridiculously long time to authorize a proper exploration of the place.

To each his own, Picard reflected, as he stepped onto his ship's raised transporter pad in his Starfleet-issue envirosuit, his helmet in hand. The few images taken by Terrance's vessel might not have inspired Terrance himself or the council, but they were enough to make the *Stargazer* captain's heart beat a little faster.

And the fact that the Federation had chosen to ignore Zebros IV for so long? That was quite all right as far as Picard was concerned. He and his crew would have an even better excuse to pick through the ruins at their leisure, as the first sentient beings in a millennium or more to handle long-buried examples of Zebrosian art and architecture.

But then, wasn't time one of the perquisites of lengthy deep-space missions like the *Stargazer*'s? If Picard and his people were really fortunate, they might even discover some bit of information that would cure a disease or enhance a Federation technology.

But even if they didn't, Picard thought, even if all they did was gain an appreciation of Zebrosian culture, that would be all right. He would still be perfectly content with the result.

After all, he had been in love with archaeology for a long time now. Since his days at the Academy, actually. And that love hadn't dimmed in all the years that had gone by since.

Yes, the captain thought, donning his helmet and locking it into place, it would be a rewarding day indeed. And eventually, if Zebros IV was as intriguing as it appeared, it might be a wonderful month. It was difficult not to smile at the prospect, but he managed.

His away team, he noticed, was less circumspect about its enthusiasm than he was. Tall, gangly Lieutenant Cabrini, for example, was grinning almost ear to ear in the transparent dome of his helmet, and dark-skinned Lieutenant M'ketwa was chuckling with pleasure. Ensigns Kirby and Moore looked—and acted, Picard thought with a bit of a frown—like Academy cadets on leave as they joined him on the transporter platform.

"I realize today's mission will be of extraordinary interest to all of us," the captain told them, his voice muffled slightly by the confines of his helmet, "but let us conduct ourselves as scientists and not as schoolchildren, shall we?"

They sobered up at once, causing Picard to regret the sharpness of his words. These were some of the brightest and most eager young people Picard had ever had the privilege of working with. Of course they were excited. They relished the opportunity to get at those ruins, just as he did.

"After all," he added on impulse, "scientists are not compelled to come in from recess."

His quip was rewarded with a surprised but pleased smile from Ensign Kirby as they dematerialized.

Chapter Two

BIN NEDRACH COULDN'T HAVE asked for a better day.

The pale green sky that arched over Melacron V
was clear and bright. The planet's two moons, Melia
and Melusha, were easily visible near the horizon.
There was no wind to speak of, no precipitation, no
thermal inversions . . . and the dark cloud, the mete-
orological phenomenon called Lai'bok that scoured
the surface of Melacron V from time to time, was not
supposed to appear for several more weeks.

He had timed it brilliantly.

From his perch on the roof of a commercial edifice
slated for demolition, Bin Nedrach shifted his position. He had been in the same spot since well before
dawn. However, having rehearsed his task repeatedly,
he was familiar with every inch of the old building.

There were three different ways he could swiftly flee once his task was completed, and four places where he could effectively hide himself in the unlikely event that all three exits were blocked. It had been a long time since he had had so many escape options.

Calmly, his two hearts beating slowly and regularly, Bin Nedrach examined his long, shiny energy rifle again. He had checked it thoroughly already, but the Melacron had learned it was always a good idea to double- and triple-check one's equipment.

The trilanium barrel was unmarred, nor was there any debris inside it which might clog the passage of the energy beam. The red safety keypad glowed softly and invitingly.

Bin Nedrach pressed it with a long, sharp-nailed finger and it changed color to yellow, indicating that the safety was off. Then he fingered it again and the safety was restored.

Good, he told himself. Working perfectly.

Faint sounds of activity wafted up from the plaza below. It was very convenient for Bin Nedrach that the officials of Melacron V had clustered all their important buildings around the same square. Of course, once his assignment had been carried out, it was entirely possible that the government would rethink that policy.

Street vendors were setting up shop, their little tents creating a colorful parade of cloth. The sweet scent of roasting shu seeds wafted up to Bin Nedrach's single wide nostril and he inhaled deeply. The more pungent aromas of grilled trusk flesh and pastries filled with a variety of berries mingled with the heady smell of the shu seeds.

They made Bin Nedrach hungry. He could do with a hot stick of grilled trusk or a bag of roasted shu seeds, he told himself. But with the iron discipline that had gotten him to the top of a dark and dangerous profession, he put aside his body's needs.

Time enough for food—good, exotic food—when his pockets bulged with latinum, he mused. For now, he had to concentrate all his faculties on the work at hand.

Little by little, the day grew brighter. There was more activity in the square below. Talk and laughter floated up to Nedrach's small, furred ears and they pricked upward, listening for more significant sounds.

There was the patter of the scarf seller, as usual. But then, he was setting up for what promised to be a brisk business with the holiday of Inseeing just around the corner. And there was the laughter of the little girl, dancing for a few coins like a leaf borne on the wind while her father played tunes on an old, battered p'taarana.

Everything reeked of normalcy. Everything was just where it should have been. And that was very much to Bin Nedrach's liking.

Abruptly, he heard the soft hum of an approaching hovertran. The sound made Bin Nedrach's hearts race. His black tongue snaked out to moisten thick, dry lips.

The hovertran, an official vehicle that could transport up to eight people at a time, shuddered to a halt and floated while the passengers disembarked. They were right on time—punctual, as all Melacron, including Bin Nedrach himself, were punctual.

As a youth, he had not realized how predictable his people were. Then, at the age of twenty, he began to plan his first assignment and he saw how everything ran by the clock.

The revelation had caused him to change his habits . . . to scramble his own comfortable routines. It would make it harder for someone to do to him what he was about to do to someone else.

One by one, in the same order as the day before and the day before that, the various heads of the Melacronai government descended into the square. The G'aha of Medicine, an older but still attractive female, headed right for the dancing girl. No surprise there.

As part of his job, Bin Nedrach had researched all the G'ahas in detail. He knew that the G'aha of Medicine had made it past her childbearing years un-Companioned and without children of her own. As a result, her weakness was her fondness for children.

It would have been simplicity itself for Nedrach to capitalize on that tendency, that vulnerability. However, the G'aha of Medicine was of no importance to him today.

He watched, noting everything, as the G'aha tossed the little dancer the same number of coins she had tossed the day before. Then the G'aha patted the child on the head and moved toward the tall, spired government building that dominated the square.

The G'aha of Finance, who could stand to lose a

few kilograms, bought a big bag of shu seeds and dusted them with a pinch of blue pepper. Then he too made his way to the government building.

Chances were, in a few seasons or so, nature would do to the G'aha of Finance what people paid Bin Nedrach to do to others. Food was the fellow's great love, his ultimate indulgence.

Parties given at his home for other high-ranking Melacron were said to be extravagant, unforgettable. What's more, his Companion and children were every bit as rotund and unhealthy as he.

But to Bin Nedrach, the G'aha of Finance was no more important than the G'aha of Medicine. They simply weren't on his agenda.

Next, he turned his attention to the G'aha of Laws and Enforcements, a slender, handsome individual who seemed rather young for his position. As Bin Nedrach watched, the G'aha stopped to purchase an embroidered scarf from the scarf vendor.

Bin Nedrach frowned deeply as his boyhood superstitions threatened to get in the way of his duty. For a moment, his mind raced, caught up in an unexpected struggle.

The rite of Inseeing was the most revered celebration among his people. It was a time to stop, retire to the peace of one's own domicile, fast for three days and think about one's life. During this period, all attention was directed inward. The ritual Inseeing scarf, translucent enough to permit vision yet sufficiently opaque to perform a symbolic blindfolding, covered one's head and face at all times.

It was said to be the height of evil to harm someone while they wore the Inseeing scarf . . . or even held it in their hands. Bin Nedrach set his jaw. *Then call me evil.* The G'aha of Laws and Enforcements had a Companion and children, he knew. Perhaps the G'aha was thinking about them as he admired the scarf, wondering about their futures.

But for the G'aha of Laws and Enforcements, there would be no wearing of the sacred scarf this year. There would be no fasting, either. Any insights he might have would come in the next few seconds, and he would regrettably have no time to act upon them.

Steadily, Bin Nedrach lifted his energy rifle. It clicked and buzzed as it automatically locked in on its target, saving him the trouble of aiming the weapon manually. He took a deep breath and pressed the safety pad, releasing the triggering mechanism inside.

The G'aha of Laws and Enforcements paid the vendor for the scarf, admired its workmanship a bit more, and reverently folded it as he headed for the black stone steps of the government building. He was the only potential customer in the plaza now, Bin Nedrach noted. The other G'ahas had already made their way inside.

No innocent bystanders would be harmed today—that was very important to Bin Nedrach. He was a professional, after all, and professionals were economical.

Still holding his breath, with a feather-light touch, Bin Nedrach's finger brushed the rifle's firing pad. Instantly, a stream of seething blue energy exploded from the weapon. It struck the G'aha of Laws and Enforcements at the base of his neck—the place where the assassin's people were most vulnerable to attack.

The G'aha arched in agony but did so silently, as Bin Nedrach had intended. He fell an instant later and tumbled down the black stone steps like a child's stuffed toy.

Bin Nedrach heard screams and wails from the square below, but he was already halfway down the rickety steps of the abandoned building. He did not have to wait to make sure the G'aha was dead. No Melacron struck with such force at the base of the neck could have survived.

The assassin's long legs flew and he jumped the last few steps to safety. By the time the stricken scarf dealer had pointed to the top of the building from whence the attack on the G'aha had come, Bin Nedrach was ensconced in his private hovertran and well and safely away.

He allowed himself a smile as he began to dismantle his weapon, just in case someone stopped him. *Mission accomplished,* he thought. *And if I am fortunate, the gods will have pity on my soul.*

The ruins of Zebros IV turned out to be unlike any Picard had ever examined. In fact, they couldn't even properly be called "ruins."

Nearly every edifice he encountered was comprised of an extremely hard, extremely durable blue material, which seemed to exist in great abundance on the planet. The result was that few of the buildings showed any significant signs of wear.

Cabrini scrutinized his tricorder readings against the backdrop of an intense orange sky. Then he looked up at the captain. "This stuff is approximately twelve times harder than diamond," he said. "We won't be able to cut it with traditional implements."

Picard nodded. "Which confirms my theory that this civilization enjoyed advanced technology, despite the deceptive simplicity of the construction." He found himself warming to the subject.

"That building there seems to be the most complex," Cabrini observed. "If we were to—"

"Ben Zoma to Picard," came the deep voice of the *Stargazer*'s first officer, interrupting the ensign's suggestion.

The captain hid a grimace. "Picard here," he said in response. "What is it, Number One?"

"You're not going to like it, sir."

"Try me," said Picard.

Gilaad Ben Zoma's voice was full of regret. "You've got a message from Starfleet Command. An Admiral Ammerman from Starbase Three is champing at the bit to talk to you."

Picard felt his heart sink in his chest. The message had, of course, been heard by his away team. They knew as well as he did what it meant and they looked at their captain sympathetically.

Don't waste pity on me, thought Picard. Unless I am mistaken, *none* of us will get to enjoy this trip.

"Understood, Mr. Ben Zoma," he said aloud. "One to beam up."

"Aye, sir," came the response.

Stepping away from the group, the captain eyed each of his people in turn. "Unfortunately," he told them, "you may not have much more time here. If I were you, I would make it count."

The next thing he knew, Picard was standing in his transporter room again. His operator regarded him.

"Short trip, sir?"

The captain scowled as he removed his helmet and pulled away his suit's collar flap. "*Too* short."

Stepping down from the transporter platform, he tucked his helmet under his arm. Then he headed for his ready room, which adjoined the *Stargazer*'s bridge.

In just a few minutes, Picard was sitting down in front of his desk, his helmet resting on the smooth, black surface beside his monitor. He thumbed the controls on his workstation and the admiral's blue-eyed, blond-haired visage filled the screen.

"Hello, Jean-Luc," said Ammerman.

The admiral was an old acquaintance. He and Picard had met at the Academy, where the older man was serving as an instructor, and continued to stay in touch over the years. Picard had been best man at Ammerman's wedding and godfather to his eldest daughter.

The fact that Starfleet had chosen Ammerman, who had such a lengthy history with the captain, to deliver what was clearly going to be an urgent message did not bode well. At least, not in Picard's mind.

28

"Hello, Admiral," said the captain, leaning back in his chair. "It's been a long time. How is Julia?"

"She's great, just great," said Ammerman. "And she sends her love, of course. But to be honest, I didn't contact you to talk about my family." He frowned a little as he took in the sight of Picard's envirosuit. "Hauled you out of an away mission, did I?"

The captain eased farther into his chair and began fiddling with the suit. "As a matter of fact," he replied, "you did. An exploration of some ancient ruins on Zebros Four."

"Damn." Ammerman looked sincerely regretful. "I hate to do this to you, Jean-Luc, but—"

"Duty calls." Picard smiled a little. "So . . . what shape has my duty taken this time, Admiral?"

The other man's expression turned sober. "How familiar are you with the Melacron-Cordracite situation?"

Picard shrugged. The names sounded familiar to him, but he couldn't place them right away. Then it came to him.

"Two powerful, unaligned species in the Kellasian sector," he said. "As I recall, they have been engaged in bitter territorial disputes over the last several years. Their governments have been trying to work toward a peaceful resolution, though there are some radical factions on both sides who don't share that goal." Something else occurred to the captain. "Unless I'm mistaken, Admiral, those factions have been responsible for some rather vicious incidents of terrorism."

Amerman nodded grimly. "That's essentially correct. Now jack up the viciousness of the attacks by a factor of ten and thin out the patience of both governments, and you've got an accurate picture of how badly things have fallen apart there."

Picard ceased fiddling with his suit. "When did all this happen?" he asked the admiral.

"Over the last couple of weeks." Ammerman rubbed his eyes. He looked tired. "It's bad, Jean-Luc."

"What about the Benniari?" the captain asked, referring to a neutral species in the sector. "It was my understanding that one of their number was acting as a mediator . . . that he had gotten the Melacron and the Cordracites to sit down together at an intrasector congress."

"That's right," said Ammerman. "His name is Cabrid Culunnh, first minister of the Benniari."

"Can't he make any headway?" Picard wondered.

The admiral sighed. "It's Culunnh himself who has contacted us, requesting Federation assistance. He tells us that the Benniari are starting to fear for their lives."

Picard was disturbed by this, but kept his expression neutral. Had the Benniari been official members of the Federation, Cabrid Culunnh would have become a highly respected ambassador by now.

Word had it that he had singlehandedly prevented war in the sector by proposing and overseeing the Kellasian Congress. For him and his government to ask for official Federation aid made it clear to Picard just how dire the situation was.

"Interestingly," said Ammerman, "it's Culunnh's

opinion that this fresh wave of terrorist incidents isn't the work of the Cordracite and Melacronai groups who've been responsible for the violence until now."

That surprised Picard. "Who then?"

Ammerman shook his head. "He's not certain, but he feels pretty strongly about it. I don't know if it's wishful thinking or what. If some third party *is* involved, flushing them into the open might help put negotiations back on track. But as it stands, the situation is pretty dicey."

Picard nodded to himself. The Benniari were a peaceful, intelligent people, but their planet was not a wealthy one. They didn't have the resources to search for an elusive third-party terrorist group—if it was even true that one existed.

"Unfortunately," the admiral told him, "your ancient civilization will have to wait a while, Jean-Luc. We want you to take the *Stargazer* to the Kellasian sector immediately."

The captain had already resigned himself. "I understand," he answered.

"Assess the situation and cool things down if you can," said Ammerman. "If you can't . . . well, the Benniari are our allies. You're authorized to do everything necessary to keep them safe."

"Acknowledged," Picard responded.

"And while you're there," Ammerman added, "see if you can find anything out about this third party. Identifying and exposing it could be the key to peace in the sector."

And, perhaps, thought the captain, the key to opening the door to Federation membership as well. But he kept that observation to himself.

"I'll have my navigator set a course for the Kellasian sector," he assured his old friend.

A somber smile played about Ammerman's lips. "Not quite yet. You need to come to Deep Space Three first. You're scheduled for a passenger pickup—someone who has firsthand knowledge of the sector."

"Cabrid Culunnh?" Picard guessed. At the same time, he wondered what the Benniari would be doing on a starbase.

Ammerman shook his head. "No, Jean-Luc. An ensign, currently serving on the *Wyoming*. Seems he's the only one in the whole damned fleet who's ever spent any time in that part of space."

The captain sat back in his chair, a little perplexed. "With all due respect, sir, why don't you simply send the *Wyoming* on this mission? Why do you need the *Stargazer?*"

The admiral sighed. "Don't you remember who's commanding the *Wyoming* these days, Jean-Luc?"

Picard remembered all right—and he could see Ammerman's point. The *Wyoming* was captained by a fellow named Karl Broadnax, whose pugnacious personality had given rise to a host of colorful nicknames—among them, "Broad-Sword" and "Battle-Ax."

To date, no one had dared inform Captain Broadnax of any of these nicknames. It wasn't considered to be worth the risk. While Picard could think of no one he would rather have at his side in the heat of battle, Broadnax's naturally confrontational attitude would be the last thing they needed in such a touchy situation.

"Karl Broadnax," said the captain, searching for words, "may not be precisely the individual the situation calls for."

The admiral smiled without reservation for a moment. "And with those words, you prove that you are becoming one of the best diplomats we have in Starfleet. Congratulations, Jean-Luc. You're the indispensable man."

Picard grunted. "We'll be there as soon as we can, sir."

Ammerman turned serious again. "Make your best speed, Captain. The Benniari will be grateful. Ammerman out."

A moment later, the screen went dark. Picard stared at his reflection in its shiny blackness for a moment.

It seemed it was not going to be a rewarding day after all.

Chapter Three

PICARD WOULD HAVE LIKED to spend an evening on Deep Space Three with Admiral Ammerman and his wife, sampling the admiral's wines and talking about old times. However, he thought—as he made his way to the *Stargazer*'s transporter room—the urgency of his mission required that he pick up his passenger and depart at once.

Partway to his destination, he saw Lieutenant Commander Jack Crusher emerge from a turbolift and fall into step alongside him. The commander was tall and cleanshaven, with a wide forehead and deepset dark eyes.

"Jack," the captain said by way of acknowledgment.

"Sir," Crusher responded.

During their off-duty hours, the younger man had become Picard's best friend. But while they were on duty, Picard preferred for them to act as captain and second officer. That way, no one would ever have reason to question Picard's objectivity.

"So," Crusher remarked, "an ensign serving aboard the *Wyoming* is the only person in Starfleet to have firsthand knowledge of this sector?" He turned to the captain. "An *ensign?*"

"Which seems a little strange to you," Picard suggested.

"That it does," the commander agreed.

The captain smiled. "It might not seem that way if you knew that this is not the first time this ensign has been in Starfleet."

The other man made a face. "What do you mean? He resigned and then joined up again a few years later?"

Picard nodded. "Precisely."

"That's strange."

"But not unheard of."

"Any idea why he quit?" Crusher asked.

"None," the captain informed him. "But you'll soon have an opportunity to ask him yourself."

They turned a corner and a set of doors hissed open ahead of them, revealing the *Sturgazer*'s transporter room. Picard nodded to the transporter operator, who deftly manipulated the controls. The mechanism whirred softly and a brightness appeared in the air above the platform.

Crusher frowned a little. "Exactly how long has this individual been out of the mix, Captain?"

Picard spared him a glance. "Fifty years."

The commander looked at him. "Did you say . . . fifty *years*, sir?"

"I did," the captain confirmed. "He served under the twenty-third-century captain Hikaru Sulu."

Crusher's forehead creased. "Then he's got to be—"

"A Vulcan," said Picard.

At that moment, the ensign in question finished materializing on the transporter pad. His erect bearing, calm eyes and cool demeanor proclaimed him a true son of his hot and hostile planet.

"Welcome aboard, Ensign Tuvok," said Picard. "Your expertise on this mission will be most useful." He indicated Crusher with a gesture. "May I present my second officer, Lieutenant Commander Jack Crusher."

Crusher was a naturally gregarious fellow. Picard could see him struggling not to step forward with hand outstretched. Instead, imitating their new temporary crewmember, he inclined his head.

"A pleasure, Ensign Tuvok," said the commander. "I must say, I'm looking forward to hearing about your service on the—"

"Captain," Tuvok cut in smoothly, "our mission, as it was described to me, is one of the utmost urgency. I suggest we dispense with"—he straightened, unable to hide his contempt for the word— "pleasantries, and call an immediate meeting of your senior staff. It will be necessary to share information and plan a strategy."

Picard was a bit surprised. Vulcans were certainly not ones for idle chitchat, but most were not quite as . . . prickly . . . as Tuvok seemed. Courtesy was actually a logical concept, as it improved relations between species and individuals, and most Vulcans practiced it religiously.

Tuvok, on the other hand, seemed to be more Vulcan than any of his fellow Vulcans. His posture had not relaxed a single iota.

"Very well," said the captain. "You make a good point, Ensign. Let's go to my ready room and we can bring everyone up to speed."

Without further ado, Tuvok crossed the room and preceded Picard out the door. As the captain and Crusher followed, their eyes met—and the commander pretended to shudder with cold.

Picard didn't want to smile, but he couldn't help himself.

The world officially known as Debennius VI had the intimidating nickname of "the Last Stop to Nowhere." Entering the shoddy establishment where he and his employer were scheduled to meet, Bin Nedrach had to admit that the ancient label was well deserved.

Debennius VI was the outermost planet in a system that in itself was not exactly a well-known destination for space travelers. Any hint of a thriving community was manifested on the other planets, with the main cultural center located on Debennius II.

Out here on the sixth planet, only the lost, the poor, and the incurably antisocial were welcomed. Bin Nedrach allowed himself a passing worry about how he was going to get out of here with both his latinum and his skin, but he quashed the thought.

After all, his employer had seen to everything thus far. No doubt, he would see to Bin Nedrach's safe departure as well.

The establishment in question—if one could dignify it with that name—had none of the orderly precision of a Melacronai equivalent. It was dark and smoky inside, and patrons were visible only as dim shapes. Apparently, the owner of the place could not afford proper lighting. That, or else he or she simply didn't care to install it.

Reflexively, Bin Nedrach's wide single nostril clamped shut against the stench of the place. He was mildly irritated by his body's automatic response, but resigned himself to breathing through his mouth until he could get out of there. It was a small enough inconvenience, considering the amount of latinum he was about to collect.

Finally, his eyes adjusted to the light. But once he got a good look at the place's "customers," his six-fingered hand fell automatically to the weapon at his side. For the first time since undertaking the mission, Bin Nedrach experienced a genuine flash of doubt.

Was it possible that someone as powerful as his

employer truly enjoyed a place like this? Or, the Melacron wondered, was this whole meeting some kind of set-up?

Nedrach knew it would be easy enough . . . hire a hungry assassin, let him undertake a dangerous mission for you, and then lure him to this "Last Stop to Nowhere." (Now that he thought about it, the nickname *did* have an ominous ring to it.) And finally, while your hungry assassin is salivating at the thought of how rich he's about to become, have another assassin dispatch him.

And who would suspect? No one.

With that in mind, the Melacron looked around some more . . . but couldn't discern any real threats. Finally, his gaze fell upon two humanoids in a dark, almost hidden corner of the room.

Ah, he thought. *He's here.* Relief flooded Bin Nedrach as he made his way as unobtrusively as possible in the direction of his employer.

By the look of him, Mendan Abbis was already half-drunk. That, Bin Nedrach had to concede, was an improvement over the first time he had met Abbis— when he was *completely* drunk.

The Thallonian's eyes sparkled as they fastened on Bin Nedrach, and he smiled a lopsided smile. Heedless of who might see, Abbis beckoned to the assassin enthusiastically.

The cold, silver eyes of the youth's Indarrhi companion seemed to bore right through Bin Nedrach. He knew that the dark-skinned, white-haired Indarrhi possessed empathic abilities.

Abbis had never introduced Nedrach to the Indarrhi, so the assassin had never learned his name. But not for the first time, he wondered how much the empath was picking up from him. Just to be safe, he calmed his thoughts, put even the most remote notion of treachery out of his mind, and approached the Thallonian with a smile on his face.

"You," slurred Abbis, making a stab at Bin Nedrach with a ruddy index finger, "are my favorite person in the entire galaxy!"

"Am I?" Bin Nedrach asked.

"Well," the Thallonian amended, pouring himself another drink from a dirty pitcher filled with a potent-looking black liquid, "at least today."

"I'm delighted that my work pleases you," said Bin Nedrach.

The Indarrhi didn't say anything. He just stared. It was unnerving, even to a hardened assassin like Nedrach.

"Your mission was a complete success." Abbis took a long drink, then wiped his mouth with his sleeve. "Even better than I had hoped. Not only was the G'aha of Laws and Enforcements an important figure, he was a very popular one as well. I'd almost go as far as to say beloved."

That was Nedrach's understanding as well.

"His murder," said Abbis, "has upset all Melacron everywhere. They're starting to murmur about going to war with the Cordracites, even the most peaceful of them."

Suddenly, he grinned and leaned in toward Bin Nedrach with an air of conspiracy. "And do you know what the best thing about this is? The most delicious thing of all?"

The assassin shook his head.

"The G'aha of Laws and Enforcements was adamantly against war with the Cordracites. Isn't that ironic?" asked Abbis. He began to laugh.

"Quite so," said Bin Nedrach.

The Indarrhi was still staring at him, his thick fingers twitching. The assassin wondered what that meant.

"You were hired with the intention of sparking a war," said Abbis. "I'd say you succeeded."

Not for the first time, Bin Nedrach wondered why Mendan Abbis, a member of a species that had nothing to do with the conflicts between the Cordracites and the Melacron, so desperately wanted to spark war between those two civilizations. Clearly, Nedrach reflected, the Thallonian had something to gain from it . . . but what could it be?

The Indarrhi's glittering eyes narrowed slightly . . . and Bin Nedrach hastily redirected his thoughts to the latinum for which Mendan Abbis was fishing in his tunic pocket. That, after all, was the assassin's only real interest in being here.

And as the Thallonian's latinum began to appear on the table in significant amounts, Bin Nedrach found it easier and easier to put the question of Abbis's motives aside.

In fact, he soon forgot about it altogether.

* * *

Crusher at first thought the lounge was empty.

After all, it was dark except for the dim glow that manifested automatically when the room wasn't in use. If any of the commander's colleagues had been there, they would have called for some real illumination.

He called out, "Computer, lights."

When the room lit up, revealing another uniformed humanoid there, Crusher nearly jumped out of his uniform. Then he saw who it was, and he forced himself to relax.

Tuvok fixed the human with his cool yet somehow piercing gaze. "Commander," he said simply.

"I'm sorry," said Crusher. "I thought the room was unoccupied. I mean . . . there weren't any lights."

The Vulcan arched an eyebrow. "Obviously," he replied with what was clearly forced patience, "you were incorrect in your assumption. I prefer soft lighting whenever possible."

The commander felt a little awkward. He had never managed to be all that comfortable around Vulcans, and this one was . . . well, as Vulcan as they came. Even so, the man was a visitor on a ship full of strangers, and Crusher didn't want to make him feel unwelcome.

He caught sight of a cup of steaming beverage on the table. From the aroma, he judged it to be Vulcan spice tea. Crossing to the replicator, he asked Tuvok, "Care for a refill?"

"No," the Vulcan said. "Thank you." His voice was every bit as icy as when he got off the transporter platform.

The commander shrugged and ordered his own drink—key limeade, extra pulpy. He'd have a synthale for his second drink, but this one made him think of Beverly. She had introduced him to it on their second date, back on Earth. He had fallen in love with key limeade and her simultaneously.

Bev, he thought. His bright, stable, yet passionate redhead. God, how he missed her. And little Wesley . . . he wondered what irretrievable moment of the toddler's childhood he was missing today.

Turning around, drink in hand, Crusher saw that Tuvok was still staring at him. He held a padd in his hands and seemed, even in his Vulcan calm, to have a shadow of annoyance on his face.

"Care for some company?" the commander asked.

"I would prefer to be alone," replied Tuvok.

Crusher ignored the comment. How was he going to get to know the ensign if they didn't speak at least a little bit?

He gestured to the padd. "Research?"

Tuvok's long fingers closed about the device ever so slightly. "No. I am fashioning a private message for my wife back on Vulcan."

The commander's eyebrows shot up. Family? *This* iceberg?

Well, it just went to prove the adage that there was a cover for every pot. Intrigued, Crusher decided to ignore Tuvok's request for solitude for a few more seconds.

Hey, he mused, everyone likes to talk about his

loved ones. Could a Vulcan be any different in that regard?

"I've got a family myself," said Crusher, slipping into the chair beside Tuvok. "A wife and a little baby boy named Wesley."

The ensign didn't say anything.

"Beverly is a Starfleet doctor," the commander continued. "I'm hoping that after my stint here is wrapped up, we can work together on a starship. It'd be nice not to have to say good-bye to the wife and kids all the time, wouldn't you think?"

Tuvok's expression didn't soften, but he did put the padd down on the table and regard Crusher steadily. "I am a father as well," he said. "I have three sons and a daughter."

Crusher smiled a gratified smile. Now we're getting somewhere, he told himself. "Miss 'em, do you?"

"Your statement implies sorrow or loneliness," said the ensign. "You should know that I experience neither."

Spoken like a true Vulcan, thought Crusher. He sighed, wondering how to get past the brick wall that had been thrown up in front of him.

"However," Tuvok went on abruptly, "I do find that I am aware of their absence. I was fortunate enough to be with my children during their formative years. It is . . . regrettable that you are on such a lengthy mission and cannot be with your son."

Surprised, the commander regarded him for a moment. By Vulcan standards, the man was positively gushing.

Crusher tried to conjure an image of Tuvok dandling an infant on his knee . . . and failed. What were Vulcan children like? Were they born with this level of control, like tiny, emotionless adults? Or were they as wild as human children—maybe even wilder, if the ancient Vulcan heritage of violent emotion was still present in their genetic code?

It was an interesting question—and one that had never before occurred to the human. He asked the ensign about it.

Tuvok shrugged. "Control must always be learned," he said flatly. "That is the primary responsibility of a Vulcan parent. However, to most of our offspring, it comes as second nature."

Crusher nodded. "I'll bet," he said sincerely, "that you're an excellent father, Tuvok."

The ensign cocked his head just a millimeter or so. "I am indeed," he replied simply.

The commander chuckled. There was no bragging in the statement, just a flat proclamation of fact.

Impulsively, he leaned forward. "I'd like your opinion on something, Tuvok. That is, if you don't mind."

The Vulcan inclined his head. "Certainly."

"I hate being away from Beverly," said Crusher. "I mean, I *really* hate it. And Wes—damn it, he's practically growing up without me. I have these nightmares about going home and finding out he's graduating from the Academy, and there I am holding a stuffed Circassian cat and looking like an idiot."

Tuvok's expression remained impassive.

"Anyway," the commander went on, "it struck me that there could be a way to accommodate crewmembers with families."

The Vulcan's brow creased ever so slightly. "Explain."

Crusher shrugged. "I thought maybe we'd take them with us."

What little openness there had been about Tuvok's features closed up.

"Think of the psychological benefits to the crew," the human went on. "We would be living full lives instead of just carrying out our assignments."

The Vulcan frowned. "It would not be wise," he said. "Starships are military vessels. They are often involved in battle and other dangerous activities. They are not places for children."

Crusher found he was eager to win Tuvok's approval—though why that might be, he couldn't exactly say. "Well, not right now, they're not," he answered reasonably. "We'd have to plan for their presence . . . take advantage of the ship's ability to separate into a primary hull and a stardrive section. Then, if we anticipate danger, we can deploy all non-essential personnel to the primary hull and get them out of harm's way."

The Vulcan's dark eyes narrowed slightly as he considered the plan. But the commander couldn't read him at all, couldn't tell if Tuvok liked the idea or thought it foolish.

Damn it, Crusher thought, I'm actually nervous! I

feel as if I were standing up in front of my third-year class back at the Academy, presenting my thesis again. . . .

"I see no flaw in your logic," Tuvok concluded suddenly.

The human felt a grin begin to spread over his face. He tried to stop it, but he didn't stand a chance. After all, it wasn't every day that one received a compliment from a Vulcan.

"I'm glad you approve," he said.

"Your approach will need some refinement, of course," said Tuvok. "And you should be aware that others may have certain emotions tied up in their analysis of your plan—unlike myself."

Crusher stood up. "But . . . it would be nice to have the family with you, wouldn't it?"

The Vulcan hesitated, then met the commander's eyes. "Yes," he said. "It would be . . . nice."

Crusher grinned again. "I've enjoyed our conversation, Tuvok. Maybe we can talk again sometime." He shrugged. "I guess I'll leave you to your message. Sorry to have interrupted."

Before he realized what he was doing, he had clapped the Vulcan on the shoulder in a display of camaraderie. Tuvok stiffened slightly—and inwardly, the commander cursed himself.

Physical contact was a violation of a Vulcan's privacy. He had just committed a terrible *faux pas*.

Oh, well, he thought, it was done.

Of course, the commander still felt an impulse to apologize. But in the end, he thought better of it. It would only make things more awkward. Instead, he turned and walked out of the lounge.

Despite his unintentional error in interspecies courtesy, Crusher felt pretty good about the conversation. In a peculiarly Vulcan way, Tuvok clearly loved his family. So did the human.

It was a start.

48

Chapter Four

As PICARD ENTERED the five-sided Grand Council Chamber on Debennius II, he decided that it was as beautiful as any venue he had ever seen. And yet, as he had been told, beauty was not its chief virtue.

After all, the chamber had been built to allow opposing forces to clash over and over again without violent incident. In that respect, it had to be a lot more than easy on the eyes.

Looking up, the captain saw the overarching, transparent dome that let the natural light of the sun shine in, albeit through a glare-softening filter. When debates continued into the evening, it was Picard's understanding that artificial illumination would be employed—but that it mimicked the sun's light so well as to be completely non-distracting.

Soft, muted colors were the rule in every aspect of the decor. Pale blues, delicate greens and purples seemed to dominate, but there was a hint here and there of a metallic hue such as silver or gold. Still, the overall effect was profoundly soothing.

Even the chamber's walls were constructed of sound-absorbing materials. And its thick carpeting was designed to feel soothing to the feet—for those diplomats and observers who had such appendages.

Picard smiled appreciatively. It was a wise collection of decorating choices for a chamber in which so many disparate voices were liable to argue over so much.

However, it wasn't just the decor that impressed the captain. Plainly speaking, the place was enormous. It easily sat the several hundred Benniari, Melacron, Cordracites and other interested species who were taking their seats for the morning's peace talks—including a few avian visitors who perched on pedestals of native woods along the walls.

The captain was impressed with the power and ingenuity of the Benniari's vision. It was for good reason, it seemed, that they were known all over the quadrant for their sensibilities in art, architecture and music.

"Some place," commented Ben Zoma, who had accompanied him there along with Commander Crusher and Ensign Tuvok.

Picard's first officer was dark and lanky with a rakish smile. He had a way with women the captain couldn't help envying and loved a good joke, but was all business when he had to be.

"Indeed," said Picard.

Jetaal Jilokh, aide to First Minister Cabrid Culunnh, looked up at the captain. At a meter and a half in height, the Benniari was somewhat on the tall side for one of his people.

"Our council chamber meets with your approval?" he asked, his Benniar voice soft and breathless to human ears.

Picard nodded. "Very much so."

"I am pleased," said Jilokh. He looked about the room with what was clearly a flush of pride. "Both the Melacron and the Cordracites were extremely generous in donating funds to build this hall. However, the design is strictly a Benniar invention.

"Before it was built," the aide went on, "the sector was headed for war. Despite the obstacles, which were many and varied, we managed to craft a foundation for peace within these walls . . . a foundation that until recently seemed as solid as bedrock." He shook his head with obvious sadness. It was an oddly human gesture, the captain thought.

"Unfortunately," Jilokh concluded, "that foundation is proving to be as fragile as blown glass."

"But that's why we're here," the captain said assuringly. "To see to it that that foundation becomes rock-solid again."

Jilokh looked at him. "Of course," he responded. With a clawlike hand, he gestured to the two-level speaker's platform at the other side of the chamber. "Let us proceed. The First Minister awaits us."

The universal translator built into Picard's communicator badge translated the Benniari's voice as thin and reedy. That, combined with his typically Benniar appearance—evocative of a small, furry Earth animal known as a koala bear—might have made those who didn't know his people dismiss them as docile and ineffectual.

The captain, of course, knew better. "By all means," he told Jilokh, "lead the way."

Turning to face the speaker's platform, the Benniari trundled down the chamber's central aisle with a rocking gait. Picard and his people followed, glancing with curiosity at the assembled delegates as more and more of them filled the chamber.

The captain noted the presence of not just Melacron, Cordracites and Benniari, but Denesthians and Shera'sha-sha and Banyanans as well. There was even a Thallonian official, a tall, poised individual dressed in expensive-looking clothes that marked him as a man of high station.

He met Picard's gaze and their eyes held for a moment. Then the Thallonian nodded cordially and took his seat.

Commander Crusher leaned closer to the captain. "Seems the Melacron-Cordracite situation has many interested observers."

"I was just thinking the same thing," Picard noted.

Jilokh looked back over his furry shoulder and chirped a couple of times—the Benniar equivalent of a chuckle, if a dry one. Obviously, he had overheard the commander's remark.

"Many interested observers indeed," he said. "Not

the least of them you yourselves, representing the Federation. And each one has his own peculiar reason for monitoring our proceedings."

"No doubt," said the captain, "they are all a little concerned."

"Quite concerned," Jilokh confirmed.

By then, they had reached the two-stage speaker's platform. Ascending to the first level and then the second, the Benniari led them to a door in the far wall. Then he touched a pad beside the door, causing it to slide into a pocket aperture.

"Please," said Jilokh, indicating with a gesture that his companions were to enter.

Picard complied . . . and found himself face to face with the renowned Cabrid Culunnh. The First Minister of Debennius II was seated behind a sleek, rounded desk made of dark wood. As he rose, the captain could see evidence of the Benniari's considerable age.

"Captain Picard," said Culunnh, as Jilokh slid closed the door to the room. He held his hands out, leathery palms exposed. "I rejoice that you were able to answer my summons."

Always aware of protocol, Picard mimicked the palms-out gesture. "I only regret we were not able to arrive sooner," he replied. He indicated his companions with a sweep of his hand. "Commander Ben Zoma, my first officer. Commander Crusher, my second officer. And Ensign Tuvok."

The First Minister took special note of the Vulcan. "You are the first of your people I have ever had the pleasure to meet," he told Tuvok. "I wish it were under different circumstances."

"As do I," said the ensign.

Picard regarded Culunnh. "I understand you are in need of some assistance, First Minister."

The Benniari chirped. "To say the least."

Reaching down under the surface of his desk, he manipulated some kind of control. A moment later, a section of wall beside the door turned transparent, affording them a view of the council chamber—although the captain had a feeling the transparency was a one-way effect.

Culunnh looked past Picard and regarded the assemblage of diplomats. "As you know," he said, "this congress's stated goal is still to try to resolve disagreements over territory. However, there are moments when it would be difficult to discern that."

"There's been discord, I take it," said Picard.

"To say the least," the First Minister responded. "Every day, we see more shouting matches, more veiled threats and accusations flung back and forth. Unless we do something, and quickly I might add, I fear we are headed for the war we built this chamber to avoid."

The captain absorbed the information. Obviously, Admiral Ammerman hadn't exaggerated the seriousness of the situation.

"If I may ask a question or two?" Tuvok suggested, asking permission of Picard and Culunnh simultaneously.

"Of course, Ensign," said the First Minister.

The captain nodded. He still felt strange hearing someone address Tuvok in that fashion, considering the Vulcan's age and experience. And yet, that *was* his official title.

"You have said," Tuvok began, "that you do not believe that this fresh wave of terrorist incidents was caused by either the Melacron or the Cordracites. However, the intervention of a third party seems unlikely, given the history of the various races in this sector."

"You wish to know if I have any proof?" asked Culunnh.

"I do," the Vulcan responded flatly.

The First Minister regarded him with a faint, hissing whistle. "You have an incisive mind," he told Tuvok. "A wonderfully Vulcan mind, I would guess. As to your question . . . I have no *real* proof. However, the methods and equipment used in the terrorist assaults are clearly not in keeping with the methods and equipment used before."

"The terrorists could be dealing with arms merchants," Crusher suggested. "If war really does break out, weapon dealers would be the first ones to reap the benefits."

"A possibility, Commander," admitted Culunnh, "but a rather unlikely one, I am afraid. We have seen weapons in these assaults from nearly every sector in the galaxy, well beyond what our local arms merchants would normally have available to them."

It was an interesting point, Picard conceded. And it seemed that Culunnh wasn't finished speaking.

"The two established terrorist presences—the Cordracite Qua-Sok and the Melacronai Me'laa'kra—have traditionally incited fear in their enemies, but have seldom actually killed anyone. They have demonstrated a preference for destroying property rather than people."

"But that has changed?" asked the captain.

"Yes," said Culunnh. "Now we are seeing brutal acts perpetrated upon beloved public figures. Public figures with families . . . even young children, I might add. This is a level of barbarism to which neither the Me'laa'kra nor the Qua-Sok ever stooped."

"I see," Picard replied.

"Previously, the terrorists wanted sympathy for their causes," the First Minister noted. "They wanted allies. None of these more recent attacks has stirred up anything but anger and hatred."

The Vulcan nodded. "And that is why you believe there is a third party involved in the attacks?"

"Correct," Culunnh told him. "Mind you, as I said, I have no hard evidence to back up my belief at this time . . . nor do I have any suspects in mind. I just look at the data and cannot help feeling as I do."

Tuvok frowned. "I understand."

Culunnh eyed him. "But you still have your doubts?"

The Vulcan nodded. "I still have my doubts."

Ben Zoma gave the captain a look. "I guess we've got our work cut out for us, sir."

"That we do," Picard agreed.

Suddenly, a gong rang loudly enough to be heard in

Culunnh's office. It seemed to reverberate in the captain's bones. He looked inquiringly at the First Minister.

"That was the three-cycle bell," Culunnh explained. "It means the morning session will begin shortly."

Jilokh spoke up. "I have set aside seats for Captain Picard and Commander Ben Zoma, First Minister."

Culunnh picked up a metal medallion on a chain and hung it from his short, furry neck. Then he glanced at Crusher and Tuvok. "And his other companions?" he asked his aide.

"They merely wished to meet with you," said Jilokh.

"That's correct," Picard chimed in. "Commander Crusher and Ensign Tuvok will be beaming back to the *Stargazer* to take the lead in our investigation."

The First Minister seemed to approve. "Our hopes go with you, gentlemen. May your endeavor be a successful one."

"Thank you," said Crusher.

Tuvok merely inclined his head.

Culunnh turned to Picard and Ben Zoma. "As you observe our meeting," he told them, "you will see for yourselves the passions raging on both sides. I think you will agree, they are considerable."

The captain nodded. "Thank you for the warning."

He watched as Culunnh toddled off on his bowed Benniar legs, followed closely by Jilokh. Both Benniari exited the room. Then Picard turned to Crusher and Tuvok.

"What I've heard from Cabrid Culunnh," he told

them, "leads me to believe his theory of a third party is worth investigating. He mentioned that the methods and equipment used in the recent terrorist incidents were different from those employed by the Qua-Sok and the Me'laa'kra. I want Joseph, Vigo and Simenon to take a look at this. And Dr. Greyhorse as well."

"Aye, sir," said Crusher.

Joseph, Vigo, Simenon and Greyhorse were individuals of uncommon intelligence and insight. The captain had no doubt that they would be able to confirm or refute Culunnh's suspicions in no time.

"Work closely with them," Picard said. "I want at least *some* useful information by the time I return to the ship."

"Aye, sir," Crusher replied again.

The captain turned to his new, rather aloof ensign. "Mr. Tuvok, I don't believe you've met our chief engineer, Mr. Simenon. You'll find he's a bit outspoken, but he certainly knows his business."

The Vulcan raised an eyebrow. "Then we should get along admirably."

Beside Picard, Ben Zoma hid a grin. Like the captain himself, he was no doubt trying to picture the tall, elegant Vulcan working alongside the cranky, arrogant, lizardlike Gnalish.

Picard held the image in his mind for a moment—the long gray face, the mobile tail, the bright ruby eyes fastened on Tuvok's implacable visage. Simenon would no doubt consider it a personal challenge to get some kind of rise out of the ensign.

The captain glanced at his second officer again. "See you back on the *Stargazer,* Mr. Crusher."

"Aye, sir," said the commander. Then he tapped his comm badge. "Crusher to transporter room. Two to beam up."

"Ready, sir," came the response.

"Energize," Crusher ordered.

Almost instantly, the commander and Tuvok were enveloped in the shimmer and sparkle of the transporter effect. A moment later, they were gone as if they had never been there in the first place.

Nodding approvingly, Picard tapped his own comm badge. "*Stargazer,* this is the captain," he said.

"Asmund here," came the voice of his efficient young helm officer. "I trust you're making progress, sir?"

"A bit," Picard told her. "Ensign Tuvok and Commander Crusher have beamed back up. As I noted before I left the ship, Commander Ben Zoma and I will stay down here in the—"

"Gladiator pit," Ben Zoma quipped with a hint of a smile.

"—Benniari's Grand Council Chamber," Picard continued evenly, without missing a beat.

He glanced at his first officer. Ben Zoma had a sometimes inconvenient sense of humor, but he was a damned fine first officer. The captain didn't begrudge him a witticism now and then.

"Acknowledged, sir," said Asmund.

"Picard out," said the captain.

Chapter Five

"RECORD MESSAGE," SAID JACK CRUSHER, leaning back in his chair.

"Recording," came the response from his workstation.

Crusher smiled at the monitor screen, imagining his wife's face there instead of a Starfleet insignia. "Hi, honey. It's me. I hope everything's working out for you and Wesley."

The commander hated like the dickens to talk to a computer screen. Unfortunately, it was the only way he could get a message to Beverly, so he put up with it.

"We're out here in the Debennius system," he said, "trying to stop a run of terrorist attacks that are bringing a couple of species called the Melacron and the Cordracites to the brink of war. My job is to check out a theory that some third party is responsible for the attacks—presumably, someone who wants that war to happen."

Crusher knew he didn't have much time. After all, the captain wanted results—and quickly—and the fact that his shift had ended an hour ago was hardly an excuse.

"I'm working with a Vulcan named Tuvok, who's had some experience in this neck of space. He's a little stiff—not unexpected, I know—but deep down, he seems like a good guy. A family man, too. I told him my idea about bringing families aboard a starship and he seemed to like it."

The commander recalled Tuvok's reaction and smiled to himself. It had given him a good feeling.

"I've never really had a lot of contact with Vulcans. Few people have. You know . . . they keep to themselves a lot." He shrugged. "But I like this guy. I think if he sticks around a while, we could become friends."

The Starfleet insignia on the screen stared back at Crusher, despite his attempts to see his wife there instead. It seemed to be reminding him that he had work to do.

"Got to go now," he said with a sigh, "but I'll send you another message as soon as I can. Love you, honey. And give Wes a hug for me. Tell him his daddy can't wait to see him."

This was the part the commander hated the most. However, he managed to get it out before the lump formed in his throat. Guess I'm getting better with practice, he told himself.

"Bye, Bev," he concluded.

Crusher instructed the computer to end the message and send it with the next subspace packet intended for headquarters. Then he got up from his chair and headed for the door.

The lounge awaits, he mused.

The sound of a gong filled the council chamber, then died.

Sitting in a seat on the second level of the speaker's platform, Picard watched First Minister Culunnh rise from his ornately carved wooden chair and approach a small lectern.

By then, all the delegates had presumably taken their seats. To the captain, the chamber looked absolutely full. There were even a few observers standing in the back.

Culunnh's small, furry head poked over the top of the lectern. His large violet eyes blinked solemnly, his shiny metal medallion glinting in the filtered sunlight.

"The four hundred and forty-first session of the Kellasian Congress is now in session," intoned the Benniari. "First Minister of Debennius II Cabrid Culunnh presiding. May I remind you that this is a place for discussion and debate—nothing else."

Ben Zoma leaned toward his commanding officer. "Not a good sign when you have to say that right off the bat."

"No," Picard breathed, "it's not."

Culunnh consulted a small screen built into his

lectern. "The chamber recognizes Sammis Tarv, Chief Delegate of Cordra Four."

Tarv, a pale-skinned insectoid with Andorian-like antennae, stood up and faced the congress. "Once again," he said in a rasping voice, "I would like to address the matter of the Melacronai colony on Tebra Six. It must be clear by now that—"

He was interrupted by a warbling cry of protest from a Melacronai throat: "I speak for the dead!"

As Picard scanned the assemblage to determine the origin of the high-pitched protest, he saw a Melacronai female come down the central aisle. She wasn't alone, either. There was a small child in her arms, an infant really, and one more on either side of her.

"G'aha Avriil cannot decry the manner of his death," the female shrilled, "but his widow can!"

"I must protest!" Sammis Tarv grated loudly. "First Minister, this woman was not properly presented to this body, nor have children ever been allowed to enter this chamber!"

Before he finished, the entire delegation of Cordracites was on its feet, adding their objections to his. Their voices sounded like a collection of rocks grinding together.

The translator installed in Picard's comm badge squealed in protest. Both the captain and his first officer winced and removed their badges. Picard scowled, having been warned that this might happen if too many of the delegates decided to speak at once.

"Silence!" demanded Cabrid Culunnh.

The Cordracites fell silent as he asked, though they

continued to gesticulate with great vehemence. But the Melacronai female chose not to heed the First Minister.

"First Minister Culunnh!" she cried out. "It seems to me that the Companion of a murdered G'aha ought to be honored within these precincts, not silenced like an unruly ta'pur!"

Her children stared wide-eyed at Culunnh. The smallest of them began to weep, his single nostril flaring and then sealing shut.

Ben Zoma shook his head. "Why do I have a feeling she and the kids didn't come here on their own?"

Picard knew exactly what his exec meant. He had no doubt the female was what she appeared to be—the spouse of a murdered Melacronai official. However, her presence there was so incendiary as to raise questions.

"More than likely," the captain whispered, "the Melacronai delegation arranged her passage here."

"To show the congress how the Melacron are suffering at the hands of the Cordracites," Ben Zoma suggested. "So in the end, everyone will sympathize with Melacronai territorial claims."

And the congress hadn't been in session for more than a minute or two. Picard had to wonder how often this type of thing occurred.

A sharp buzzer sounded, interrupting the G'aha's widow. Cabrid Culunnh's tufted ears lay flat against his round head, a sure sign of irritation. "Madam," he responded, "I grieve for your great loss—"

A roar of protest went up from the Cordracite delegation. However, the First Minister barreled on.

"—and I am certain everyone here does the same. We have never condoned and *will* never condone the assassination of an elected official under any circumstances at all."

He glared at the entire assembly. Picard hadn't thought it possible for a Benniari to glare, but Culunnh was doing it.

"However," said the First Minister, "it is true that you did not petition to be heard, and that your children are not permitted at these debates. I levy two rounds of silence against the Melacronai delegation as a penalty for violating the established rules of conduct for this congress."

"I object!" trilled a Melacron. "We had no more warning than you did that this female would seek to address the Congress!"

"Perhaps not," Culunnh allowed, whether he believed it or not. "However, it has long been a policy here to hold delegates responsible for the actions of their people. The decision stands."

The Melecronai delegation warbled their complaints, but to no avail. The First Minister buzzed them a second time and a third. Eventually, they sat down and fell silent.

"Sammis Tarv," said Culunnh, "you had the floor before the proceedings were interrupted. Please go on."

However, when the Cordracite got up again to speak, he was shouted down by a group whose species Picard was unable to identify. And when they were silenced, the Melacronai delegation objected, citing some obscure and seemingly useless rule of protocol.

The First Minister denied the Melacron their objection, but they continued to voice it loudly and at great length. Culunnh buzzed them; it didn't help. Then the Cordracites began to speak at the same time, their deep, scratchy voices grating on everyone present.

Before long, it was a free-for-all.

The captain scanned the crowd, trying to discern who was attacking or defending whom. However, alliances seemed to shift from moment to moment, making it impossible for him to learn anything.

He did make one intriguing observation, however. The Thallonian nobleman appeared to remain silent throughout the conflict. He sat back in his seat observing the ebb and flow of charges and accusations with eyes that didn't seem to miss a thing.

Ben Zoma grunted. "You know, I'm amazed that war didn't break out a long time ago."

"That makes two of us," Picard muttered.

"Captain Picard?" said a soft, fluttery voice.

The human turned and saw that it was the First Minister who had called his name. The Benniari's large, violet eyes looked at him pleadingly, though Picard didn't have any idea what would be asked of him.

But he wouldn't have to wait long to find out.

"Yes, Minister?" the captain replied.

Culunnh turned to the congress. "Captain Picard of the Federation has agreed to honor us with his advice on these matters."

Picard blinked, but otherwise did nothing to reveal his surprise. He had believed that he and Ben Zoma were there to observe the proceedings, not make speeches to the congress.

However, he had been charged with reestablishing the peace in this sector in any way that made sense. If the First Minister of Debennius II thought he could help to calm this assembly, who was he to refuse?

For a moment he wondered if some faction or other would object, saying that the captain had not been properly "presented." However, the shouting appeared to die down as soon as he stood up and approached the lectern. Clearly, at least some of the delegates wished to hear what a Federation official had to say for himself.

"I would be honored to address this august body, First Minister," Picard said in his smoothest, most diplomatic-sounding voice. He straightened the red tunic of his dress uniform and approached the lectern. At the same time, Culunnh took a few steps back.

The captain was concerned that he would look silly standing behind a meter-high lectern. However, as he got closer it automatically rose to the height of his chest, removing at least one problem.

It was a good thing, Picard reflected soberly. After all, there were so many other problems to deal with.

He gathered his thoughts as he surveyed the sea of people sitting before him. From the insectlike Cordracites to the small, fuzzy shapes of the Benniari to the long, tentacled forms of the Shera'sha-sha, every sentient race in the sector seemed to have a representative here.

That was good, the captain told himself. He would start there.

"My name is Captain Jean-Luc Picard," he said, "of the Federation starship *Stargazer.* I was invited to this planet, this congress and"—he smiled a little—"to this podium by the First Minister of the Benniari. May I take this moment to salute Cabrid Culunnh for his tireless efforts to secure peace in this sector."

The sounds of accolades followed. Culunnh nodded slightly, receiving Picard's compliment with grace and dignity.

The captain's ears strained for sounds of resentment from the audience, but none came. It was a good sign. When parties in conflict turned their attention to attacking their mediator, whether verbally or physically, it was usually time to prepare for war.

"I am pleased to be present at these historic talks," Picard continued, "and pleased to see that, unless I am mistaken, every species in the Kellasian sector has a representative at this congress. What that tells me is that everyone here cares deeply about avoiding an armed conflict. That gives me, and the United Federation of Planets I represent, reason for optimism that a peaceful conclusion will be achieved in due time."

"Not until those who murdered my Companion are caught and punished for their crime!"

The outburst from the widow of the Melacronai G'aha was unexpected. So was her sudden rush toward the stage. After all, the female had already been escorted from the chamber with her children.

Picard didn't think she posed a threat, however. So he stayed where he was and let the Benniar guards deal with the woman.

Under different circumstances, the thought of Benniari guarding anything effectively might have seemed ludicrous. Fortunately, they didn't have to rely on their physical size. A touch of a button on their baldrics immobilized the woman's limbs, if not her voice.

"Justice, Picard of the Federation!" she screamed. "Justice! Help us find the Cordracite killers of my Companion!"

The captain swallowed. "Those responsible for the terrorist attacks will be caught and punished, I assure you," he said in the most tranquil voice he could muster, hoping desperately that fate would not prove him a liar. "But so far we have no proof that the Cordracites—"

"Who needs proof?" came the gurgling, hissing voice of one of the Shera'sha-sha. Its pale green tentacles waved frantically. "We all know what the Cordracites are! We all know what they do!"

"The Cordracites defend themselves against the aggressions of the Melacron, nothing more." The flat voice of the skeletal-looking Tikraat who had spoken made the words a statement more than a defense.

No translation device ever devised could convey the emotions of the Tikraata. The best they could do was serve up the words, uttered in a mechanical, atonal voice. "It is the Melacron who—"

"Let us have order in this hall!" Picard cried out. His voice carried and the arguments ceased. For the moment, he thought darkly.

"Listen to yourselves!" he told the assemblage. "Squabbling like children tearing at a new toy! You are diplomats, every one of you. You represent the highest virtues your people have to offer. I understand that tempers are running high, but let us move forward with our eyes open—so that we may truly see and understand what is taking place!"

"The Melacronai murderers are getting away with it, that's what's taking place!" someone shouted.

Picard felt his jaw muscles clench. He held his hands up in a call for quiet, but no one would pay any attention to him. Abruptly, the clear, pure sound of the Benniari gong sliced cleanly through the melee.

"Let us recess for a few cycles," said Cabrid Culunnh, who had taken up a position beside the captain. "As Captain Picard sagely counsels us, it is wiser to proceed thoughtfully and deliberately than to rush forward in the heat of emotion."

The congress muttered its dissatisfaction, but it was obvious that nothing more could be accomplished that morning. The delegates rose and dispersed, still arguing among themselves.

The First Minister turned to Picard. "Thank you for trying, Captain," he said in a soft, resigned voice. "Now you have some idea of the obstacles that confront me here."

"Indeed I do," Picard replied sincerely. He shook his head. "I doubt that Hercules had a more difficult time."

"Hercules?" Culunnh echoed. He cocked his head, obviously curious about the captain's reference.

"A great hero from one of my world's mythologies," Picard explained. "He was charged with seven supposedly impossible tasks. But in the end, he managed to complete them all."

Understanding flitted over the Benniari's furred face. Culunnh chirped once, and then again.

"Your Hercules," he said dryly, "never had to get a Melacron and a Cordracite to stop arguing. Otherwise, he might still be at it."

Picard acknowledged the truth of the comment. "Perhaps he would at that, First Minister." He watched the delegates continue to filter out of the chamber, still contending bitterly. "Perhaps he would at that."

Chapter Six

PICARD HAD NURTURED A HOPE that the afternoon session of the Kellasian Congress would be more productive than the morning session. That hope was dashed when the Cordracite delegation announced that it was absenting itself from the afternoon proceedings.

"For what reason?" Cabrid Culunnh asked.

"To protest the repeated admission of the Melacronai female," was the indignant answer supplied by Sammis Tarv.

The captain sighed as he watched the Cordracites file out of the chamber with their heads bowed, to the disgust of some observers and the rather vocal approval of others. Clearly, they would not solve a territorial dispute with only one of the disputants present.

"Those Cordracites sure know how to ruin a party," Ben Zoma observed in a voice only Picard could hear.

The captain nodded. "I imagine they've had lots of practice. But then, the Melacron seem no better."

The afternoon session went ahead without the Cordracites. But as Picard had predicted, it didn't get very far. In fact, it seemed to him that it took a few steps backward.

Tempers were running too high, the captain observed. Racial hatreds, some old, some new, had replaced rational objectives. No one was listening, everyone was talking, and poor Cabrid Culunnh seemed to get older and more exhausted by the minute.

The Kellasian Congress had become a joke. He could see that clearly now. Perhaps it had been effective before this latest wave of terrorist attacks, but it was effective no more.

Picard sincerely hoped his research team aboard the *Stargazer* was making headway. He and his first officer certainly weren't.

At the midafternoon recess, the captain and Ben Zoma departed the podium. Their intention was to use the allotted seventeen cycles—approximately a half-hour of Earth time—to stretch their legs. Debennius II was a lovely planet, after all. Picard believed a brief walk beneath a soft blue sky might clear their minds a bit.

It was not to be, however. No sooner had Picard descended to the chamber's central walkway than the large Thallonian he had observed earlier appeared suddenly at his side.

"Captain," said the Thallonian in a smooth, cultured voice.

The human turned to him. "Yes?"

"Permit me to introduce myself," the delegate told him. "I am Governor Gerrid Thul, here at the congress representing the interests of the Thallonian Empire." Thul extended a large ruddy hand, demonstrating that he was familiar with human customs.

Picard shook the Thallonian's hand. His grip was strong and firm, a rarity among aliens who attempted the handshake ritual.

"Jean-Luc Picard," said the captain, though by now he was certain everyone knew precisely who he was. He indicated his companion. "And this is Gilaad Ben Zoma, my first officer."

Thul shook Ben Zoma's hand as well.

"We have seventeen cycles before the war of words begins again," Thul told Picard. "Might I have a moment with you?" His eyes flickered to the first officer, then back to the captain. "In private?" he added.

Picard turned to Ben Zoma.

"Go ahead," said the dark-haired man. "I should call up to the *Stargazer* anyway. I need to check on some things."

The captain nodded, aware of at least some of the matters Ben Zoma would be checking on—all mundane but necessary aspects of ship's business. Then he turned to the Thallonian. "Very well. Shall we speak outside? Or do you have somewhere else in mind?"

"Outside will be fine," Thul told him.

Together, they made their way through the doors of the Grand Council Chamber and walked out into a beautiful, sunny day. Picard had to blink as his eyes adjusted to the brighter light.

In front of them, white stone steps led down to a circular pool with a fountain. The Thallonian approached it and peered into the sparkling depths. As the captain followed suit, he caught a glint of color—some kind of marine life, he realized.

A small bowl filled with some gray-green, crumbly matter stood on a nearby pedestal. Thul reached a big, red hand into it and began to sprinkle the surface of the water with the gray-green stuff. At once, the fish—if they could be called that, for they resembled no fish Picard had ever seen—darted to the surface and snatched at it.

The captain laughed as he realized what the stuff on the pedestal was. "Fish food," he said.

The Thallonian glanced at him and smiled. "Indeed," he said. He finished feeding the aquatic creatures, meticulously dusted off his hands, and turned to face Picard again.

"You asked to speak with me," the captain noted, acutely aware of how little time they had before the session resumed.

"I did," Thul agreed. He held his hands out, palms up. "Let me be blunt. How much do you know about our problems in this sector?"

Picard replied with equal bluntness. "Very little, I'm afraid. Only what's generally known to all those assembled. But I assure you, I intend to learn a good deal more."

The governor clasped his hands behind his back and stared into the depths of the fish pool. "Truly," he said, "it is a shameful spectacle. Supposedly, it is over territory. But of course, it has become a great deal more than that in recent weeks."

"You've been here that long?" asked the captain.

Thul nodded. "Too long, as you can imagine. I would much rather be back at my outpost, doing some real work. I need not tell you that attending these sessions has taken its toll on me." He glanced at Picard. "But then, I'm sure there is somewhere else you would rather be as well."

The captain grunted, thinking of the ruins on Zebros IV. "The same could probably be said of everyone in the congress . . . except perhaps the Cordracites and the Melacron themselves."

"Except them," the Thallonian agreed. "And they are closer than ever to an armed conflict—one which would take place precariously close to my emperor's borders. As you can imagine, the revered Tae Cwan does not wish to see such a conflict. That's why I'm here, a loyal servant of my master—to see to it that a war never takes place."

Picard was glad to hear that at least one delegate was approaching the matter with a cool head. He said so.

"One delegate, by himself, can do very little," Thul

pointed out. He eyed the captain. "However, judging by what I heard from you this morning, it sounds as if your Federation and my Empire seek the same sort of outcome to these talks."

"It does at that," Picard agreed. By then, he could see where the Thallonian was going with his comments. "You're suggesting that we join forces, I take it?"

"I am," Thul confirmed, his dark eyes blazing resolutely. "Let us work in concert, Captain. Then perhaps we can put an end to this war of words before it becomes a war in truth."

"We could pool our knowledge," Picard said.

"And back each other up during the talks," said the governor. He smiled. "Certainly, we have nothing to lose."

The captain hesitated a moment before replying. He didn't know very much about the Thallonians. Hardly anyone in the Federation did.

However, Thul seemed genuine in his desire to end the enmity between the Melacron and the Cordracites. Nor had it escaped Picard's notice that the governor was one of the very few delegates not crying out for blood in the Grand Council Chamber.

The one thing the captain knew for certain was that the Thallonian Empire was a powerful entity. Perhaps if he and Thul worked together here and now, their unity would not only improve the present situation but influence future negotiations with the governor's people.

"You make a compelling case," said Picard. He

smiled as well. "From now on, we'll work together as closely as possible."

Thul clapped him on the shoulder. "I am pleased," he told the captain. "I am pleased indeed."

Crusher leaned back in his seat and surveyed the faces of the others who had joined him in the lounge.

Phigus Simenon, the ship's lizardlike chief engineer. Pug Joseph, the baby-faced head of security, who was straddling a chair in front of the room's computer workstation. Carter Greyhorse, the big, broadshouldered Native American who served as chief medical officer. Vigo, the strapping blue Pandrilite in charge of the *Stargazer*'s weapons systems.

And, of course, Ensign Tuvok, who was standing off to the side with his arms folded across his chest.

"Well, Ensign Tuvok," said Simenon, eyeing the Vulcan with slitted, blood-red eyes as he switched his scaly tail from one side to the other, "you're the expert on the Kellasian sector. Why don't you tell us who this mysterious third party is already, so we can all go have a nice snack and put our feet up?"

Caught off balance, the ensign looked quizzically at the Gnalish. "I beg your pardon?" he said.

The engineer stopped and returned Tuvok's scrutiny. "We backtracked all the way to Starbase Three to pick you up, didn't we? I thought that you might know something."

Tuvok frowned ever so slightly. "I know quite a bit. However, it will require considerable investigation to determine if there is a third party—and if so, to uncover his identity."

"Investigation," Simenon hissed, his eyes gleaming with humor. "Now why didn't I think of that?"

"Pay no attention to him," Greyhorse told the Vulcan.

"The doctor's right," said Joseph. He had turned around to face his workstation and was tapping away. "Our friend Simenon doesn't always work and play well with others."

"Doesn't *ever*," Greyhorse amended.

Crusher knew that the Gnalish could be irascible in the extreme. The human had long since given up trying to beat him in a game of one-upmanship, since he never seemed to get anywhere.

Simenon smiled to himself. "My apologies, Mr. Tuvok. I didn't know your feelings were hurt so easily."

The ensign's brow creased. "I do not have feelings," he shot back. "I am a Vulcan. And if it is your intention to bait me, I would advise you to spend your time in more gainful pursuits . . . for instance, adjusting the magnetic switching controls in the plasma distribution manifold."

The Gnalish's head snapped around. "What are you talking about? There's nothing wrong with the magnetic switching controls."

The Vulcan lifted an eyebrow. "That is correct. It was merely . . . an example," he said archly.

It took Simenon a moment to realize that the tables had been turned on him, but when he did he hissed with delight. After all, he liked nothing better than when someone matched him blow for blow.

"Thataway," he told Tuvok with a surprisingly paternal tone in his voice. "Don't take guff from anyone—even me."

Crusher nodded approvingly. It seemed Tuvok was going to be able to hold his own on the *Stargazer*—even against the likes of the Gnalish.

"Now," he said, as the ranking officer in the room, "let's put the sharp part of our wits to the problem instead of each other."

"Here's a start," Joseph told them. He swiveled around in his chair again. "I've taken the liberty of pulling up all pertinent information on terrorist incidents in the sector."

"You mean the latest wave?" asked Greyhorse, his expression a characteristically grim one.

"No," said the security chief. "All of them, including the ones attributed to the established terrorist groups."

"The Quack-Socks and the Melly-Craw," snorted Simenon.

The Vulcan opened his mouth to correct the Gnalish's deliberate mispronunciations, but Crusher caught his eye and shook his head. Realizing he was being baited again, Tuvok remained silent.

"Gather 'round," Joseph advised his colleagues. "Don't be shy."

They all complied. Even Simenon.

"Now, as I understand it," the security chief went on with his colleagues looking over his shoulders, "the First Minister has two reasons for suspecting the intervention of a third party. One is a change in the methods used by the terrorists. The other is a change in the equipment they used . . . in other words, the weapons."

Crusher nodded. "That's right."

"Okay," said Joseph, tapping his monitor screen with a forefinger. "This is a catalogue of the terrorist incidents that took place between a year and six months ago."

One by one, scenes of carnage filled the screen, lingered for a moment, then faded . . . only to be replaced by others. Crusher shook his head as he looked at a bombed-out building in one scene, the desecration of a graveyard in another, the remnants of some ancient statuary in a third.

What a heartbreaking mess, he reflected. He couldn't understand how people could be so bent on destruction.

"All right," Joseph told them. "Now let's take a look at the incidents that took place in the last couple of weeks."

Again, scenes of carnage filled the screen. As Crusher watched, a series of dead Cordracites were pulled from a ragged hole in the ground. A moment later, a bound Melacron was executed with a directed-energy weapon. More Cordracite corpses, scattered across a playground. More Melacron corpses, floating on an expanse of blue-green water.

"I would say these are of a distinctly more bloody nature," Greyhorse noted with an air of disapproval.

Simenon slid a ruby-red eye in his direction. "Is that your professional opinion, Doctor?"

Greyhorse frowned at the Gnalish. "If you like."

"So," said Crusher, "so far, Culunnh seems to have a point. The terrorists' methods *have* changed."

"What about their weapons?" Vigo asked.

"Coming right up," said Joseph.

With that, he pulled up a set of objects depicted against a white background. They included hand weapons, blades of various shapes and sizes, and a couple of undetonated bombs.

"Each of these was used in a terrorist incident between a year and six months ago," the security chief remarked.

"They're all rather standard," Vigo observed.

"Nothing from outside the sector?" asked the Gnalish.

"I'd be surprised if it were," said the weapons officer.

Tuvok pointed to one object in particular—a long, scimitarlike affair. "What is this?" he inquired.

"Have you seen it before?" Greyhorse asked him.

The Vulcan shrugged. "I am not certain."

Joseph magnified the weapon and the legend beneath it. "It's the ritual slaughter blade of the Me'laa'kra," he explained. "All the sacred burden beasts in the incident on Cordra Four were killed with it."

"Twenty-two in all," said Simenon, reading off the screen. There was no hint of sarcasm in his voice anymore. "Absolutely sickening."

"Twenty two?" Tuvok asked. "Are you certain?"

Joseph looked at the ensign. "Positive. Why?"

"Twenty-two is a lucky number in the view of the ancient Cordracites," Tuvok informed him without emotion. "It is associated with the acquisition of wealth and power."

The security chief looked impressed with the observation. "Interesting, Ensign. But why murder burden beasts?"

Tuvok considered the question for a moment. Then again, he spoke dispassionately. "In primitive times, the Cordracites used these animals to sow their fields. In some regions, they were elevated to the status of harvest gods—deities who presided over the cultivation of land."

Crusher nodded. "So these animal slaughters might have been symbolic—a ritual objection to the Cordracite drive for territory."

"A drive matched meter for meter by our friends the Melacron," Joseph pointed out with a frown.

"Which, in a naaga shell," said the Gnalish, "is why they're at each other's throats all the time."

"More significantly," the Vulcan went on, "it seems the Me'laa'kra see their activities as a holy crusade, striking at the mystical symbols of the Cordracite belief system—and not at the Cordracites themselves."

"Indeed," said Simenon.

"But as we've already seen," Crusher noted, "recent incidents have clearly been designed to generate Cordracite fatalities."

"Which lends a bit more support to the third party theory," the chief medical officer told them.

"At least among the Me'laa'kra," said the Vulcan. "Perhaps we could examine a Qua-Sok weapon."

The security chief reduced the ritual slaughter blade to its previous size and gave them a view of the entire collection. Tuvok studied it again, but nothing seemed to pop out at him.

"Pick something anyway," Greyhorse encouraged him. "We had good luck with your last choice."

Vigo planted a big, blue forefinger on the screen. "Here," he said. "I'll do it for him."

As before, Joseph magnified the object—a small, black undetonated bomb. He glanced at the Vulcan. "Anything?"

Tuvok shook his head. "No. Perhaps if we were to see the aftermath of the incident, however . . ."

"Your wish is my command," the security chief told him. As Crusher watched, he tapped out the requisite command on his keyboard.

A tableau came up showing a half-destroyed power relay station on Melacron VI. The ensign extended a dark index finger and pointed to a scrawled message on a broken wall.

"Would you please magnify this?" Tuvok requested.

Joseph did as he was asked. Abruptly, the message became large enough to take up most of the screen.

"What does it say?" asked Crusher, who had no idea.

"I do not pretend to be an expert in Cordracite

languages," said the Vulcan, "but I believe it credits the destruction of the relay station to the 'fierce and terrible Qua-Sok,' who only acted in 'the most upright and justified' fashion. Or something to that effect."

"Worried about their image, are they?" asked Simenon.

"Culunnh said they were," Crusher pointed out.

"What's more," Tuvok added, "they claimed responsibility for the incident. We should determine if anyone claimed responsibility for any of the more recent crimes against the Melacron."

Vigo nodded. "Good idea."

They went over each of the incidents—three of them in all. There was no sign of any scrawled messages at any of the sites. In fact, the perpetrators seemed to have gone out of their way to avoid leaving traces of their having been there.

"Another significant difference," Simenon noted.

Finally, Joseph tried to call up a visual inventory of the weapons used in the previous two weeks. But after a moment, he sighed and sat back in his chair, an expression of bemusement on his pugnosed face.

"What's the matter?" asked Greyhorse.

"They don't have any pictures of the weapons employed recently," said the security officer. "Whoever used them took them along with them."

"Sounds like the work of professionals," Vigo observed.

"But the Melacron must have speculated as to what was used," Crusher suggested.

Calling up the data, Joseph nodded. "They did. Unfortunately, they weren't able to get very specific. They weren't familiar with the energy signatures they found."

The Pandrilite weapons officer grunted. "Even *more* like the work of professionals," he maintained.

"Well," said Simenon, "the evidence—or lack of it, in this case—seems pretty clear. The First Minister is right. There *is* a third party involved in these attacks."

"Trying to pick up where the Qua-Sok and the Me'laa'kra left off," the security chief expanded.

"That would be my guess as well," said Tuvok.

Crusher recalled that the Vulcan had disagreed with Culunnh's conclusions down on Debennius VI. However, he now seemed quite willing to agree with them. *I guess that's one of the benefits of being without emotions,* the commander mused. *You never get too attached to a particular point of view.*

He could see how the Vulcan's bland yet somehow arrogant demeanor might seem a bit unsettling at times. But if Tuvok knew the Kellasian sector as well as he appeared to know it, Crusher would put up with his quirks from morning to night.

"Of course, that begs a question," Vigo pointed out.

Joseph nodded. "If there's a third party . . . who is he? And what does he hope to gain by killing innocent people?"

No one answered him, at first.

Then the Gnalish spoke up. "Arms merchants?" he suggested.

"I mentioned that as a possibility," said Crusher, "but the First Minister told us he didn't think so. He seemed to think the incidents involved weapons from all over the galaxy—a wider variety than arms merchants could get their hands on."

The Vulcan nodded. "Let us dismiss them for the time being."

"So," said Simenon, rephrasing the question, "who's busy killing all those Melacron and Cordracites?"

The six of them exchanged uncomfortable looks.

"Aye, there's the rub," the engineer commented cheerfully, as if nothing made him happier than pronouncing doom. "Your Shakespeare did have a way with words—especially violent ones."

Crusher stroked his chin. "Let's try another angle. I'm willing to bet that whoever killed the G'aha on Melacron Five wanted to get away as quickly as possible. Let's call up a list of everyone who left the planet between the time of the assassination and today."

Joseph provided them with a list on his monitor screen. "Unfortunately, it's pretty long," he told the others.

Crusher inspected it and fought back a sigh. "So it is."

"Exactly what are you hoping to find?" inquired the Gnalish, his crimson eyes bright with curiosity.

Crusher shrugged. "I just thought something might—"

But Tuvok stopped him with a gesture, his

eyes locked onto the screen. "Fascinating," he murmured.

"What is?" Vigo asked him.

The Vulcan pointed to one of the names on the screen. "That is." Then he looked at Crusher. "I believe I may have something, Commander."

Crusher smiled. "That's great. But what is it?"

Tuvok told him.

Chapter Seven

NEARLY TEN HOURS after his away team first beamed down to Debennius II, Picard tapped his communicator badge and contacted the *Stargazer*. "Two to beam up," he told Crusher.

"Aye, sir," said the second officer.

The captain regarded Ben Zoma, noting inwardly that his exec looked as weary and frustrated as he himself felt. It took its toll, sitting in a room full of angry, argumentative people. What's more, the food offered them by the Benniari had been less than appealing. Neither of them had been driven to eat very much of it.

"I don't know what I want to do first," said the first officer, "gorge myself or find someplace quiet to collapse."

Picard frowned. "Unfortunately, we're not going to get the opportunity to do either, Gilaad. We need to discuss the progress of our investigative team as soon as we get back."

Ben Zoma grunted goodnaturedly and turned a weary smile on his superior. "Slavedriver," he said.

Then they were surrounded by the transporter effect. A moment later, they materialized in the *Stargazer's* transporter room.

Glancing at the transporter console, the captain noticed that his chief engineer was working the controls. Simenon's sharp, lizardlike face split into a grin that showed pointed teeth. What's more, his tail lashed back and forth in what Picard had come to learn was an expression of eagerness.

"Progress?" the captain asked.

Simenon shrugged his narrow shoulders. "Some," he replied, almost perverse in his terseness. "We're all waiting for you and Commander Ben Zoma in your ready room, sir—though I should warn you, none of us is dressed as nicely as the two of you are."

Picard pulled down on the front of his dress tunic and gestured to the sliding doors. "Lead the way, Mr. Simenon—and be glad I didn't ask you to beam down as well."

The engineer hissed to show his amusement. Then, complying with the captain's command, he made his way out into the corridor and found the nearest turbolift. In less than a minute, the three of them were walking out onto the *Stargazer's* bridge.

As Picard turned right and passed the communications station, he nodded to Cadwallader. The young
woman smiled and nodded back—and didn't say
a word, vituperative or otherwise. It was good to be
out of that damned council chamber, the captain
reflected.

The doors to his ready room slid aside for him.
Crusher, Tuvok, Greyhorse, Vigo and Joseph were
clustered inside, no doubt discussing some element of
their investigation.

"Sir," said Crusher, turning to acknowledge Picard,
"I—"

The captain held up a hand for silence. Then he
crossed to the room's only replicator and punched up
two plates full of bread, fruit and cheese, along with a
couple of glasses of sparkling water.

Ben Zoma, who was right behind him, smiled as
the orders materialized. "Thanks," he said. "I don't
think I could have lasted another minute."

"Think nothing of it," Picard responded.

Bringing his plate over to his desk, he laid it down
on the sleek, black surface and sat down beside it.
Then, slicing an apple and a piece of sharp cheddar,
he downed them both at a single bite.

At the same time, Ben Zoma dug into his own
food. Watching him, the captain believed his exec
really *couldn't* have lasted another minute.

Picard's officers waited patiently for their superi-
ors to finish. But the captain didn't want to wait that
long. He signaled for the team to proceed with their
report.

As the ranking officer on the assignment, it fell to Crusher to outline their progress. "As far as Culunnh's theory about a third party goes, sir . . . we seem to have found some corroborative evidence."

Picard was interested. "Go on."

Crusher described the weapons found at the sites of the earlier incidents—and the dearth of weapons found at the later ones. He also spoke of the relative levels of violence.

The captain nodded. "So the First Minister wasn't too far off base after all, was he?"

"We don't believe so, sir," said Crusher.

"What's more," Simenon added with a grin, "our friend Mr. Tuvok has come up with a lead as to the identity of the third party."

Picard turned to the Vulcan. "Tell me more, Ensign."

Tuvok's forehead wrinkled. Obviously, he was more than a little discomfited by the Gnalish's attitude. "Unfortunately," he said, "it is what you humans might call a long shot."

"If I may say so," Joseph chimed in with undisguised eagerness, "it's better than a long shot, Captain. It's a legitimate lead."

With his upturned nose and close-cropped, sandy hair, some people often tended to underestimate Pug Joseph. Picard wasn't one of them.

Crusher smiled at the security chief. "Maybe we should let the captain decide for himself, Mr. Joseph."

The chief nodded, chastened. "Whatever you say, sir."

The captain regarded Tuvok. "Ensign? Is someone going to tell me about this or not?"

The Vulcan's nostrils flared as he began. "A Melacron named Bin Nedrach was listed as a passenger on an intrasystem transport vessel departing Melacron Five approximately two point four hours after the assassination of the G'aha of Laws and Enforcements."

Picard turned to Ben Zoma, who was washing down his hastily eaten food with some sparkling water. "That would be the spouse of the female we saw in the council chamber this morning?"

The first officer nodded. "I'd imagine."

The captain returned his attention to Tuvok. "Go on."

"At first glance," said the Vulcan, "it may appear that Nedrach's departure was merely a coincidence. After all, he had no criminal record. There would be no good reason to suspect him of wrongdoing."

"Except?" Picard supplied.

Tuvok remained as deadpan as ever. "Except that fifty-five years ago, when I was visiting this sector for the first time, there was an infamous Melacronai crime clan in existence. It had all but claimed the furthest planet in the system, Debennius Six, controlling who came and went, who was allowed to open and run businesses—everything. It was during this time that Debennius Six became known as 'the Last Stop to Nowhere.' "

"I see," said the captain, "but—"

The Vulcan went on as if Picard hadn't opened his

mouth. "One of the clan's top 'bosses,' " he noted, "if I am using the term correctly, was an individual named Bin Nedrach."

The captain's eyes narrowed. "The same man who departed Melacron Five on that transport?"

"He would have to have been pretty advanced in years," Ben Zoma remarked between bites. He glanced at Simenon. "And the Melacronai don't live as long as *some* species do."

"I wondered about the same things," said the ensign. "Digging a little more deeply into the passenger manifest, I discovered that it was not the Bin Nedrach who had held the Melacronai in an iron grip fifty-five years earlier. It was his grandson."

Picard was growing more and more interested. So much so, in fact, that he pushed his plate of food aside.

"The fact that Melacronai crime clans place a high value on familial relationships," Tuvok continued, "and that this younger Bin Nedrach left less than three hours after an assassination, suggests that this may be a worthwhile lead." He lifted an eyebrow. "And if I may speak frankly, Captain, at the present moment, it is the only lead we have."

Joseph chuckled, obviously proud of the Vulcan's deductive abilities. In fact, it seemed to Picard, he couldn't have been prouder if Tuvok were a longstanding member of the crew.

"What a memory!" said the security chief.

Tuvok glanced at him. "I am a Vulcan, Mr. Joseph.

Please do not attribute to skill what is merely the result of genetics."

"Still," the chief rejoined, "to remember a name for that long—and to be able to link it to this Bin Nedrach—all I can say, Ensign, is it's too bad you're not a security officer. You'd make a damned good one."

Tuvok appeared to take the compliment in stride. "I will keep that in mind," he told Joseph.

In the meantime, Picard thought, they had something to go on. It wasn't a great deal, but it was something.

The captain stroked his chin, mulling over their next step. "Do we know where this Bin Nedrach is now?" he asked.

Joseph shrugged. "We can make a guess, but—"

"I cannot afford to guess," said Picard. He turned to Crusher and the Vulcan. "Jack, Tuvok—I'm putting you two on this. I want you to go undercover and try to locate Bin Nedrach."

"And when we find him?" the second officer asked.

The captain shook his head. "Don't bring him in immediately. One man, even if he is an assassin, could not be doing everything by himself."

"Someone's pulling his strings," Ben Zoma translated.

"That is right," said Picard. "And that's the someone I want."

"Aye, Captain," Crusher and Tuvok responded at precisely the same time.

The captain saw them glance at each other. They were good men, both of them, he reflected. They would work together just fine, despite the essential differences in their natures.

At least, he hoped so.

"In the meantime," Picard said, "Commander Ben Zoma and I will continue to monitor the situation on Debennius Two."

The first officer grunted. "I think Crusher and Tuvok have the easier assignment by far."

Picard allowed himself a hint of a smile. "We will see about that." He considered the second officer and the ensign. "Dismissed, gentlemen." He turned to Simenon, Joseph, Greyhorse and Vigo. "You too."

He waited until the six of them had left his ready room through the sliding doors. Then he regarded Ben Zoma. "I know what you're thinking," he told his exec. "Tuvok seems like the type who works better on his own."

Ben Zoma dismissed the suggestion with a wave of his hand. "That may be so, Captain—but we don't know Tuvok the way we know Jack. We couldn't very well have sent him out there by himself."

Picard nodded and pulled his plate closer again. "I suppose not," he said. And as he sliced another piece of apple for himself, he focused on what lay ahead in the council chamber.

It was midafternoon on Cordra III.

Dar Shabik knew that his face would appear calm

and composed if anyone happened to glance in his direction. After all, he had spent many years learning to keep it that way.

Not a twitch of an antenna, nor a dilation of his faceted pupils betrayed him as he hurried through a sea of his fellow Cordracites, looking like any other worker heading home to his family after a long day in the capital city of Kiwanari.

This was the busiest hour. By law, every business shut down at the same time, though opening times were permitted to vary widely. The public transports were always crowded now. No one paid much attention to his fellow commuters. Everyone had one goal—getting home.

Except for Shabik.

He was dressed as the other workers were, in the long black mantlecoat that served a purely decorative function on bodies sealed and protected with a chitinous shell. And like many of the others, he was carrying a small collection of packages.

Many Cordracites purchased foodstuffs from the vendors who set up shop near the major business centers. This was especially true during the harvest season, when fresh fruits and vegetables were at their peak.

Of the three sacks in Shabik's arms, one was full of the delicious, juicy fruit of the jaami tree. The second contained an assortment of leafy green vegetables; he had been careful to allow their tops to peek out of the bag, allaying any suspicions that might have arisen.

The third bag was full of death.

At a corner he had chosen ahead of time, Shabik stopped and waited for the hover shuttle. There were seven other Cordracites in line ahead of him already, females as well as males, but he wasn't concerned about securing a place on the vehicle.

He had spent more than a week planning this, accumulating all the information he might need and then some. He knew how many seats were likely to be available on the shuttle this afternoon. He knew when it was likely to arrive at this corner—in another minute at the outside. He even knew the color of the driver's eyes.

His fellow commuters didn't need to be concerned with such things. However, Shabik did. Because, in truth, he wasn't one of them. His actions were dictated by an entirely different agenda.

Twenty seconds after he began waiting for the shuttle, it turned a nearby corner and headed his way. Forty seconds after he began waiting, it stopped and allowed additional passengers to board.

And as luck would have it, there was a seat available for each and every one of them.

Shabik sat down in one of them. Then he leaned back and went over what he had to do. It was simple, really. But then, even simple plans had the potential to go awry.

Less than a minute later, the shuttle began to slow as it approached its next stop. Shabik rose. As the vehicle lurched to a halt and the door opened, he made his way through the thick press of bodies.

In the process, he exaggerated the awkwardness of his packages. Unfortunately, he played his part too well and he got himself wedged between one of the other commuters and a vertical bar.

"Excuse me?" he said pointedly.

"Oh! Terribly sorry," the female apologized, turning her body so that Shabik could get by.

For an instant, their eyes met and he got a good look at her. She was lovely, her flesh a delicate shade of gray, her eyes as large and as yellow as their world's magnificent sun.

Pity, Shabik thought. But what he said was "Thank you."

As he made his way toward the door, the third package slid down his body and plopped onto the floor of the shuttle. He pretended not to notice, of course. As quickly as he could, he exited and disappeared into the crowd on the street.

But as the shuttle doors slid closed, he heard the female cry out. "Wait!" she said. "You dropped something!"

Shabik looked back again—and again, their eyes met. Silently, he cursed her. If her comment gave him away—

No, he assured himself. It won't. There won't be enough time. Turning and picking up his pace a little, but not too much, he buried himself more deeply in the safety of the milling throng.

Shabik didn't look back at the female or the shuttle, but the muscles beneath his shell were tight in anticipation. Come on, he thought. It should happen any—

Suddenly, there was an explosion.

Like everyone else, he stopped for a moment and watched the shuttle go up in a ball of wild, red flame. He allowed the heat of it to lick at his face like a lover. Then he drew a breath, put the cries of terror behind him and made his way to his private vehicle . . .

Mission accomplished.

Chapter Eight

"MELACRONAI BEASTS!" RASPED SAMMIS TARV. "Is there no depth to which you will not stoop in your madness?"

On the two-level podium, Picard winced at the Cordracite delegate's choice of words. They were not the sort he had hoped to hear at the Kellasian Congress's morning session.

A moment later, the insult was joined by others. It was several cycles before Cabrid Culunnh could get the room silent enough for everyone to understand exactly what had happened.

There had been another terrorist attack. This time it was a bomb, not a political assassination—and it was on Cordra III, not Melacron V. However, the captain reflected, it was essentially the same old story.

His hopes sagged as he scanned the chamber. All he saw were angry faces. Frightened faces. Under the circumstances, he supposed they had a right to feel that way.

Picard hoped that Crusher and Tuvok would find what they were looking for—and quickly. Otherwise, the Congress was in danger of deteriorating into a name-calling competition.

"Innocents!" another Cordracite voice grated. "Workers on an afternoon shuttle, going home to mates and offspring—"

Another voice trilled to meet it and clash with it. "And our G'aha was not innocent?" asked a Melacron. "He had no Companion? No children?"

"Order!" Cabrid Culunnh demanded.

But the accusations didn't stop. In fact, other voices rose up to support the first bunch.

Picard's jaw clenched. Out of the corner of his eye, he caught a glimpse of someone standing amid the chaos. It was Gerrid Thul, the Thallonian. And he was glaring at the captain, obviously as unhappy about this turn of events as Picard was.

"What is it?" asked Ben Zoma from the seat beside him.

The captain frowned. "It's time to see whether our alliance with Governor Thul is going to get us anywhere."

"Order!" the First Minister called out—again, to no avail.

Making sure the Thallonian was still paying attention to him, Picard jerked his head in the direction of Cabrid Culunnh. Thul's eyes narrowed. Then, as understanding seemed to set in, he nodded.

A moment later, the captain of the *Stargazer* left his seat and positioned himself beside the First Minister. At the same time, Thul advanced to the podium and ascended to the higher level, then placed himself on the Benniari's other side.

"Order!" Picard called out, speaking as one used to having his commands obeyed. "We will have order in this room!"

Something in his tone of voice pierced the chaos. The cries of outrage subsided. And before the turmoil could begin again, the Thallonian added his voice to the captain's.

"We have no proof that the Melacron were responsible for the bombing," he thundered, "any more than we have proof that it was a Cordracite who assassinated the G'aha!"

Like Picard, he had a way of getting people's attention. The captain gave Thul room to maneuver.

"We don't even know yet what kind of bomb it was!" he went on. "Are we nothing but frightened children, to leap to such conclusions? Or are we the bearers of wisdom our people trusted we would be when they dispatched us to this momentous congress?"

Picard suppressed a smile. He couldn't have put it better himself. In the wake of the Thallonian's remarks, Culunnh stepped forward. There was dignity in every line of his small body.

"This is our sector," the First Minister said quietly, but in a voice that carried throughout the chamber. "These are our planets. Our people. And yet, see who must remind us of our mission here—a Federation starship captain and a Thallonian governor. I, for one, am ashamed."

The assemblage had the grace to look embarrassed by Culunnh's words—embarrassed and repentant. For the first time that day, they gave the Benniari their undivided attention.

"See what fear and hatred have done to us," he said, "that only outsiders can see our problems clearly." He lifted his head. "Rest assured, reports will come in throughout the day. We will be able, I hope, to trace the origin of the bomb, and perhaps that will give us the answers we seek. In the meantime, let us conduct this congress like the civilized beings we are!"

Picard glanced at Thul. The governor nodded, obviously as relieved as the captain was that the congress had settled down.

Culunnh turned to the two of them. "Gentlemen, I thank you for your intervention. Please take your seats again. I trust I can call upon both of you to speak later in the session."

Picard nodded. "Of course."

"It would be my great pleasure," said Thul.

As the Thallonian left the podium for the time being, Picard returned to his seat as well. He saw that his first officer was impressed.

"Quite a performance," Ben Zoma whispered.

"For the governor too," the captain noted.

His first officer quirked a smile. "Actually, sir, it was the governor I was talking about."

Picard chuckled a little. Then he leaned back in his chair and watched the First Minister try to move the meeting forward. Even with order restored, it wasn't an easy task.

Find something, Jack, the captain urged silently. Find something before we run out of tricks.

Sitting cross-legged at the navigational controls of his new space vessel, Jack Crusher wished the Benniari were just a little bigger and a little more humanoid-shaped.

Not that he was complaining. It had been generous of the First Minister to lend them a ship in which to travel to Debennius VI. It would be a whole lot less noticeable than one of the *Stargazer*'s shuttles, and would therefore raise fewer questions.

However, because the Benniari were small and . . . well, differently shaped than either humans or Vulcans . . . some emergency retrofitting had been necessary. Actually, quite a bit of emergency retrofitting. For instance, while the Benniar ship—a compact vehicle by any standard—granted them enough room to stand up, the seats had needed to be completely removed for Tuvok and Crusher to access the controls.

The second officer had to laugh. "I feel a little silly," he confessed to the Vulcan.

Tuvok didn't even favor him with a glance. "We were able to make this ship serve our needs. There is nothing silly about that."

It seemed to Crusher that his companion spoke with a touch more severity than was required—a little extra dollop of dignity, as if he too were somewhat unsettled by the position he was forced to assume.

Methinks the Vulcan doth protest too much, the commander reflected. But in the end, of course, Tuvok was right. They had been able to make the ship work for them, and that was all that really mattered.

"We are now entering orbit around Debennius Six," said the ensign.

"The Last Stop to Nowhere," mused Crusher.

Tuvok frowned as he worked at his controls. "That is the sobriquet by which it is known, yes."

"And this is where we'll find Bin Nedrach," said the commander.

"That is indeed our hope," the Vulcan rejoined.

Fortunately for them, Nedrach hadn't bothered to cover his departure from Melacron V. With no criminal record to set him apart from the other passengers, he apparently hadn't believed it necessary to obtain a pseudonym or a set of falsified documents.

But then, Nedrach hadn't taken the estimable Ensign Tuvok into account. It helps to have someone with a ridiculously long memory on your side, Crusher told himself.

Because of the nature of this planet's "society"—or

lack thereof—there was no one to contact for permission to land. The commander was reminded of Earth's late nineteenth century, the "wild, lawless West," where a gun was all a man needed to get where he wanted to go.

The ease with which they found a place to land and hide their small craft, all within a few kilometers of a main city, was actually rather unsettling.

"Any disreputable type can sneak onto this planet," Crusher said.

"But then," Tuvok told him as they concealed their ship with loose foliage, "so can a team of Starfleet officers."

The commander looked at him. "In other words, I shouldn't look a gift horse in the mouth."

The Vulcan appeared perplexed—and maybe a little annoyed as well. "The reference escapes me," he said.

"What it means," Crusher explained, "is that you shouldn't question good luck. You should just run with it."

Tuvok sighed a little. "I see."

"Don't you have any colorful Vulcan expressions?" asked the human.

The ensign glanced at him. "No," he said flatly. And he dragged a few last branches full of leaves up against their vessel.

Crusher brushed off his hands. "Looks like we're done."

"Indeed," said Tuvok. He gestured. "The city is that way." And he began to walk toward it.

The human had no trouble catching up with him. "Impatient, aren't we?" he asked his companion.

Tuvok stopped and turned to him, obviously a little surprised. "Not really. I simply saw no reason to delay."

Crusher smiled at the ensign's expression. "My fault. You're absolutely right—there isn't." And as he started walking again, he reminded himself that he couldn't joke with the Vulcan as he might Joseph or Simenon—not even about the clothes they had to wear.

Gone were the tailored, maroon tunics that marked them as members of Starfleet. Also gone were the ribbed, white turtleneck pullovers they were used to wearing underneath.

Crusher was now clad in a multicolored vest and black trousers—both of them made of high-quality material and pleasant to the touch, marking him as a man of means. And the style, he had been assured, was the most up-to-date for the system.

Unfortunately, the boots were new and pinched him a little, and the voluminous red shirt he wore beneath the vest made him feel a bit like a pirate from Earth's turbulent fifteenth century. But on the bright side, the full sleeves of his shirt actually turned out to be a bonus; Crusher found they were handy for concealing pouches bulging with latinum, not to mention a small, handheld phaser.

Tuvok was clad in a tight-fitting jumpsuit of black and gray. His belt bristled with weapons, none of them Starfleet issue—but unlike Crusher, he made no attempt to hide them. The unforgiving cut of the garb accentuated his lean, powerful muscles, pointed ears and dark skin.

People would talk to Crusher—but they would be wary of his grim-looking companion. At least, that was the plan.

"Fascinating," said Tuvok as they came in sight of a low, dark building that seemed on the verge of falling apart.

"Fascinating?" the human echoed. For the life of him, he couldn't see what the ensign found intriguing about the place.

"Yes," said Tuvok. "Last time I visited this sector, this was a gaming establishment called The Den."

Crusher grunted. "Lovely."

The Vulcan spared him a glance. "At the time, Commander, it was a well-known meeting place for the members of the crime clan to which Bin Nedrach's grandfather belonged." He eyed the ramshackle structure again. "Although the Melacronai species is short-lived in comparison to my own, this edifice has changed little in more than fifty years."

"It *always* seemed to be on the verge of collapse?" Crusher wondered.

"Indeed," came the reply. "I must confess, I marvel that it has not completed the process."

"That makes two of us," said the commander. "Well, come on, Sulak. It looks like we've found our first stop."

Tuvok frowned at the use of his pseudonym. "Of course . . . Marcus."

As they approached The Den, Crusher took a deep breath. Relax, he thought. If there's trouble, you'll be able to handle it. That was what the phaser was for, though he wouldn't use it if he didn't have to.

Assuming an air of boldness, even arrogance, the commander pushed open the door. It was dark and musty inside The Den, and he had to pause for a moment to let his eyes become adjusted to the light. Then he went in. Naturally, his companion followed him.

Noise that was undoubtedly meant to be music assaulted Crusher's ears. Smoke from various burning substances attacked his nose, his eyes and his mouth. But instead of giving into an urge to choke on it, he forced himself to inhale deeply and fashion a grin.

The commander was glad of Tuvok's solid presence behind him as he made his way through the room. The place was a lot bigger than it had looked from the outside, he reflected.

"Dabo!" came a cry from some corner, followed by a chorus of groans and cheers. "All right, everyone," said the same voice, "double down, double down, let's get this game going!"

In another corner, a handful of Orion traders were playing a heated game of dom-jot, which was similar to Terran billiards. The Orions looked up at Crusher and the Vulcan as they passed by, their sparkling green eyes wary in their green-skinned faces.

Casting about for someone to speak with, the commander spied a gangly, beetle-browed humanoid standing behind a bar, busy pouring drinks for patrons and wiping away spills. The fact that he had four long arms made his task a bit easier.

There didn't seem to be anyone else in charge, so Crusher made his way through the crowd and slipped into a wobbly chair at the bar. He gave the bartender a dazzling smile.

"What'll it be?" asked the four-armed specimen, training a dark, protuberant pair of eyes on the human and Tuvok.

"Information," Crusher said. "I'm looking for a Melacron named Bin Nedrach. Seen him around lately?"

The dark eyes narrowed to slits and the alien paused for a moment, indicating to Crusher that he wasn't all that quick on the uptake. "Who wants to know?" the bartender rumbled warily.

"Someone who wishes to offer him employment," the Vulcan replied.

His clipped tone made the commander wince a little. "Lucrative employment," Crusher added quickly.

The bartender stared at Tuvok for a moment, his brow creased down the middle. Then he began to wheeze alarmingly. It took the commander a few seconds to realize that the alien was laughing.

"You want to employ Nedrach, do you?" he asked, exaggerating the words in a mocking tone of voice. "Well," and his voice dropped to an unfriendly growl, "you won't find Nedrach around here. Go find someone else."

Crusher didn't like the way the conversation was going. He had to do something about it, he told himself, or he and his Vulcan partner would soon find themselves stymied in their investigation.

Before the bartender could turn away from them, the commander reached up with a casual bravado he didn't feel and seized the grimy material of the alien's tunic front. Then he hauled the bartender's face down to within an inch of his own.

Silence fell all around him. By that, Crusher knew everyone present was taking in the scene. It was fine with him. In fact, it was exactly what he had been hoping for.

"I don't think you understand," Crusher growled, smiling a wolfish grin. "My friend Sulak here said we wanted Nedrach. We don't want anyone else." The human tugged harder on the bartender's shirtfront. "Only Nedrach will do. Maybe you understand that now?"

The alien was big enough and muscular enough to pound the commander to a bloody pulp. However, as Crusher had gambled, he was also too slow-witted to be sure of his chances in a fight.

Crusher held the bartender's gaze for just long enough before releasing him with an air of disdain. Then, flicking his wrist, he let a few pieces of latinum slip from his sleeve onto the wooden bar.

Staring into the alien's dark, angry popeyes, the commander repeated, "Do you understand now?"

The bartender's thick, hairy brow lowered at the sight of all that latinum gleaming on his bar. This much, at least, he clearly understood. He reached out a thick-fingered hand for the latinum, the slender slips of yellow-white metal looking tiny in his big mitt.

But before he could close his fingers about the latinum, Crusher deftly plucked them from his palm.

"Hey!" the bartender exclaimed indignantly.

"I don't give something for nothing, friend," the human told him.

For a moment, the alien looked as if he was about to vault over the bar and do some pulping after all. But Crusher stood his ground as if he weren't the least bit concerned about that possibility.

At last, the bartender jerked his massive head. "Back here," he said, lowering his voice so only the human and the Vulcan could hear him. "Too many eyes and ears out here, you know what I mean?"

Crusher knew what he meant, all right. It seemed that everyone in the Den was watching as they followed the alien's hulking figure to a tiny, smelly back room. The barkeeper opened the door, closed it behind the three of them, then glanced around carefully before speaking.

"Like I said," he grumbled at last, "Bin Nedrach doesn't come around this place anymore."

"Do you know where he *does* go?" the commander inquired.

The alien shook his head from side to side. "No idea."

Crusher glanced at Tuvok. The Vulcan shrugged. Turning back to the bartender, the commander said,

"In that case, I fail to see the purpose of this conversation—which means no more latinum."

Again, a reference to the precious metal seemed to work wonders with the alien's powers of concentration. "Wait!" he howled, holding up all four of his long-fingered hands. "I don't know where Nedrach is, but I can tell you who *would* know."

"And who's that?" asked Crusher.

"His rider," came the reply. "And *him* I know how to find."

The commander wasn't familiar with the term "rider," but it wasn't difficult to guess what it might mean. A steed or a mount, a beast of burden who did the work, needed someone to tell him where to go and what to do.

"And where can we find Nedrach's rider?" Crusher asked.

Languidly, keeping his eyes on the bartender's face, he again shook out the three slips of latinum—this time, into his palm. He ran his thumb over the shiny metal and waited for the alien to speak.

"There is a klaapish-klaapish'na house not far from here," said the bartender, his dark popeyes glued to the latinum. "The name of the place is The House of Comfort."

Jack kept his expression as neutral as possible. He wasn't sure what a klaapish-klaapish'na house was, but with the name The House of Comfort, he could make a pretty good guess.

Already, he was formulating his next message to Beverly: Hi, honey. Hope you and Wes are well. My most recent assignment took me undercover to an alien brothel. Hope you understand the sacrifices an officer has to make in the line of duty. . . .

"You'll want to find a Melacron named Pudris Barrh," said the bartender. "You tell him you know he's Nedrach's rider and he'll have to be the one to tell you yes or no."

Crusher nodded. He had gotten what he came for. With a flourish, he dropped two slips of the latinum into the alien's outstretched hand.

The barkeeper looked up with an angry expression on his face. "There were three on the counter," he snarled.

"Three to put me in touch with Nedrach," the human said, conscious of maintaining the hardnosed reputation he had established minutes earlier. "You didn't do that. You only told me how to find his rider."

The alien seemed about to object. Crusher smiled up at him. "Two slips of latinum—and keeping your pretty face from being rearranged. I'd call that good for a few moments' work." He bowed almost insultingly. "Thank you for your time. Nice place you run here."

Then, without another word, the commander opened the door and stepped back into the main gaming room. With a last glance at the sullen bartender, Ensign Tuvok followed.

"So far, so good," the human muttered.

The Vulcan didn't comment.

Some of the customers shot them bold, appraising

glances as they crossed the floor. But Crusher met each of the looks with equal boldness. Then he and Tuvok opened the front door and walked outside.

"Progress," the commander said triumphantly as they strode away from The Den. "Now we . . ."

He noticed that the Vulcan was giving him a look that could only be classified as a glare.

"What?" asked Crusher.

Tuvok didn't answer.

"Come on," said the commander, "you're obviously upset about something. What is it?"

"I am not upset," came the reply. "I am a Vulcan."

Crusher rolled his eyes. "All right, then. Let's just say you seem to disapprove of something."

Tuvok frowned at him. "I *do* disapprove."

"Well, why?"

"You took a clearly unnecessary risk with the bartender," the ensign explained with a hint of annoyance in his voice. "Your implied threat and your extravagant display of latinum accomplished nothing except to draw unwanted and perhaps dangerous attention to us."

The commander was stung by Tuvok's disapproval. "That's not true at all," he said. "It got us exactly what we wanted—information on how to get hold of Bin Nedrach."

"Perhaps," the Vulcan responded. "However, we could have obtained the same information in a far less public and confrontational fashion. Surely there were others here who knew of Nedrach and his rider. We could have approached them quietly. Subtly."

Crusher stifled an impulse to put a comradely arm around Tuvok's stiff shoulders. "That's a logical approach, all right," he admitted. "Damned logical. Just one problem—hardened criminals and the dregs of society seldom appreciate that kind of logic."

The Vulcan grunted scornfully.

"All they respect is force and power," the commander explained. "Back there, I let everyone know that I had both. I was willing to rough up the barkeep if I needed to, and I had the latinum in my sleeve to give the impression that I had connections."

Tuvok still didn't look convinced.

"People form impressions very quickly," said Crusher. "When you spoke to him politely, the bartender laughed at you. If we'd let him get away with that, don't you think every two-bit thug in the place would have treated us the same way?"

The Vulcan turned away.

"Nobody would have been willing to talk to us," the commander continued. "We would still have gotten noticed, but for an entirely different reason. Your way, we would have been objects of ridicule, pariahs. My way, they couldn't help thinking we were just like them." He paused. "Do you see what I'm talking about?"

Tuvok regarded him again, but refrained from speaking. Crusher's explanation had satisfied him enough, apparently, for him not to pursue the matter any further.

But the frown remained.

Chapter Nine

TRICIA CADWALLADER EYED the heaping plate of sturrd across the rec room table from her and tried not to grimace.

Vigo, who had brought the sturrd to the table, looked at her face and winced in sympathy. "Sorry, Cadwallader," he said in his deep, rich voice. "I forgot the effect that sturrd has on you."

The ensign dismissed the need for an apology with a wave of her hand. "It's what you eat, Lieutenant. I mean, you don't complain about watching me eat barbecued shrimp."

The weapons officer shrugged. "That's because I don't mind the sight of barbecued shrimp."

Cadwallader smiled at him. "But even if you did, you wouldn't say anything because it wouldn't be polite. That's why I'm not going to say anything about your sturrd . . . even if it does look like beach sand and ground glass with maple syrup thrown over it."

Vigo studied her for a moment. Then he got to his feet and picked up his plate. "I'm going to get something else," he told her.

"No!" said the ensign, drawing stares from her colleagues at other tables. "Don't you dare get rid of that. I want you to sit here and enjoy it." Suddenly, she remembered the difference in their ranks and blushed. "I mean . . . enjoy it, *sir.*"

The Pandrilite frowned as he considered his course of action. It must have seemed to him that he would trouble her no matter what he did.

"Please?" Cadwallader added.

With a sigh, Vigo put his plate of sturrd back on the table and sat down again. "If you insist," he told her.

"I do," the ensign confirmed.

For a while, the two of them sat and ate in silence, and Cadwallader managed not to listen too hard to the crunching sounds in her companion's mouth. Then Vigo spoke up again.

"Care for a game of sharash'di later?" he asked.

The ensign looked at him askance. "You know your problem, Lieutenant? You've beaten everyone on the ship so many times that no one wants to play with you—including me."

Vigo tapped his fork on a particularly hard piece of sturrd. "Commander Crusher plays with me every chance he gets."

"If I may say so," Cadwallader replied, "Commander Crusher sometimes finds it difficult to let go of something once he's sunk his teeth into it—which, I suppose, is one of the qualities that makes him a good officer."

The Pandrilite gave it some thought. "He does tend to hold onto a single sharash strategy too long, now that you mention it."

The ensign smiled. "There you go."

Vigo shook his head. "I wish I was out there with him."

Cadwallader could empathize. "Me, too," she said. "Sitting up here in orbit is the worst part of being in the fleet."

Actually, the worst part was watching the Pandrilite eat his lunch. However, she refrained from returning to that topic.

"It's not just that," Vigo told her. "It's that they're working undercover in a place they don't know very well. I'd feel a lot better if the captain had sent me to watch over them."

The ensign nodded. "We all would. However, big fellows like you tend to attract attention. Besides, Tuvok's a Vulcan. From what I've been given to understand, those people can take care of themselves."

The weapons officer smiled without much enthusiasm. "You're talking about that neck pinch they use?"

"That," said Cadwallader, "and other things. I'm just saying that Tuvok will be able to provide all the

120

muscle they need. And if it comes to that, Commander Crusher's no slouch either."

Vigo grunted. "I suppose you're right." He paused. "So there's no chance at all that you'll play a game? Not even one?"

The ensign shook her head. "I wouldn't be much competition, sir. I figure I'm beaten before I start. Look, why don't you find someone you *haven't* played yet? Someone who doesn't know how badly they're going to lose?"

The Pandrilite nodded his big, blue head. "Maybe you're right."

Just then, someone came to stand by their table. Looking up, Cadwallader saw that it was Gerda Asmund with a tray of food in her hands.

"Do you mind if I join you?" asked the tall, blond navigator.

"Not at all," said Vigo, his eyes narrowing craftily.

"Have a seat," the ensign told her.

Gerda put her tray down on the table and pulled out a chair. Then she glanced at her companions. "So," she asked with her usual blunt efficiency, "what are we talking about?"

The Pandrilite considered his words for a moment. Then he said, "Tell me, Lieutenant . . . have you ever played sharash'di?"

Picard sat back in his ready room chair and sipped appreciatively at his hot, steaming drink.

"What is the name of this delightful beverage?" Thul asked from the other side of the captain's desk.

"Earl Grey tea," Picard replied. "It is named after the man who crafted this particular recipe."

"Wonderful!" the Thallonian remarked. "When these talks are concluded, I must negotiate with you to bring a supply back to my Emperor. I am certain he would enjoy it as much as I do."

The captain smiled at his ally's enthusiasm. "Governor," he said, "if you and I can manage to conclude these negotiations without any blood being spilled, I will replicate and send you more tea than your entire Empire can consume in a year."

Gerrid Thul chuckled at that. Then he sat his cup down in his lap and regarded Picard with a sly smile.

"Despite the drama in which you and I find ourselves embroiled," he said, "I must say getting to know you has been an unexpectedly pleasant turn of events. We work well together, I think."

The captain returned the smile. The delicate, tart aroma of the bergamot in the tea teased his nostrils.

"I agree, Governor. Perhaps our teamwork on this matter will translate into something more momentous . . . say, a diplomatic relationship between your Empire and my Federation."

"Perhaps," Thul replied pessimistically, "but I would not place a very large wager on the possibility. My Empire is—shall we say—a good deal more insular than I am."

"That is a pity," Picard told him. "Still, I am pleased by the way the talks are going now. Did

you see the G'aha of Finance and the First Elected of Kiwanari Province actually laughing together?"

It was the first real sign of hope that the captain
had received since his arrival on Debennius II. It
is difficult, he mused, to sit down and share a
laugh with your enemy and fire upon him the next
day.

"The improvement is remarkable," the governor
agreed. "And it's your efforts that have made it so."

"*Our* efforts," Picard amended. "There are those in
the congress who couldn't care less about some distant Federation. But the Thallonian Empire . . . that
appears to be a different story."

Thul shrugged. "And in some cases, the reverse is
true. Perhaps we should say we have both contributed
and leave it at that."

The captain nodded. "I would agree to that."

For a moment, the two of them sipped their tea in
silence. Then the governor spoke up again. "You have
a fine ship here, Picard. I wouldn't mind seeing a bit
more of it."

The captain sighed. "And I wouldn't mind showing
it off. Unfortunately, Starfleet regulations prevent me
from doing that."

Thul's brow furrowed. "Regulations . . . ?" Then
understanding dawned. "I see. It is a security matter."

Picard nodded. "I'm afraid so."

The Thallonian dismissed the apology with a flip of
his hand. "It's probably a wise policy, now that you
mention it. You must have all sorts of visitors on your

vessel from time to time. You can't be expected to discern the honest from the dishonest."

"Then you take no offense?" the captain asked.

"None at all," his guest assured him. He reached into a vest pocket and removed a flat, latinum-plated chronometer. "But if there's no guided tour today," he said, consulting the device, "we should probably return to the planet's surface. It's impossible to tell how many brushfires may have begun in our absence."

"Done," Picard responded.

Taking a last sip from his tea cup, he got up and retrieved Thul's as well. Then he brought them both to the replicator.

"This way," he told the governor, indicating the exit.

"After you," Thul told him.

Together, the captain and his guest left his ready room and walked back to the *Stargazer*'s transporter facility. En route, Picard wondered how Crusher and Tuvok were doing.

He hoped they were all right—and that they were making some kind of progress in their quest for the truth.

Ulassi's heart pounded hard in her chitin-shelled chest.

The daughter of a high-ranking government official, she had been indulged and cosseted and sheltered all of her young life. However, she had never done anything even vaguely significant or lasting.

Though others envied her and she had taken a bit of pleasure in that, her station in life had always felt like a burden to her.

Now, at last, Ulassi was acting on her own. She was doing something she believed in, instead of something she was expected to do. It was a remarkably heady sensation.

She opened her mouth as she climbed, panting to release some of the body heat she had built up. Her body, slim and attractive but unused to such exertion, would ache the next day. She was sure of it.

But that was all right. In fact, the prospect was thrilling to her in a way. Until that moment, she had only used her physical form for her own selfish pleasure. The stiffness she would feel tomorrow would be a welcome reminder of the worthy work she had performed today.

Finally, muscles quivering from the strain, Ulassi reached a plateau. She sat there for a moment, trying to catch her breath, and surveyed the terrain below. The perspective was impressive to say the least, but Ulassi was in no mood to appreciate the natural beauty of the place.

Mountains, forests, the pure expanse of water that stretched out beyond them . . . what good was any of it when her people were enslaved? How could she find joy in the view when she knew the price her father and others had to pay for it?

Once, Cordra III had been independent, able to sustain its people with the bounty of its fields and its forests. Now, the once-proud Cordracites needed trade, negotiation, commerce. And with whom?

With Melacron V. The very thought was revolting to her.

Some Cordracites, Ulassi's well-born father among them, were still trying to bring about peace with the Melacron. They were trying to smooth over their considerable differences. But the notion made Ulassi's stomach roil like a giant grub worm.

Peace, she thought, with that ugly, violent, inferior race? How could anyone in their right mind even consider such a thing?

Spurred by the thought, Ulassi resumed her climb down the treacherous rock face. Halfway to her destination, her feet slipped and she gasped in fear. Stones tumbled beneath her, striking off the cliff walls as they fell and finally splashing in the water below.

She had almost been killed, she realized. She had almost lost her life in the pursuit of something noble. By the gods, she thought, this was exciting! This was living!

Trembling with fervor, trepidation and joy, Ulassi finally made her way to the rocky outcropping she had been aiming for all along. Only then did she stop to rest.

For a long moment, she gazed into the water just below her. She studied her gray, antennaed reflection, found renewed faith in the determination that was plain on her own golden-eyed face.

Armed with it, fortified with it, Ulassi closed her eyes for a long moment. Then slowly, almost reverently, she brought forth the vial of death that she had safely packed in her waist pouch.

Strange, she thought, holding it in the sunlight. It was so small a thing—just a few milliliters of liquid—and yet it would eventually bring about the deaths of thousands . . .

And in time, a great and terrible war.

Squatting, Ulassi opened the vial and poured its contents into the water. Only a few drops per thousand liters of water were necessary to achieve the desired goal. There was something sacred in the potency of the poison, she thought dreamily. Something wonderful and outrageous, like the judgment of a wronged, angry god.

For now, sadly, it was her own people, the Cordracites, who would have to perish. She was sorry about that, but there was little she could do about it. Sacrifices were needed if she was to bring about the changes that would save her planet as a whole.

And soon enough, Ulassi thought . . . soon enough it would be the disgusting, single-nostriled Melacron who would be dying. Then Cordra III would disentangle itself from the grip of Melacron V and stand, proud and whole and independent once more.

As the thick black poison dissolved into the city's water supply, she said a prayer . . . for herself, for her father, for all those whose deaths would bring about her world's liberation. She prayed that they would die quickly and without pain.

"Long live Cordra III!" Ulassi whispered aloud, tears filling her eyes at the righteousness of her cause.

Then, with a start, she realized what she had become. She was a hero now, wasn't she? A hero like Risaab of Golluk or the Sisters Noraddis or the Ten Warriors of Hitna'he. Someday schoolchildren would sing songs about her and old people would write her name in their graves.

The thought made Ulassi smile as she climbed back up the face of the cliff and started back to her father's domicile.

Chapter Ten

"WELL," SAID COMMANDER CRUSHER, mainly to break the uncomfortable silence into which he and Tuvok seemed to have fallen, "there she is, in all her bacchanalian glory."

"The House of Comfort," the Vulcan observed warily.

"The House of Comfort," the commander confirmed.

"It does not," said Tuvok, "look very comfortable."

For the briefest of seconds, Crusher wondered if the ensign had made a joke. Then he dismissed the notion. As usual, it seemed, Tuvok was simply being literal.

Viewed from outside, The House of Comfort looked every bit as dark, dilapidated and unappealing as The Den had looked—maybe even more so, though he wouldn't have thought that possible. The commander hoped that the interior would prove more attractive.

Like an actor assuming a role, Crusher set his jaw and again began looking at things as "Marcus" would. A Starfleet officer might feel uncomfortable about entering a house of prostitution, but Marcus wouldn't hesitate. Marcus, if he actually existed, would probably be comfortable in this sort of environment.

At the very least, he wouldn't have a wife and a small son back in Federation space, the thought of whom made him feel guilty. Putting the thought aside, the commander walked forward and flung open the door.

A wave of moist, warm air rushed out to meet him. It was saturated with a variety of alien scents—many of them surprisingly pleasant, some a good deal less so.

Crusher wondered at the high level of humidity in the place, but chalked it up to the idiosyncrasies of the patrons. The same for the soft, cloying music of unknown origin that seemed to waft its way around him. In any case, he had to admit that the ambiance was a welcome change from the rank, hostile environment of The Den.

"Welcome to The House of Comfort," said a soft, husky voice.

The human turned and saw where it had come from—an attractive female half a head taller than either himself or Tuvok, with a tight-fitting golden gown and skin as purple as the lush carpeting underfoot.

The proprietress? he wondered.

As she moved closer, Crusher got a better view of the golden eyes and thick, indigo hair, the high cheekbones and the full lips. The female lacked a proper nose and had a set of ears three times the size of a human's, but he didn't imagine she would have any problem getting someone to buy her a drink at a starbase lounge.

"Do you have a room reserved or is someone waiting for you?" she asked him and Tuvok.

The commander felt the betraying heat of a blush in his face. He hoped the woman would attribute it to the warmth of her establishment, or perhaps a flush of anticipation at the "comforts" to come.

He didn't speak immediately, wanting to make certain his voice was under control. And when he did speak, he chose his words carefully.

"We're here to meet someone," he said. "I was told that a Melacron named Pudris Barrh enjoyed visiting this establishment."

The alien smiled. "Oh, I see . . . you're one of Barrh's boys," she remarked with a knowing lilt.

Barrh's boys? Crusher asked himself. What did she mean by that? He experienced a moment of alarm but kept his composure.

"If you can get past Old Scowly there," the female continued, "you can join Barrh at his pleasures if you like." She raised a long, slender arm and pointed to a gilded door to her right.

Standing guard there was one of the biggest, ugliest, most dangerous-looking humanoids it had ever been the commander's misfortune to see. The moniker "Old Scowly" seemed more than appropriate. The fellow was three meters tall if he was a centimeter.

He only had two arms, but they were heavily muscled and covered with skin so callused that Crusher wondered if a phaser would do it any damage. Twin sets of horns, one at his temples and one protruding from a mouth crowded with yellow teeth, had been sharpened and decorated with carvings the commander had never seen before.

Small, porcine eyes glittered beneath an overhanging brow ridge as Old Scowly turned his oversized head in their direction. Large, round nostrils flared with a grunting sound.

The commander glanced at Tuvok, whose expression—naturally—had not changed an iota since they entered the establishment. Forcing a grin, Crusher swaggered over to Old Scowly and took the bull by the horns—figuratively speaking, of course.

The commander wondered how they would ever get past such a specimen. With an effort, he banished the thought. After all, failure was not one of their options. Inside that room, at his so-called "pleasures," was the man they needed to see—and see him they would.

"We're here to meet with Pudris Barrh," Crusher told Old Scowly.

The behemoth scowled, his lips writhing in a way

the human had never seen before. "I do not know you," he rumbled, his voice both exceptionally deep and exceptionally ominous.

Crusher continued to smile, undaunted. "But you *will* know me," he assured the alien. "You see, I'm here to conduct some mutually profitable business with your employer."

Expertly he flicked a slip of latinum down from his sleeve into his palm. He was getting pretty good at it, too.

"Extremely profitable," the commander emphasized.

Old Scowly's face twisted even more. Crusher would not have thought it possible, but there it was.

The enormous alien straightened to his full, imposing height. "I serve Barrh for reasons other than profit," he rumbled.

"Really," said the commander. He wondered what those reasons could be. Loyalty? Fear? Debt? Unable to figure it out, he shrugged and the latinum disappeared again up his sleeve.

"Whatever you say," he responded casually, "but I still think Barrh would be interested in seeing me."

The tiny eyes peered at him.

Ensign Tuvok was not pleased.

He had disapproved of his companion's flamboyant methods from the outset. The Vulcan had accepted the necessity of their charade in deference to Picard, but it seemed to him that Crusher drew far too much attention to himself and their mission.

Of course, the human was still a youth by the standards of Tuvok's people. No—less than a youth. An infant. And yet, in the eyes of Starfleet, Crusher was his commanding officer.

His *superior.*

Inwardly, Tuvok shivered. Humans, he thought.

He had been around them far too long in situations that were far too volatile. He longed for the crystalline stillness of Vulcan's deep meditation chambers, the tranquility of a walk in a sunwashed, crimson desert, the sense of balance and well-being that enveloped him when he sat down to harmonious meals with his family.

And yet, after so many years, something had pulled inexorably at Tuvok to rejoin Starfleet. Duty had struggled with duty, and no entity living could win such a battle.

He watched with a mounting sense of apprehension as the conversation between Crusher and the guard called Old Scowly unfolded. Clearly, he told himself, the commander's scheme was leading them into trouble.

Finally, Old Scowly agreed to approach his employer. With some difficulty, he slipped his hulking frame inside the gilded door—whereupon Crusher leaned closer to Tuvok and spoke quickly and quietly.

"I don't know for certain what kind of establishment this is," said the commander, "but I can make a pretty good guess."

"Unfortunately," the Vulcan whispered back with sincere and undisguised revulsion, "so can I."

"Still, we may have to go along with it." Crusher regarded Tuvok. "Would that . . . pose a problem?"

"Naturally," the Vulcan replied.

The commander grunted. "I was afraid you would say that."

"And knowing what I do of human marriage customs," said Tuvok, "I would imagine it would pose a problem for you as well."

Crusher looked lost. "Maybe we could just play along for some of it . . . for the sake of—"

"My master will scc you now," said Old Scowly. He had reappeared before the Vulcan knew it. "You may enter through the changing room, remove your clothes, and join Pudris Barrh at his pleasures."

Tuvok kept his disgust to himself. His companion maintained control over his expression as well, though the visible darkening of his cheeks seemed to betray him. The Vulcan hoped that Old Scowly was unfamiliar with the physical manifestations of human emotions or, as Crusher might be inclined to phrase it, "the jig" would be "up."

"Excellent," Crusher replied heartily. He turned to Tuvok. "Sulak, you'll accompany me."

"You will divest yourselves of your weapons as well, of course," growled Old Scowly.

The commander winked knowingly. "Of course."

The gilded door opened again and they went inside. As the door closed behind them, the Vulcan saw that they were in a dressing room of some sort—or more accurately, an *un*dressing room.

The walls were paneled with dark woods and there

were lockers made of the same material. The only other pieces of furniture in the room were a couple of long benches.

Crusher uttered an earthy human phrase with which Tuvok was not unacquainted. "What the hell do we do now?" he sighed.

The Vulcan didn't answer, of course. The question was clearly a rhetorical one.

Frowning, the commander sat down on one of the benches and began to remove his boots. He didn't look happy.

As it happened, Tuvok wasn't happy either. If he didn't know better, he would have said that the uncomfortable sensation in the pit of his stomach was apprehension. Of course, that was impossible. His control over his emotions was impeccable.

And yet, the sensation remained.

"There must be another way," said Crusher.

"There is no other way," the Vulcan told him. "This is the situation in which your plan has placed us." He knew his words sounded biting, but he didn't wish any of them back.

The human ran his hands through his thick, dark hair. "Damn it," he said, "if Beverly ever . . ."

"Finds out about this?" the ensign suggested.

Frowning, Crusher nodded. "But as you say, there's no other option open to us. I guess we'll just deal with whatever comes as best we can." He grunted. "The things we do for king and country."

Tuvok looked at him. "We do not pay homage to a king, nor does Starfleet ally itself with any provincial governments," he pointed out as he unstrapped his weapons belt.

Crusher darted an amused glance at him. "I'm glad you're along for the ride, Ensign."

This was not a ride, but a mission. Nonetheless, the Vulcan saw no point in correcting his companion at this juncture.

He remained silent while he and Crusher disrobed. It was not a particularly pleasant experience for Tuvok.

Vulcans, after all, were intensely private people and he was no exception. While it was illogical to be ashamed of the way one's body happened to have formed, neither was Tuvok in the habit of divesting himself of his clothing at the drop of an invitation.

He went through a quick mental exercise to quiet his unusually charged thoughts and reestablish calm. It helped, though not as much as the ensign would have liked.

When both he and Crusher had finished undressing, they glanced at each other's face—carefully avoiding the possibility of glancing elsewhere. The commander cleared his throat.

"Well," he said, "let's go." Then he crossed the room and opened the door in the far wall.

Steam rushed out and enveloped them, and for a moment Tuvok couldn't see. Then he made out some shapes in the warm mist and realized what he and Crusher could expect there. A wave of relief washed over him.

The House of Comfort was not a house of prostitution, the Vulcan told himself. It was a *bathhouse*.

The man he presumed was Pudris Barrh was loung-
ing in a steaming pool of what appeared to be green
slime. However, as the Melacron shifted his position
in the pool, it became obvious that it was merely
water that had been treated with something—Tuvok
couldn't be certain what.

When the air cleared for a moment—a byproduct
of their entrance—the Vulcan was able to get a better
look at their host. He was rather corpulent for a
Melacron, it seemed, and more pale-looking than
most.

As thick, sludgy ripples made their slow way out-
ward from Barrh's generous torso, he waved to
Tuvok and Crusher. "Please, gentlemen, join me.
We've not met yet, but there are few better places to
get to know someone than in The House of Comfort!"

Barrh threw back his head and laughed loudly at
his joke. The commander laughed as well.

"No weapons, of course," the Melacron told them,
wagging a chubby forefinger in their direction. "No
distractions of any kind. Just good fellowship, engaging conversation, and business."

"Of course," Crusher responded.

He and Tuvok exchanged a quick glance. Taking a
deep breath, the human walked up the carpeted stairs
and placed first one foot, then the other, into the hot,
liquid muck.

The ensign had little choice but to follow suit. He
assured himself, as he sank up to his chest in the
thick, surprisingly pleasant-smelling stuff, that there

was really no logical reason T'Pel ever had to become acquainted with this misadventure.

Besides, he reflected, there was quite a good chance that the majority of his and Crusher's actions would be classified. He had to confess that he found some comfort in the prospect.

"Now," said Barrh, surveying them with slitted eyes, "my associate says you have something profitable to offer me?"

"That's our hope," said the human. He let the liquid lap at his chin for a moment before continuing. "My name is Marcus. I'm told by someone who should know that you're the rider of one Bin Nedrach."

The Melacron rumbled deep in his throat. Casually, Tuvok lifted his arms out of the water and placed them on the back of the tub, just in case he had to reach for Barrh quickly.

"If you had come a few weeks ago," said the Melacron, "you would have been right. I am no longer the bastard's rider."

"Problem?" Crusher was almost cheerful.

"You could say that," Barrh replied with a note of bitterness in his voice. "We had a little . . . disagreement over a commission. I don't keep steeds I can't control, Marcus. Surely you understand that?"

Crusher nodded. "Naturally. Still, it's a pity."

"But he's not the only steed in my stable," their host continued. "I've several who will—"

The commander affected a look of disappointment and shook his head. "No, I'm afraid it's a special job. It's got to be Nedrach."

Barrh shifted his considerable bulk in the water. "Then you might as well enjoy the soak, friend Marcus. You're out of luck."

Crusher chuckled and fixed the Melacron with a look—alerting Tuvok that they were in for more of the same nonsense displayed at The Den. He felt the familiar sensation of disapproval stir within him. Humans were irksome, no question about it.

"No, I don't think we *are* out of luck," the commander told Barrh.

The Melacron looked at him. "What do you mean?"

Crusher shrugged. "Someone's got to be riding Nedrach. Who would let a steed of that caliber go unsaddled for long?" He leaned toward Barrh. "I'm willing to bet you can tell me who that someone is."

The Melacron laughed out loud at Crusher's brazen behavior. Tuvok thought of Old Scowly, standing just behind the gilded door, ready to burst in at a moment's notice. It would be bad enough for them to be shown the door, he reflected. To be shown the door without the benefit of their clothing would be even less acceptable.

"It is obvious to me, friend Marcus," said Barrh, and this time there was a distinct edge to his words, "you don't place much value on your life or the life of your friend, or you wouldn't be threatening a fellow who handles assassins for a living."

Crusher fell still for a moment. He smiled easily, but his eyes had gone quite hard and cold.

"It is obvious to me, friend Barrh," he replied, "that

you don't place too much value on your life either, or else you wouldn't be threatening a man with the wealth to hire assassins in Nedrach's price range . . . not to mention the precaution of a Vulcan bodyguard."

Tuvok was startled by the comment and the sudden hard look Barrh gave him, but he played along with the commander's charade. He tilted his head and cast a sidelong look at the Melacron. Let Barrh make of the gesture what he will, he thought.

The Melacron looked from the Vulcan to the human and back again, his eyes sharp and alert. Finally, he sighed.

"Bin Nedrach has caused me sufficient irritation," he said. "He's not worth ruining a good, hot soak over."

Crusher nodded. "That's the spirit."

"The fellow you want," Barrh continued, "is Bidrik Onaggh. He's a Benniari. He runs a dance hall on the other side of the city—just the thing to entertain a gentleman after spending some time at The House of Comfort."

"Onaggh is Nedrach's rider?" the commander inquired.

"No," said the Melacron. "But he speaks with him from time to time. He'll know more about Nedrach's whereabouts right now than anyone."

Tuvok was surprised to hear that a Benniari was involved with crime on this depressing planet. The Benniari were known for their culture and gentleness, after all.

Then again, he reminded himself, even a Vulcan occasionally forsook logic and turned to unsavory pursuits. Given that, Barrh's revelation wasn't necessarily all that surprising.

Crusher rose from the pool. Green slime clung to his body for a moment, then oozed off and plopped back into the clogged bath water. As he reached for a large towel on a nearby wall rack, he said, "Thanks, friend Barrh." Wrapping the towel around him, he turned around slowly to meet the Melacron's gaze. "Of course, if you've lied to us, we'll be back."

"Naturally," said Barrh.

The commander gave his host a perfunctory smile, tucked the loose end of the towel into the area around his waist, and nodded brusquely to Tuvok. However, the Vulcan hesitated for a fraction of a second before he followed Crusher out of the pool, and therefore saw what the human did not: a subtle change in their host's expression.

It had started out as affable as when they entered. But for a moment, it was clearly filled with scorn.

Making note of it, Tuvok rose, secured another towel and wrapped it about himself, then trailed Crusher out of the room. Before long, he found himself back in the dressing facility—and relieved to be there indeed.

To his dismay, the commander seemed inordinately pleased with himself. "We got what we came for," he crowed, discarding his towel and reaching for his clothing. "Now it's on to the dance hall."

"I wonder," the Vulcan replied stiffly. "You shamed our host—and he appears to be a proud man."

142

"I didn't *shame* him," Crusher responded, stepping into his trousers and belting them. "I just called his bluff. We talked business."

"On the contrary," Tuvok said, "it is my belief that we have made a powerful enemy in Pudris Barrh."

The commander frowned. "Look, I'm only doing what needs to be done. These people play rough."

The Vulcan raised an eyebrow. "That is precisely my concern."

Crusher began to pull on his boots. "Trust me, Tuvok—I know what I'm doing. Barrh and his colleagues treat each other like yesterday's garbage." He jerked a thumb at the door that led to the bath. "Look at how they refer to their employees. They call them steeds—as if they're fit for nothing more than getting them where they want to go."

"The reference did not escape me," said Tuvok.

"If we don't act as tough and dangerous as they are," the commander went on, "they won't show us any respect. If you want to worry about something, worry about that."

The Vulcan disagreed. He said so—to Crusher's surprise and chagrin, apparently. "You have put us in unnecessary danger," Tuvok observed. "When this assignment is completed, I will make note of that in my report. And I will add that you are motivated, at least in part, by the pleasure you take in acting out your role."

The human stared at him. "You think I enjoy this?"

"I do," the ensign replied honestly.

Crusher turned an angry shade of red. "That's fine,"

he said, glancing at the doors to make sure no one was eavesdropping on them. "You can think what you want. You can even report what you want. Just remember that while this mission is in progress, you follow my orders—no matter how many years you've got on me. Is that understood?"

Tuvok was inclined to retort, but he refrained from doing so. After all, the human was correct in his assessment of the Vulcan's responsibilities. Tuvok had voiced his objection—he could do no more.

"I will do as you say," he agreed at last.

That seemed to take the edge off Crusher's anger. Taking a breath, the human continued getting dressed. But now and then, he threw a searching look in the Vulcan's direction.

Crusher wished to be his friend, Tuvok noted. He had recognized that from the moment they met. The Vulcan had even acknowledged that he and the commander had something in common—families they cared for a great deal, though they were far away.

However, every move Crusher had made on this planet had irritated and alarmed Tuvok—and placed their mission in jeopardy. Mentally, the ensign began drafting his report.

He only hoped that he would live long enough to record it.

Chapter Eleven

Mendan Abbis was a happy man.

The Thallonian ale in his goblet was surprisingly good today. It had even been served at room temperature to bring out the tartness in it. Even his Indarrhi friend Wyl was in a pleasant mood, having had his fill of Mephylite pleasure pods.

But most importantly, thought Abbis, Melacronai and Cordracites were dying in obscene numbers, and no one had the slightest idea why. Everything was going just as he had planned.

Abbis had even learned to like Debennius VI, the irreplaceable "Last Stop to Nowhere." For the rest of his long and exceedingly powerful life, he would look upon these days and this place with great fondness.

Even The Den had its good points, he reflected as

he looked around. It was almost always dark and crowded, and people left one alone. It smelled a bit, of course, but what was that but a minor inconvenience?

"He's here," said Wyl in his high, nasal voice.

Abbis straightened a bit. The Indarrhi's empathic abilities might be rudimentary, but the Thallonian trusted him to be able to pick out a single Cordracite in a crowd. Wyl's silver eyes were fixed on the door, and by concentrating Abbis could make out the pale, insectoid form half-hidden by bodies and smoke.

Smothering a grin, the Thallonian waved down a waiter with a tray full of empty ceramic drinking vessels. "Another goblet!" he demanded.

A chipped specimen was plunked down on the dirty table in front of him. With great anticipation, Abbis uncorked a new bottle of Thallonian ale and poured to the goblet's brim. Then he poured some more for himself as well, spilling a little.

He chuckled at his clumsiness. No doubt, his reflexes were dulled a bit by the liquor and—

"You're an easy man to find," came the rasping voice of the Cordracite, his faceted eyes blinking at him.

Abbis glanced up at him. "I have no reason to hide . . ." *What was the name?* he asked silently.

He is called Shabik, Wyl supplied just as silently.

"No reason at all, my good friend Shabik. Sit down and join me in a celebratory cup!" Abbis demanded.

He tried to push the overfilled goblet of ale in the Cordracite's direction without spilling it. It wasn't a very successful maneuver. *Oh, well,* he thought. *I can afford another bottle or three.*

"Thanks, but I don't drink," said the Cordracite. He didn't make any move to sit down, either. He just stood there, blinking. "I'll take my money now, if it pleases you."

"It would please me if you would do me the honor of sitting at my table," said Abbis, his voice rising.

The Cordracite frowned at the remark. Still, he sat down on the crude bench opposite his employer.

"There," the Thallonian said approvingly, "that's better." He fumbled in his pocket and produced a pouch full of the agreed-upon sum in slips of latinum. "Your work was excellent, incidentally."

"Of course," said Shabik.

His tone was supercilious; it grated on Abbis's nerves. He watched as the Cordracite opened the pouch and counted the slips of latinum. Then he looked up at his employer.

"Will there be additional jobs?" he asked.

Abbis took a sip of his Thallonian ale. "Not at the moment," he said. Recalling something he'd just learned, he couldn't help chuckling. "Actually, you may be out of business soon."

Shabik blinked again. "What do you mean?"

Abbis shrugged. "I guess you haven't heard. The water supply of the capital city on Cordra Three was poisoned by a fanatic—and for free!" He laughed again, this time with greater vigor. "If this keeps up, it may be I won't have to part with latinum anymore!"

Shabik didn't look amused. His antennae bent forward, as rigid as lances. Leaving his ale untouched, he got up from his seat. "If you change your mind, let me know. If not, we've never met."

And he left without another word. For a moment, Mendan Abbis watched the assassin make his way through the crowd. Then he grunted, drained his goblet and reached for the one the Cordracite hadn't bothered to taste.

"It *is* remarkable," he told his companion. "Now even the victims have victims. Truly, war can't be far away."

Wyl narrowed his eyes as he smiled. "I am pleased for you," he remarked. "I hope you are pleased with yourself."

The Indarrhi had a habit of spouting cryptic phrases that meant nothing to Abbis. Was he pleased with himself? He sprawled in the chair, the alcohol warming him, and thought about it.

Yes, he decided, he was *very* pleased. He was pleased with Bin Nedrach, he was pleased with Shabik, and he was pleased with all the other professionals busily executing his orders.

He was doing the job he had set out to do. He had chosen his henchmen well. His timing had turned out to be impeccable. So what was there *not* to be pleased about?

Abbis drained the goblet that had been scorned by Shabik and filled his own again. His world was growing warmer and fuzzier around the edges when a big, ungainly-looking alien brushed against his table and knocked over one of his ale bottles.

An empty one, the Thallonian noted. But it didn't keep a spurt of anger from filling his throat. He was on his feet and his sword was in his hand even before he realized he'd drawn it.

"Oaf!" Abbis bellowed at the alien. "In your clumsiness, you knocked over an entire bottle of Thallonian ale!"

Though large, the alien clearly wasn't the belligerent sort. He shrank away from Abbis, lifting appendages that were not quite paws and not quite hands in front of his mottled, nearly shapeless face.

"Humblest apologies!" he wheezed. "The room is crowded, you see. I was jostled and I—"

The Thallonian felt his whole body thrumming with excitement. It had been too long since he'd had the pleasure of an all-out fight. Brandishing his blade like the expert he was, he rose and closed the distance between himself and the alien.

Abbis could smell his victim's terror. It was a heady perfume, and his drunkenness only seemed to magnify it.

"I did not see your table, I swear it!" the alien moaned. "Please, sir, allow me to repay you for your—"

"I'll say you're going to pay!" cried the Thallonian. In an instant, the naked tip of his sword was at the alien's soft, fleshy throat.

One quick push, he thought—ah, so easy—and The Den's manager would have a very large and bloody body to haul away. The alien closed his eyes and whimpered softly, no doubt seeing the same end for himself.

But before he could make his thrust, Abbis felt his anger begin to cool. And cool some more. There was no challenge for him here, he realized, nothing to be gained. Not even a little fun.

The alien's toppling of the bottle had obviously been an accident. And even if it weren't, the Thallonian told himself, the thing was empty. So what was the point of taking offense?

Abbis thought of his last conversation with his father, and what Thul had said about true valor. He thought of all the assassins who answered to him. He thought of war, only another incident or two away.

He had accomplished a great deal during his short stay on Debennius VI. There was no need for him to prove his manhood by taking the life of a fat, defenseless fool.

The Thallonian stuffed his sword back into his belt and looked down his nose at the alien. "Yes," he repeated, "you'll pay. Another bottle of The Den's best and we'll call it even."

The alien opened his eyes, saw that he was not going to die and exhaled a huge, trembling sigh of relief. "Yes, yes, of course," he breathed. "Thallonian ale, was it? Happy to do so, sir, happy, yes, happy!"

Abbis withdrew and lowered himself onto his bench again. The silence that had descended when he first unsheathed his sword began to fill in with sound. The buzz of conversation and the clicking of ceramic goblets resumed. Little by little, the erstwhile customers and staff of The Den turned their worthy attention elsewhere.

Wyl, however, was staring at him. It bothered Abbis.

"What are you looking at?" he asked his friend.

"You," came the reply.

The Thallonian snorted. "I might have guessed that. But why?"

"You have never walked away from a fight in all the years that I've known you," the Indarrhi observed.

Abbis scowled. "Is that a problem?"

Wyl smiled. "Quite the contrary, I would say. I see a bright future ahead of you, Mendan Abbis. After all, the only thing that ever really stood in your way was yourself."

Just then, the waitress came over with another bottle of ale. Without a word, she plunked it down on the table and left. The Thallonian looked around. Finally, he caught the eye of the big alien. Pointing to the bottle, he nodded. The alien seemed happy, yes, happy.

"A bright future indeed," said the Indarrhi.

The Thallonian shot him a look of disdain. "You're telling fortunes now? Stick to what you do best."

But Abbis's words belied the pride he felt. And his companion being what he was, he would know that.

Wyl leaned back in his chair. "Sometimes," he said, "predicting the future is not all that difficult."

Picard was sitting on the Council Chamber's podium in his usual spot, watching a Melacronai diplomat address the afternoon session, when Jetaal Jilokh entered the room with a look of anxiety on his furry, round face. The Benniari's ears were pressed flat against his head and his violet eyes were enormous.

By that, the captain of the *Stargazer* knew that the news was bad. Of course, he had no idea *how* bad.

Culunnh's aide trundled down the central aisle and ascended the podium. Then he approached the First Minister, who was seated against the wall opposite Picard, and whispered something into his tufted ear.

As he listened to the message, Culunnh's mouth opened and he seemed to shrink in size. He muttered something in return, but the captain couldn't make it out.

From his seat next to Picard, Ben Zoma leaned over and whispered a grim "This is not a good thing."

"I'm afraid you're right," the captain sighed.

The First Minister waited until the Melacron had finished, then took his spot at the lectern. "I have some distressing news from Cordra Three," he said, his voice solemn and hushed.

The chamber fell silent.

"I have just been informed that . . ." Culunnh swallowed. ". . . that more than two thousand Cordracites in the capital city of Mailoc have been poisoned by a contaminated water supply. Four hundred have already died. The city council suspects . . ." He winced. ". . . tampering."

Picard was already on his feet when the silence was shattered by long wails of grief and fury. Before it could get any worse, he joined the First Minister at the lectern.

"We do not know for certain that it was an act of

terrorism!" The captain had to bellow to be heard above the din. "We need to learn the results of the investigation first!"

He glanced down at Culunnh. The little Benniari looked broken. In his soft violet eyes Picard read the truth: the city council of Mailoc was not ready to officially announce that the reservoir had been deliberately poisoned, but everyone involved knew that was the case.

Suddenly Gerrid Thul was by the human's side, his towering presence a reassurance. "Captain Picard has the right of it," the Thallonian thundered. "Let us give the city council a chance to do their jobs."

There were cries of protest from the Cordracites and their allies. And to Picard's consternation, they were just as loud as before.

He conceded that the Cordracites had reason to be angry. Indeed, he would have been furious if he were in their place. But he couldn't allow that anger to sabotage the proceedings.

"We cannot act without reliable information," the captain said.

"Let us resume our talks tomorrow," Thul advised. "By then, we should have a better understanding of what took place."

"We have come so far," Picard told the delegates, appealing to their reason with a voice that rang through the chamber like a bell. "We have made so much progress here in the last few sessions. We must not let something like this undo the work we have done!"

For a long, tense second or two, he had a feeling that their pleas to wait, to be rational, would be ignored by the assemblage. The captain would not have been shocked if the delegates rose, picked up their chairs and hurled them at the podium with murderous intent.

But they didn't.

To Picard's surprise, the congress of diplomats—for that was what they surely were, in that moment—began nodding in agreement. Slowly but surely, the sentiment spread from one end of the chamber to the other.

Then Sammis Tarv rose to speak for the Cordracite delegation. "We will postpone any radical action until we have a better understanding of the tragedy," he announced gravely.

"Thank you," the captain said earnestly.

"A wise decision from a wise delegation," the Thallonian added with a hint of relief in his voice.

Unfortunately, it wouldn't take more than a day for the official report to come in from Cordra III. The captain didn't want to think about what would happen then.

He turned to face Thul. "Time is running out," he observed in a low voice, with unavoidable solemnity.

The governor didn't disagree.

Chapter Twelve

As Crusher and Tuvok approached the entrance to the dance hall, the commander was feeling pretty good about their chances of success.

It seemed to him they were a hair's breadth from locating Bin Nedrach. And once they did that, they would be able to get some idea as to who was behind the terrorist incidents.

Of course, Tuvok's criticisms back in the dressing room still rankled a little—not to mention his threat of filing a report. It was too bad, Crusher thought. At the outset, he had liked the Vulcan and valued his opinions. But now he saw that Tuvok was more of a hindrance than a help.

After all, what did someone of the Vulcan's background know about bluff and bluster, or what motivated scum like Barrh? When had one of Tuvok's people ever won a hand of five-card draw?

Crusher glanced at the Vulcan, but Tuvok didn't glance back. He seemed to be in a world of his own.

Now that the commander thought about it, it had probably been a mistake to have the Vulcan accompany him in the first place. In fact, any of the *Stargazer*'s command officers would have been better suited than Tuvok to achieving their objective—even if the ensign *did* have some experience in this star system.

Like The Den and The House of Comfort, the dance hall looked slovenly and run down from the outside. Even the wooden sign by the door was so weathered as to be illegible.

With all the money that seemed to be floating around Debennius VI, the commander wondered that the owners of these establishments were so willing to let their places look dilapidated. Then again, for all he knew, it might be a sign of status, some kind of peculiar Benniar ranking system. Perhaps the more wealth you had, the worse you let your place appear—an indication that you didn't have to go to the trouble of courting any new customers.

Or maybe the people who owned these places just didn't give a damn. That was a possibility as well.

Before Crusher or Tuvok could open the door to the dance hall, it opened for them and a gangly Shaidanian pushed his way out. All four of his eyes looked bleary and red-rimmed with too much alcohol, including the two on the long, slender stalks protruding from his forehead.

Music, slow and sultry and played by someone who knew what he was doing, floated out of the place. The commander was more than a little surprised. Maybe the floor show would be of the same quality, he mused, though he certainly wasn't counting on it.

He and Tuvok walked inside, allowing the door to slam shut behind them. The dance hall was dark and crowded and filled with alien smells—in many respects, a first cousin to The Den.

On the rounded center stage, however, illuminated by brightly colored lights, a lithe Orion slave girl danced. And contrary to Crusher's expectations, her performance was a compelling one indeed.

The slave girl's long, lean muscles rippled smoothly under her green skin, which changed color as she moved in and out of the lights. Her cascade of black hair seemed to coil and uncoil as if it had a life of its own, and the smoke swirling about the place caressed her body as she moved in time to the slow, sensuous pipe music.

Breathtaking, the commander thought. It was almost impossible for him to take his eyes off her. But then, she had been bred from birth to achieve just such an effect.

At one point, the slave girl bent her knees and, arms undulating, bent backward so far that her hair swept the floor. As she writhed, beads of perspiration glistening on her skin, she arched her belly upward and flexed her abdominals with uncanny control.

Abruptly, her bright green eyes fixed on Crusher,

sending a jolt of electricity up and down his spine. No, he thought, she can't be looking at me. Not with all the lights blinding her.

And yet, the slave girl's gaze seemed to linger. Well, the commander mused, maybe she can see *despite* all the lights. But why was the Orion looking at Crusher in particular? Or was it just part of the show for her to meet a customer's gaze now and then?

The latter, no doubt. Still, part of the commander wanted desperately for it to be otherwise.

Suddenly, the slave girl broke eye contact and turned her attention elsewhere—to another patron, he imagined. Crusher felt vacant, oddly disappointed. Then she returned to an upright position again and moved away, disappointing him even more.

Breathtaking, he thought again.

"Commander," said a familiar voice.

Crusher turned and saw Tuvok standing next to him. Somehow, he had managed to forget that the Vulcan was there.

"Let's find someone in charge," Crusher said, shaking off the effects of the slave girl as best he could.

He looked about for someone who might have some authority. As in The Den, no one popped out at him, so he went to the bar. The Vulcan followed dutifully, as always. Seating themselves, they ordered drinks.

As he partook of his beverage, the commander scanned the crowd. His eyes fell on a tall, sallow individual with an elongated head and a narrow thread of dark fur that ran from his crown down the back of his neck. Crusher wasn't familiar with the species, but the being appeared to move through the throng with confidence, greeting several people and occasionally leaning over to whisper in someone's ear.

This individual might or might not have been in charge of the place, the human acknowledged. However, it was a good bet that he could steer them where they wanted to go.

Crusher pointed out the alien to Tuvok. "Let's go," he said, starting in the requisite direction.

The Vulcan didn't seem particularly enthused, but he didn't lodge any complaints either. He simply got off his seat and followed the commander through the crowd.

When Crusher reached the being with the elongated head, he tapped him lightly on the shoulder. The alien turned gracefully, fastening small, emerald-green eyes on him.

"You are not regular patrons here," he observed in a high-pitched whistle of a voice.

The commander smiled affably. "No," he conceded, "we're not. But from what we've seen," and he indicated the Orion on the stage with a tilt of his head, "we'll be sure to come back some time. At the moment, however, my friend and I are here on business."

"Oh?" said the alien.

"That's right," Crusher told him. "I'm looking for a Benniari named Bidrik Onaggh. I believe this is his—"

The commander felt the threat of moving bodies before he actually turned and saw them emerge from the shadows. There were six or seven of them, he counted at a glance, all big and dangerous-looking. Lousy odds at best, he told himself.

It was obvious now to Crusher that their arrival had been expected. It was also obvious that this reception had nothing to do with sharing mutually beneficial information about steeds and riders. It had to do with the way he had treated Pudris Barrh.

Tuvok had been right, it seemed. The commander had made a mistake. He only hoped it wasn't too late to make up for it.

Making eye contact with the Vulcan, he shook his phaser pistol out of its hiding place in his voluminous sleeve. It fell with easy convenience into his waiting palm.

Unfortunately, Crusher didn't get a chance to fire it. The big blue hand of a Pandrilite clamped down suddenly on his wrist, its thick, blue fingers squeezing his bones like a metal vise. Groaning in pain, the human dropped the energy weapon.

But as he did so he also launched a kick at his captor's knee. It must have struck with considerable force, because the Pandrilite screamed and let go of Crusher's wrist.

Grunts, curses and the sound of bone striking bone told him that Tuvok was fighting hand-to-hand beside him. The commander saw at least two bodies hit the floor in quick succession—one a Melacron and the other someone from the same species as Old Scowly. Clearly, Crusher reflected, the Vulcan nerve pinch had been employed with at least some success.

But he didn't take the time to think anything more. Not when his phaser was lying on the floor, still up for grabs.

Diving for it, the commander reached out and closed his fingers around its barrel. Then he flipped over onto his back and began firing. In this press of bodies, he reasoned, he was bound to hit someone. He did. Twice, in fact.

But before he could hit a third adversary, an exceedingly ugly Banyanan sprang on him with a yell. Crusher tried to spear his adversary with a phaser beam, but the alien was too quick for him.

Knocking the commander's weapon hand aside, the Banyanan raised a dagger that was as unsightly as he was. For an instant, Crusher could almost feel the pain of the serrated blade penetrating his unprotected throat.

But remembering his training, he shot the heel of his hand into the alien's angular chin, making the Banyanan's head rock back. And before he could recover, the human had wrested control of the knife.

The alien grunted in surprise, unsure of what to do next—giving Crusher all the opportunity he needed. Clenching his jaw, he drove the dagger into the side of the Banyanan's neck.

As the alien clutched at his wound, trying to draw the bloody dagger out, the commander pushed him away and made an attempt to get to his feet. Halfway there, something hit him.

Hard.

Peering up from the bottom of a deep, red well,

where the sounds of battle seemed much too far away, Crusher tried to make out his adversary. A being who could have been Old Scowly's twin hauled him upward, nearly yanking the human's arm out of its socket in the process.

For a moment, he stood there, his knees too weak to support him for long, and attempted to fire his phaser—only to realize that he had managed to lose it again. Bad, Crusher thought. Very bad.

Then he saw the alien's mammoth fist come at him in what seemed strangely like slow motion. He watched, fascinated, as it made inexorable progress in the direction of his face.

Very bad, the commander repeated inwardly, bracing himself for the inevitable, devastating impact.

Lir Kirnis was bored.

A master scientist, she was the head of a small band of Melacron who had dared to leave the worlds of their home system to explore the frontiers of science—which was little more than a fancy way of saying they were stuck out here on a distant rock, far away from friends and kin, and had been for a long, long time.

Sitting in her lab above the colony's enclosed, hundred-meter-long main thoroughfare, Kirnis could see the comings and goings of her colleagues and their families. Somehow, they always seemed happier than she was.

But then, her colleagues had been wiser than she, bringing along their Companions and their childen for company. Lir had always been Companioned to her work, not to another living being.

Back on Melacron V, that had been enough to sustain her. But here at this lonely outpost surrounded by a forbidding landscape and volatile weather, there were no fields through which she could stroll while puzzling out a problem. There were no restaurants with good food and wine to satisfy her physical needs, no entertainments to divert her mind.

Nothing but dark, barren mountains and her fellow scientists and the microscopic organisms that continued to elude her scrutiny.

Kirnis heaved a sigh. The creatures had been such a lure at first, such an irresistible temptation. The G'aha of Medicine had approached her with the first findings, taken from an unmanned Melacronai probe. The tiny life forms embedded deep within the rocks boasted a gene sequence that no scientist had ever observed.

Preliminary tests indicated that there might be a way to turn these microscopic entities into instruments of medicine in much the same way that, some three hundred and fifty years earlier, her people had been able to turn common bacteria into cures for a variety of diseases.

The whole prospect was wonderfully exciting. And of all the master scientists at work on Melacron V, Kirnis had been asked to head the expedition.

That was four years ago, she reflected. Four long, frustrating years. Where in the gods' names had the time gone?

Sighing again, Kirnis called up the latest report and watched it appear on her monitor screen. The log indicated that sample 857230-KRA, obtained from the heart of the volcanic range located at forty-two point four degrees latitude and thirty-seven point zero degrees longitude, had been just as disappointing as all the other samples taken before it.

It simply refused to survive in laboratory conditions. How could one study a microscopic organism if it refused to live any longer than a day—and for no reason anyone could discern?

Four years here, she thought, and all their efforts had been in vain. It wasn't a record Kirnis was proud of, especially in light of the high expectations that had accompanied her voyage here.

She glanced over at her bright green-and-scarlet scarf, folded reverently, awaiting her. At least Inseeing would begin at sunset tomorrow; she could console herself with that. It was her favorite holiday.

Normally, a Melacron purchased a new scarf every year and wore it only for the period of Inseeing. Then it was burned in accordance with the ancient sacraments. She and her team, however, had already been stuck at their outpost two years longer than they had planned. As a result, they had been unable to purchase new scarves.

Tradition held that it was bad luck to preserve the scarves and not burn them. But Kirnis had always held a sneaking suspicion that "tradition" had been started by scarf-makers. Besides, she couldn't bear the prospect of having no scarf at—

Behind her, the colony's advance warning monitor began to beep. Apparently, she told herself, the sensor mechanisms orbiting the outpost had detected the approach of something.

Adrenaline flooded Kirnis. She hadn't expected a Melacronai vessel to show up for several months yet. Whirling, she checked the monitor. Then her eyes went wide as she read the information couched there—the impossible, heartstopping and yet undeniable information.

Status: vessel approaching. Bearing: two six four mark two. Vessel type: Cordracite warship third class, weapons systems armed.

"No," she breathed. Of course there had been a history of bad blood between the Melacron and the Cordracites, but that was no reason for an armed warship to bear down on an isolated outpost.

"There's nothing here," she complained, though none of her colleagues was in the room to hear her.

Gritting her teeth against panic, Kirnis flipped a switch on her communications console. Abruptly, the image of the approaching vessel appeared on her screen. It was indeed a Cordracite warship, bristling with weapons ports and full of terrible purpose.

She would contact them, she decided. She would convince them that they were making a mistake.

"Master Scientist Lir Kirnis to Cordracite vessel," she said in a voice that shook. "This is a Melacronai research outpost populated only with scientists and their families. Repeat, this outpost is populated only with scientists and their families. The results of our research are available to all. There is no need for an attack." She swallowed in a painfuly dry throat. "Please respond and we will discuss the situation further."

Then Kirnis punched a brightly lit button on the console and waited for the Cordracites' answer. To her horror, none came.

Trembling, her two hearts thumping, she repeated the message, adding, "We have no weapons here, no tactical systems. Ours is a purely scientific venture. Please respond, Cordracite vessel. Your orders to attack this facility must be in error."

There was silence across the vastness of cold space. Nor did the ship turn away. It continued to bear down on them.

Kirnis glanced at the main thoroughfare, where her colleagues and their families continued to make their way from place to place. Clearly, they were oblivious of the danger facing them.

She wondered if she should tell them what was about to happen. She wondered if she would want to know, if their positions were reversed—and decided not to say anything.

If these were their last moments, as seemed increasingly likely, why tear them apart with fear? Why not let the Melacron there go on as though nothing were wrong, enjoying each other to their last breath?

Kirnis turned to the monitor again. Numbly, disbelievingly, she watched the vessel's weapons stations flash a bright green—and being a scientist, knew what that meant.

"This can't be happening!" she shrieked into the console's communications grid. "Hold your fire! Cordracite vessel, you've made a mistake! There are no weapons here, nothing of value." She felt her stomach muscles clench. "There are children . . . children, damn it! Come down and see for your—"

Then it was too late to protest, too late for anything, because the sky was ablaze with a hideous emerald fire. The last thought that went through Kirnis's mind was, absurdly, that not burning her Inseeing scarf for two years in a row had brought her very bad luck indeed.

Chapter Thirteen

"THIS CAN'T BE HAPPENING!" Lir Kirnis screamed. "Hold your fire! Cordracite vessel, you've made a mistake! There are no weapons here, nothing of value." She licked her lips. "There are children . . . children, damn it! Come down and see for your—"

Jean-Luc Picard watched in horrified silence— along with the rest of the Kellasian Congress—as Melacronai Master Scientist Lir Kirnis frantically tried to dissuade the attack that ultimately destroyed her.

Kirnis stared up at something, her eyes wide, her face bathed in a sickly green light. Her mouth moved, but it didn't produce any words. Then the image on his screen went blank.

The captain's teeth ground together. After all, he

had seen the terror in Kirnis's expression. He had seen the damning sensor data downloaded from the colony computers, which somehow survived the attack. And he had seen the list of those who had perished.

As Kirnis had indicated, there had indeed been children at the outpost—a great many of them, it seemed. And they had all fallen victim to the Cordracite war vessel.

"There can be no error!" shrilled the Melacronai G'aha of Finance, his eyes wide with fury. "On the eve of our most sacred and holy time, the Cordracite monsters appear like demons out of legend to massacre the young, the helpless and the innocent!"

"No!" countered Sammis Tarv, on his feet now, his antennae bent forward with indignation. "This is not just an error—it is a cold, calculated attempt by the Melacronai government to blame the Cordracites for their tragedy! These—these *creatures* murdered their own scientists and made it look as if we did it!"

"We would kill our own?" The G'aha was stunned by the accusation. "And we would do this on the eve of Inseeing? Trust a Cordracite to think of something so irrational . . . so abominable!"

"Trust a Melacron to *do* something so abominable!" came a rasping reply from one of the Cordracites.

And then it happened. The assemblage's carefully built foundation of diplomacy and reason shattered like fine crystal under the impact of a level-ten phaser barrage. The Cordracite Elected One charged the

Melacronai G'aha, his jaw pincers extending from his mouth as he hissed the ancient blood cry of his people. Just as eager for a confrontation, the G'aha bellowed and met the Elected One halfway.

Picard couldn't allow it. Leaping down from the podium with Ben Zoma on his heels, he made a beeline for the combatants.

As it turned out, Gerrid Thul reached them first. He threw his body between them and struggled to keep the delegates from killing each other—no easy task. Fortunately, others arrived to help, the captain and his first officer among them.

The Cordracite was the more formidable of the delegates. His pincers and his clawlike fingers tore clothing and flesh alike.

"Peace! Peace in these halls, I beg you!"

Cabrid Culunnh's voice was shrill with grief—over the murders of innocents, over the violence displayed in a hall meant to nurture peace, over the looming specter of war and even more death. He hastened down from the stage, his small, round face expressing his apprehension as eloquently as any words he might utter.

"The First Minister is right!" said Picard, raising his voice to be heard over the uproar. "These halls are meant for dialogue, not defamation . . . debate, not indictment!'

The combatants glowered at each other, their chests heaving and their faces flushed with emotion. But it seemed that, for the moment at least, the fight had gone out of them.

"You are right, Captain Picard," said Sammis Tarv.

There was blood on the front of his tunic—though the captain couldn't tell whose it was. "This chamber is for discourse. It is not for combat."

Then, before anyone could stop him or even guesss what he was about to do, the Cordracite darted forward and slashed the G'aha's face with his hand. And as quickly as he had attacked, he stepped back.

"That is an informal declaration of hostility," Tarv spat at the Melacron. "Rest assured that a formal declaration will be dispatched from my government in due time."

"Cordracite excrement!" howled the G'aha, clapping his hand to his wound. His eyes were enormous with anger. "And to think I once believed that peace with your people would be a worthwhile goal. The Sakari area of space is ours—and if we have to take thousands of your worthless lives to claim it, then so be it!"

The Cordracite made a rasping sound in his throat. "You took the words out of my mouth," he said.

Picard shook his head. His worst fear had come to pass. Despite his best efforts, it seemed, there would be war.

There was no more fighting after that. The two delegations simply turned away from each other and marched out of the hall. The other species represented in the council chamber muttered and exchanged glances, no doubt mulling their options.

Some seemed to stream after the Melacron. Others appeared to follow the Cordracites. Before long, none of the delegates remained.

Only a few lost souls still stood there in the mammoth chamber, looking shellshocked and perplexed: Picard, Ben Zoma, Gerrid Thul, Cabrid Culunnh, and a few of his Benniari attendants. The place seemed to ring with ghostly cries and threats even after those who had uttered them were gone.

"It will destroy us," Culunnh said softly.

Picard didn't have the wherewithal to argue with the Benniari, though he wished it were otherwise.

"At first," the First Minister went on, "it will only be a conflict between the Melacron and the Cordracites. But one by one, the other species in the sector will choose sides."

"Perhaps . . ." Jilokh began.

Culunnh held up a hand. "No . . . don't hold out false hope, Jilokh." He eyed the captain, Ben Zoma and then Thul. "You have all seen the beginning of it today. Caught in the middle, as always, the Benniari will be the victims." He shook his head. "We have failed. I am ashamed."

"You did everything you could," Picard assured him. "You kept both sides talking far longer than anyone had any right to expect. I would not consider that a failure."

"It does not matter what went before," said Culunnh. "The Cordracites and the Melacron have left with the heat of war in their hearts."

"Which may yet cool," the Thallonian put in.

The First Minister smiled wanly at him. "I did not know Thallonians were such optimists."

"Not optimists, no," Thul conceded. "But the first

virtue among my people is courage, my friend. And that means more than how well you conduct yourself in a fight."

"Once the first official attack begins," said Culunnh, "courage will be needed by all of us. I pray that we find it."

Picard sighed. He had hoped to make an optimistic report to Starfleet Command. He had hoped there would be some good news. It didn't appear that that was a possibility anymore.

Commander Jack Crusher had once had a headache more painful than this one. But only once.

He was young back then, only twenty-two, attending a bachelor party for a fellow cadet. There were women and dancing and loud music, and some remarkably smooth Romulan ale that had been smuggled to Earth somehow.

Crusher had drunk too much and danced too much and his friends had tried to convince him that he had done other things as well. Unfortunately, he didn't remember any of them. What he did remember, and would never forget, was the exquisite torture of a hangover that had all the force of a Klingon disruptor barrage behind it.

This headache was a close second.

He tried to push himself up into a sitting position, and it was only then that he realized his hands had been tied behind his back. He winced as pain awakened unexpectedly in his face.

His nose hurt worst of all. It felt flattened so badly

he probably could have given Old Scowly a run for his money in the ugly department. Then again, he doubted it was anything Greyhorse couldn't fix in his sickbay.

Unfortunately, the commander wasn't *in* Greyhorse's sickbay. He looked around the room he *was* in, trying to ignore the bruises and the dried blood and the stiffness in his limbs. The place was small, cold and dingy, he observed. There were no windows and only a single door.

A silhouette beside him, dark against the greater darkness, had to be Tuvok. His face was turned away, so Crusher couldn't gauge the extent of the Vulcan's injuries. But from what he could tell, Tuvok was breathing all right, and that was the most important thing.

Abruptly, the human heard a ripple of voices from outside, though he was unable to make out the words, and a harsh, quick burst of nasty laughter. It was probably at his expense, he told himself.

Crusher cursed softly. He supposed he deserved some abuse. Though it was too late to do anything about it, he remembered the strange look the Orion dancer had given him. He had flattered himself into thinking she was just appreciative of his boyish good looks. He realized now that it had been the woman's way of warning him about the impending trap.

"You are awake," came Tuvok's voice, remarkably crisp despite the beating he had taken.

The commander glanced at the Vulcan, who had turned to face him. His features too were swollen and caked with dried blood, but the dark brown eyes were as implacable as ever.

"I wish I wasn't," Crusher told him. "And how did you wind up? No serious injuries, I trust?"

"Nothing life-threatening," Tuvok reported disdainfully.

"Me either," said the commander, though he was well aware that the Vulcan hadn't asked. "I don't suppose you've used your remarkable powers of observation to find a way out of here?"

"There *is* no way out except through the door," Tuvok informed him coolly and efficiently. "It is undoubtedly locked and there appear to be two guards. Escape will be difficult if not impossible . . . unless, of course, an opportunity presents itself."

He didn't sound hopeful that it would.

Crusher flexed his fingers. They were all but numb and the attempt at movement set sharp pains rushing through their joints. Despite them, he tried to twist his wrists and loosen his bonds, but the knots held.

"We'd better start working on that unexpected opportunity," he said.

His companion cast him a withering look. "There would be no need to depend on the unexpected if you had taken my advice to heart."

The commander didn't like the tone of Tuvok's voice. "I'd say that's water under the bridge, wouldn't you?"

"You humans have a saying," the ensign noted. "Those who do not learn from history are doomed to repeat it."

Crusher felt a surge of resentment. "In other words," he said, "you'd rather look back than ahead."

Tuvok's eyes narrowed. "In other words," he responded coldly, "one cannot look ahead with confidence until he has gained an understanding of what came before. In the current instance, for example, I warned you that you were taking unnecessary risks. However, you chose to ignore me. You decided to intimidate Pudris Barrh in his home territory."

The human frowned. He had to admit that it wasn't the best idea he'd ever had—but only to himself.

"Had you exercised restraint," the Vulcan went on, "he would not have arranged to have us beaten and bound." He sighed. "You are careless, Commander Crusher—careless with your life, with your mission and with the subordinate officer under your command, not to mention the requirements of your wife and your young child . . ."

The mention of Beverly and Wesley caught Crusher off guard. "My wife and child . . . ?" he echoed.

"When you exchanged vows with your mate," Tuvok explained, "you made a commitment. When you impregnated her, you made a commitment to your son. By pursuing an illogical, reckless course of behavior, you have violated both of those commitments."

The commander made a face. "Now wait just a—"

But the Vulcan forged on, undeterred. "If you die here," he said, "your spouse will no doubt grieve your loss. However, she is a mature adult; she will recover from the experience. Your child, on the other hand, may not. Humanoid offspring require input from both parents to achieve their full potential. Your actions here have all but ensured that your son will be deprived of your input."

Crusher was getting more annoyed by the minute. "We're not dead yet," he reminded Tuvok. "And don't accuse me of not caring about my wife and son, all right? They're the most important people in the universe to me."

"One would not know it from your actions," the Vulcan insisted.

The commander's jaw clenched. "Listen to me, dammit. I'm a Starfleet officer. So's my wife. And for that matter, so are you."

He glanced at the door. He had to be mindful of the guards outside it, despite the wave of emotion he could feel crashing over him.

"When we accepted our commissions," Crusher went on, "we accepted everything that goes along with them—the bad as well as the good. As a Starfleet captain said a long time ago, risk is our business."

There was a flicker of recognition in Tuvok's eyes. Obviously, he too had heard the reference.

"Now," said the commander, forcing himself to put the matter in perspective, "I'm not saying you don't have a point . . ."

The ensign raised an eyebrow.

"In this particular instance, I mean," Crusher added quickly. "I maintain that my overall strategy was a good one. After all, it worked on the bartender at The Den, didn't it? It just didn't work on Pudris Barrh."

Tuvok frowned.

"All right," said the human, "it backfired horribly when I tried it on Pudris Barrh. But that doesn't mean I'm going to stop taking chances if I think they're reasonable. And it doesn't mean—"

He stopped abruptly and gazed at the Vulcan. Suddenly, he realized what was going on. The revelation chased the heat of indignation out of him and left only compassion in its wake.

"Oh, man," said Crusher. "I'm sorry. I understand now."

"Understand what?" asked Tuvok.

"You're a Starfleet officer," the commander explained. "You feel that responsibility as intensely as anyone. But you're also a family man, with a wife and children—and you don't think you're going to make it home to them. You think that you've somehow let them down."

The Vulcan didn't confirm Crusher's observation. On the other hand, he didn't deny it.

"And since it's not appropriate for one of your people to feel guilt, you're projecting that feeling—that conflict—onto me," the commander concluded. "You're accusing me of abandoning my family because you can't contemplate the idea of accusing yourself."

Still, Tuvok said nothing. He just stared.

"But there's no need to beat yourself up about it," Crusher insisted. "You did what you had to do—just as I did. And we're both going to have to hope our loved ones understand that."

For the first time since the beginning of their conversation, the Vulcan looked away. The commander saw that Tuvok needed some time to think. He gave it to him.

Finally, the Vulcan turned back to him and spoke again. "I was . . . as you humans put it . . . out of line."

Crusher didn't reply right away. He sensed there was something more Tuvok wanted to say.

"It is unsettling indeed," the ensign continued, "to consider that your interpretation of my actions may be correct in some respects. I cannot deny that there is a conflict within me between my duty to Starfleet and my duty to my family, and it is certainly possible that this conflict has colored my view of the situation."

It was a truly remarkable admission for a Vulcan. Tuvok might as well have admitted a yen for cotton candy . . . or the Romulan ale that Crusher had run afoul of as a cadet.

"However, we should be concentrating our efforts on escape," the ensign pointed out, no doubt hoping to change the subject. "After all, we *do* have a mission to complete."

The commander smiled, though it hurt him to do so. "All right," he said. "What about that unexpected opportunity you mentioned?"

Chapter Fourteen

Captain's log, supplemental. Despite the efforts of myself, Commander Ben Zoma and others, including First Minister Culunnh and Governor Thul of the Thallonian Empire, we have failed to hold the peace talks together. The congress on Debennius Six has disbanded, perhaps for good. Also, we are no closer to discerning who is behind the terrorist assaults than we were before. All we know is that they are cold-blooded murderers, acting with a purpose and a plan—as evidenced by the fact that each incident is more brutal than the last. First a political assassination, then the bombing of a commuter vehicle, then the poisoning of a reservoir . . . and now the destruction of an entire colony, damn their—

PICARD PAUSED. His anger at the atrocities was beginning to color his log. Taking a deep breath, he deleted the last two words.

As he was about to resume his report, the door to his room chimed softly. Looking up, the captain wondered what new bit of bad news Ben Zoma might be bringing him.

"Come," he called.

Then he remembered that he wasn't in his quarters back on the *Stargazer.* He was in a suite First Minister Culunnh had obtained for him on Debennius II so the Benniari could reach him at a moment's notice, and the door mechanism wouldn't respond to his voice.

Rising from his chair, he crossed the room and touched a pad built into the wall beside the door. A moment later, the panel moved aside with an exhalation of air, revealing his visitor.

It wasn't Ben Zoma, either. "Governor Thul," said Picard.

The governor smiled. "Captain . . . may I come in?"

"By all means," Picard responded, moving to one side so the Thallonian could enter the room.

"I've become persona non grata among both the Cordracites and the Melacron," Thul observed as he came inside.

"As have I," the captain noted, as the door hissed closed again. "Which makes it rather difficult to talk sense into them."

The Thallonian took the seat against the wall,

opposite the one where Picard had been sitting. "I'm afraid that peace-mongers are not much appreciated at the moment."

Picard grunted. "So it would appear." He indicated a transparent decanter full of bright yellow liquid sitting on a wooden endtable. "Would you care for some wine, Governor?"

"Wine?" Thul replied wonderingly. "I thought tea was your beverage of choice, Captain."

Picard smiled without humor. "Cabrid Culunnh had this sent up here a couple of hours ago. He said he hoped it might give me some consolation."

"And has it?" asked the Thallonian.

The captain shrugged. "I've barely touched it."

"Then let us rectify that oversight," said Thul.

Picard nodded and poured two glasses of the stuff. Then he gave one of them to his visitor.

"To peace," the Thallonian noted. As he raised his glass, it sparkled in the light.

"To peace," the captain agreed, raising his glass as well. "May it be more than the empty illusion it seems at the moment."

Together, they sipped the dry, tart beverage in silence. The wine wasn't to Picard's taste, exactly, but it wasn't awful either. His father's vineyards back on Earth had occasionally produced worse.

Staring into the depths of his wine, Thul spoke. "I cannot get it out of my head, Captain. There will be war soon. So many millions of innocents . . . what a waste of life."

Picard didn't answer. His mind's eye was filled

with images of the soft-spoken, wise Benniari. Because of their presence in the disputed territories, they would no doubt be among the first to perish— just as the First Minister had predicted.

"I'm tempted to intervene," said the governor. "To stop it, somehow. And not just on behalf of Culunnh's people. After all, there are Thallonians in danger as well—those who serve the Emperor in various ways outside the borders of the Empire."

"I envy you that liberty," the captain answered sincerely. "Unfortunately, my hands are tied."

Thul looked at him. "What do you mean?"

"You spoke of the first virtue among your people," Picard said. "We of the United Federation of Planets have a central tenet as well. We have vowed not to intervene in conflicts among other civilizations, unless we are asked to do so by one of the combatants—and clearly, neither the Cordracites nor the Melacron have asked for our aid."

"The Benniari have," the Thallonian pointed out.

"Yes," the captain agreed, "and we will protect them if they are attacked. But beyond that . . ." He shrugged again.

"That must be terribly frustrating," said Thul.

Picard smiled wryly. "You have no idea. But those are my orders and I will obey them."

The governor finished his wine, then got to his feet and stretched. "I thought we might come up with something . . . an idea. But I find I'm too tired to do much thinking. Maybe I should just call it a night."

"As you wish," said the captain.

"Thank you for the wine," Thul tossed back over his shoulder as he crossed the room.

"Anytime," Picard told him. "May it help you sleep better."

The Thallonian stopped at the door. "I'll see you tomorrow," he said, "assuming the council chamber is still standing then."

"Tomorrow," the captain replied.

And with that, Thul made his exit.

Picard watched the doors slide closed behind him. Then he raised his glass again and watched the way the light filtered through the wine. The stuff wouldn't help *him* sleep better, he remarked inwardly. At that moment, he doubted anything would.

But he poured himself another glass, just in case.

After what seemed like an eternity of wrestling with his bonds, Jack Crusher arrived at the frustrating conclusion that they had been tied by the all-time expert.

"I've been at this forever," he growled, half to himself.

"You have only been conscious for one hour, twelve minutes and seventeen seconds," Tuvok corrected him. "And you have only spent seventy-six percent of that time attempting to free yourself."

The commander opened his mouth to make a less-than-pleasant retort, when he heard scuffling sounds on the other side of the door. He glanced at Tuvok, who had obviously heard them too. They fell silent.

A moment later, they heard the grating sound of a bolt being lifted. Then the door was pushed open.

Crusher recognized the alien who stood in the doorway as a Thallonian, though he had never spoken to one before. The tall, red-skinned being surveyed them with bright eyes.

"My name is Mendan Abbis," he said haughtily and incautiously. "I understand you've been sniffing around my steeds. Tell me, my friends—what do you *really* want with Bin Nedrach?"

"Ah," said the commander, trying to act as if he weren't in such a disadvantageous position. "So you're the elusive rider we've been hearing about. I can't say I much like the way you do business."

The Thallonian didn't smile at the jest. "I asked you a question," he reminded the human.

"What would *anyone* want with him?" Crusher replied as nonchalantly as possible. "We want to hire him, of course. We've got a job for him—if he's the best assassin around, as people say."

Abbis's gaze never left Crusher's face. "That sounds plausible. If it's true, it'll be confirmed soon enough. Then perhaps we can do business." He tossed a look over his shoulder. "Wyl!"

A tall, slender figure stepped into the room. His skin was dark, his hair white and tightly curled, and his deepset eyes glittered like silver. He seemed to look to the Thallonian for guidance.

"My friend Wyl here is an Indarrhi," said Abbis. "Perhaps you've heard of what they can do." A satisfied pause. "Rest assured, he'll get the truth out of you."

"Torture?" asked Crusher as calmly as if he were inquiring if the Thallonian took milk and sugar in his coffee.

Their captor chuckled. "You can resist torture, if your will is strong enough. Wyl has . . . other ways."

He nodded in Tuvok's direction and the Indarrhi approached him. Kneeling beside the ensign, he extended a hand and placed thick, ungainly fingers on Tuvok's temple. The silver eyes closed in concentration.

Though his expression remained utterly neutral, it was clear to Crusher that the Vulcan didn't like the idea. However, under the circumstances, he could hardly put up a fight.

"Now then," Abbis told Tuvok, "I ask you again— and you'd better answer if you value your life—what do you want with Bin Nedrach?"

His voice flat and lifeless, the Vulcan replied: "We wished to hire him to perform an assassination."

The Thallonian turned to his friend. "Wyl? Is he lying?"

The Indarrhi shook his curly, white locks. He looked confused, his dark brow creased. "I . . . I can't tell!"

Abbis's eyes narrowed. "What?"

Wyl rocked back on his heels, looking at Tuvok with a look of mingled awe and annoyance on his face. "This one," he said, "doesn't seem to have any emotions. At least, I can't sense any."

Abbis frowned—rather petulantly, Crusher thought. "Curse him," he said. "Try the other one, then."

As the Indarrhi knelt beside him and stretched his fingers out to touch his face, the commander called on all the techniques for mental calm he'd ever known. He tried to think about something, anything, other than the true reason he and Tuvok had come . . .

A thick rare steak. A good beer. A hot fudge sundae with sprinkles. Kissing Beverly for the first time.

The pain in his bladder right now.

"Can you feel *his* emotions?" asked the Thallonian.

The Indarrhi nodded. "He'll do."

Abbis turned his attention to Crusher. "What do you want with Bin Nedrach?" he demanded.

The commander tried to feel irritation. "How many times do we have to say it? We want to hire him!"

The Thallonian tilted his head to one side, still wary. "Tell me who you want killed," he said.

Fear thrust up a white wall in Crusher's mind. Then he asked, "Why should I tell you anything before we've struck a deal? When you find out who it is, you might jack up the price."

Abbis's lip curled. "What is your relationship to this other man?" he inquired, indicating Tuvok with a flick of his wrist.

Damn it, thought the commander, he was merciless.

"He's my bodyguard. Can't be too careful in my profession." Crusher forced a laugh; it sounded false, even to him. "I can see you have an appreciation for such things."

"He's lying," said the Indarrhi firmly. "He and his friend are most definitely not here in search of a steed."

Abbis approached the commander and towered over him. "If you're not here to hire Bin Nedrach . . . why are you here?"

Crusher didn't utter a word in response. He simply met the Thallonian glare for glare.

Abbis sighed. "Under the circumstances," he said, sounding reluctant, "I'm afraid I'm just going to have to kill you both. Though I confess to a great deal of curiosity about your true mission, I can't afford to indulge it. It would be too risky."

Casually, he reached for a directed energy weapon at his belt. With a quick flick of his fingers, he had it in his hand—its business end pointed at a spot between the commander's eyes.

I love you, Beverly.

"Wait." It was Tuvok. "There is no need for bloodshed. I will freely tell you what you wish to know."

Abbis hesitated for a second. Then he lowered his weapon.

Crusher glanced at the Vulcan, trying to keep his expression neutral. He wondered what kind of elaborate fantasy Tuvok was about to weave to throw their enemies off the trail.

"My name is Ensign Tuvok," he said. "This is Lieutenant Jack Crusher. We are officers in Starfleet, operating under the aegis of the United Federation of Planets."

Surprise and anger flared in the commander. What the hell did Tuvok think he was doing?

"We are attempting to find Bin Nedrach," the Vulcan went on, "because we believe him to be responsible for the assassination of the Melacronai G'aha of Laws and Enforcements."

The commander couldn't believe what he was hearing. He wanted to cry out, to tell Tuvok to shut his mouth, but that would only confirm the truth of the Vulcan's statements.

Tuvok continued gamely with his confession. "We are operating in a clandestine mode under orders from our captain. Our mission is to identify and stop those who are behind the incidents of violence on Melacron Five and Cordra Three—incidents which are propelling the Cordracites and the Melacron toward war."

"In other words," Abbis concluded, "you're trying to keep this war from taking place?"

"That is correct," said the ensign.

Hurt and anger flooded Crusher. He wished Tuvok had never returned to Starfleet. Clearly, he didn't belong there.

"This is the truth?" asked Abbis.

"The truth," Tuvok agreed. "If you do not believe me, you are free to have your Indarrhi friend examine Commander Crusher again. He will confirm what I have said, whether he wishes to or not."

The commander could only stare in dismay. He wasn't looking forward to dying, of course, but he would have embraced death if it meant carrying out their mission. After all, this wasn't just a walk in the park. Millions of innocents in the Kellasian sector would die if the Melacron and the Cordracites went to war.

Earlier, Tuvok had said he was torn between family and Starfleet. Clearly, the traitorous bastard had chosen the former. His life for millions of lives—damned poor logic, in Crusher's opinion.

The commander was so full of righteous anger, he almost didn't hear what Tuvok said next. And even when he did, he didn't have the slightest idea what the Vulcan was talking about.

"Your father is playing you for a fool," Tuvok told Abbis.

The Thallonian looked at him. "What did you say?"

"Your father is playing you for a fool," the Vulcan repeated evenly.

Clearly, the words had hit home. Abbis's face was even ruddier than usual, his eyes screwed up small and tight.

"Explain yourself," he told Tuvok, "before I punch a hole in your skull and let you watch your brains spill out."

"We know all about him," the Vulcan said calmly.

Crusher listened as intently as the Thallonian. *What do we know?* he wondered. *And how the devil do we know it?*

"We have discovered that your father, Governor Gerrid Thul, is the one behind the assassinations and the other terrorist incidents," Tuvok continued. "He is acting through you, his illegitimate son."

Abbis looked shocked—but he didn't seem able to

deny it. Therefore, the commander figured, it was true.

"We also know his goal," said the Vulcan. "He wishes to set himself up as Emperor of a new empire, made up of the systems situated between the Thallonian worlds and the Federation."

The Thallonian exchanged glances with the Indarrhi. The one named Wyl shrugged his shoulders.

"Such a goal," Tuvok noted, "will be far easier for Thul to accomplish if most sentient life in the sector is eliminated. Hence, a war between the Melacron and the Cordracites, instigated by your father and attributed to terrorist groups on both sides."

Abbis's expression was one of respect. "I'm impressed," he said.

So was Crusher.

"It is an ideal plan," Tuvok observed, "nearly flawless in its logic. The Kellasian sector will destroy itself, each species thinking the other one responsible, and the Thallonian Emperor will have no idea that it is all your father's doing."

Abbis nodded. "Yes," he said slowly. "It *is* an ideal plan. And I'm proud to be part of it."

"However . . ." the Vulcan added, letting his voice trail off as if he had thought better of revealing something.

"However *what?*" the Thallonian spat.

"What you do not know," Tuvok continued unperturbed, "is that Thul is only using you. Once you have done what he wishes you to do, you will no longer be a necessary component of his plan. Indeed, you will be a hindrance—which is why he plans to kill you."

Abbis's brow creased in disbelief. "You're insane," he breathed.

"Thul is nothing if not logical—and logic clearly indicates that you will be a danger to him," the Vulcan maintained. "After all, you know too much. You could betray him to the Thallonian Emperor." He shrugged. "Why would he let someone like that continue to live?"

"Because I'm his son," Abbis told him, trying to affect an air of confidence, even disdain. "I'm his flesh and blood, damn it." But the tremor in his voice gave him away.

"In addition," said Tuvok, "your father has dreams of founding a new imperial line. He does not want a bastard for his heir. He craves a son of pure and noble blood. Surely that is why he asked for the hand of the Emperor's sister in marriage."

For the briefest of moments, Crusher found himself feeling sorry for the young Thallonian. He had a mercurial face, and it was difficult for him to conceal his emotions.

Then he remembered the weapon in Abbis's hand, and how he had planned to kill the commander with no more remorse than he might feel squashing a bug. Abruptly, Crusher's pity evaporated.

"You asked for the truth," the Vulcan told the Thallonian. "I have given it to you."

Abbis's mouth twisted with anger, and for a wild moment Crusher feared the youth might use his weapon after all. But instead, he turned his back on his captives and went to the far wall.

Leaning against it, he took long, slow, deep breaths. He looked as if he was trying to calm himself, trying to come to terms with the devastating impact of what Tuvok had revealed to him.

His Indarrhi friend joined him and put a hand on the Thallonian's shoulder. But with a snarl, Abbis batted it away. Shrugging, Wyl withdrew to the center of the room.

Just then, a slight rustling sound caught Crusher's attention. He glanced at the Vulcan and realized what it meant—that Tuvok had freed himself from his bonds. But the Thallonian seemed to have heard it too, because he turned back to them with widened eyes.

What happened next took only a fraction of a second, but it seemed to the commander that it occurred in slow motion.

As Abbis raised his hand weapon and took aim, the Vulcan launched himself across the room and grabbed the shocked Indarrhi. Then he spun Wyl around and used him as a shield against the blue bolt of energy the Thallonian unleashed at him.

The bolt struck Wyl in the chest and the Indarrhi spasmed horribly under its influence—then slumped in Tuvok's arms. There was no question in Crusher's mind that Wyl was dead.

"Wyl!" Abbis cried out, horror etched into his every feature.

The hurt in his voice made Crusher's chest ache in

sympathy. He suspected, if even part of what Tuvok had said was true, that the Thallonian had just murdered the only being who ever really liked him.

Before he could fire again, Tuvok was on him like a panther. A quick contraction of the Vulcan's fingers on a nerve in his adversary's neck and Abbis crumpled without a sound.

Tuvok recovered the Thallonian's weapon and tucked it into his belt. Then he listened for an intrusion from outside. When none materialized, he came around behind Crusher and began loosening his bonds.

"An unexpected opportunity," he remarked casually.

Crusher thought he saw a glint of humor in the dark brown eyes. "Is that a joke, Ensign?"

Tuvok looked at him, as inscrutable as ever. "Vulcans do not joke," he pointed out.

At last, Tuvok crossed the room again and placed his pointed ear to the door. "Abbis must have dismissed the guards for the moment," he noted. "I still do not hear anyone out there."

As Crusher got up and rubbed his wrists, restoring circulation to them, he said, "Can you tell me what the hell just happened? For a second I thought you were turning traitor or something."

"A necessary ploy," Tuvok noted.

"And that business about Abbis's father . . ." the commander asked. "Where did you get all that?"

"The Indarrhi's empathic connection worked both ways," the ensign explained—though it seemed that only half his attention was focused on the explanation. "When he attempted to sense my emotions, our minds were linked. It was not difficult to examine his thoughts and extract something useful from them. And the rest——" He hesitated.

"The rest . . . ?" Crusher prodded.

Again, Tuvok's dark eyes seemed to glimmer with the faintest hint of mischief. "The rest," said the Vulcan, "I made up."

Crusher grinned at him. "Tuvok, you son of a mugato. I didn't know you had it in you."

The ensign's brow wrinkled ever so slightly. "There is much you do not know about me, Commander. Perhaps we will have the chance to rectify that at a later time. For the moment, however, I suggest we address ourselves to the question of regaining our freedom."

He had barely gotten the words out when a series of loud grunts and other noises beyond the door alerted them to the guards' return. Thinking quickly, Crusher whispered an idea to Tuvok.

The Vulcan nodded his approval, changed the setting on the Thallonian's hand weapon and turned it over to his companion. Then they returned to the chairs to which they had been tied, sat down and placed their hands behind their backs.

Here goes nothing, thought the commander. "They killed each other!" he cried out at the top of his lungs. "Somebody help us! Oh, God, the blood—get them out of here!"

At once the door was flung open and Old Scowly's twin—the one whose mammoth fist had pounded

Crusher's face—rushed into the room. He was brandishing a weapon that seemed puny in his hand.

Behind him, glaring at the prisoners with his single eye, was the Banyanan. He, too, was armed.

"There!" the commander yelled, his voice high and—he dearly hoped—filled with convincing terror. "The two of them killed each other right in front of our eyes!"

Crusher watched as Old Scowly's twin knelt beside the bodies. Then he exchanged glances with Tuvok. There was a brief instant when both alien guards took their eyes off the prisoners in their desire to see what had become of Abbis and his friend.

"The Indarrhi's dead," snorted the Banyanan. "But the Thallonian doesn't even look injured."

A tribute to Tuvok's skill, the commander thought.

Then he whipped his weapon out and fired it at the Banyanan. At the same time, the Vulcan sprang for Old Scowly's twin.

Struck squarely in the chest, the Banyanan went flying backward and hit the wall behind him. He was unconscious before he slumped to the floor. Old Scowly's lookalike took a bit more attention, but in the end Tuvok was able to disable him as well.

Crusher and the Vulcan looked at each other, gratified that their plan had borne fruit. All their differences, it seemed, had been put behind them.

As Tuvok stripped his adversary of his weapon, the commander dropped down at the side of the Banyanan and did the same.

"Two down, a few dozen more to go," he said.

"Indeed," was the Vulcan's only reply.

A few moments later, armed with three directed energy pistols and a couple of sharp, wicked-looking daggers, the Starfleet officers were ready to pursue their escape. Cautiously, Crusher advanced to the door, twisted its archaic-looking metal knob and pushed it open a crack. Then he craned his neck and peered out of the room . . .

Into the splendid, knowing eyes of the Orion slave girl.

Chapter Fifteen

THE GOLDEN-HUED SHACKLES on the slave girl's arms and legs gleamed luxuriantly against the rich green of her flesh. Stunned by the sight of her, Crusher couldn't think of anything to say.

Fortunately, he had the presence of mind to pull the Orion inside the room. Her skin felt warm and supple to the touch—unnervingly so.

"So," she said in a husky and not unpleasant voice. She took in the sight of the fallen Thallonian and his friend. "It seems you are Federation spies after all. They thought you might be."

"You . . ." said the commander, finding his voice again. "You tried to warn us, didn't you? When you were dancing?"

She tossed her black mane of hair and smiled, pursing her dark, full lips. Crusher was uncomfortably aware of the fact that the girl's outfit didn't cover very much.

"Yes," she said in answer to his question. "But you were too absorbed in your charade to notice."

The human's first inclination was to object, but he didn't think he would get very far. "Yes," he conceded, "I was."

"Commander . . ." said Tuvok.

Crusher held up a hand. His gut was telling him that this girl might be useful. She'd already tried to help them once. . . .

"That was risky," he said, trying to sound her out. "What you did on the stage, I mean."

She laughed softly. "Not that risky. No one would suspect me of being intelligent enough to betray my master. I know what we are called, after all . . . Orion *animal* women. I also know that in Federation space, the kind of slavery our masters practice is illegal."

The intensity of her stare was doing something to Crusher's stomach—and regions slightly lower. The slave girl moved closer to him on her bare feet and gracefully raised her chains to the level of his face.

"I can help you escape," she said invitingly, whether she had intended that kind of effect or not. "Take me with you. Free me."

Her eyes, he thought, were pools of obsidian, the kind a man could get lost in forever. And that mouth. . . .

"Commander," Tuvok repeated, this time in a

slightly more forceful tone of voice. "We only have so much time at our disposal."

"I know," said Crusher. He regarded the girl. "What's your name?"

She looked surprised. "I—I don't have one," she replied. "The Master simply calls me . . ." and she uttered a word that was a local epithet regarding certain female body parts.

The commander winced. That did it.

"From now on . . ." he said, recalling how beautifully she had moved, how strong and graceful she had been, "from now on, you're Grace. That is, until you choose a name for yourself."

The slave girl seemed delighted. Her eyes shone gratefully. "Grace," she repeated as if it were a toy.

Crusher couldn't help smiling a bit as well. "So what kind of plan did you have in mind . . . Grace?"

She told him.

As the door to his guest quarters on Debennius II hissed shut behind him, Gerrid Thul smiled to himself.

After all, the foolish human captain had told him everything he needed to know. The Federation was a toothless beast unless asked to fight, and right now, both the Cordracites and the Melacron were hot for each other's blood. They would not ask anyone to help them stop it.

Everything was going splendidly, the Thallonian told himself. There was only one more thing that needed to be done before the Cordracites and the Melacron went hurtling over the edge into a full-blown war.

Thul removed his oval-shaped communicator from his tunic and spoke into it. "This is the governor," he said.

"Kaavin here," his second-in-command replied crisply.

"I wish to return," he told her.

A moment later, the air around him with filled with swirls of golden light. The next thing the Thallonian knew, he was standing on a raised pentagon in his vessel's transporter facility.

The transporter technician inclined his large, hairless head. "My lord," he said dutifully.

Thul didn't say a thing. But then, he didn't have to. On his ship, as in the colony he governed, he could do anything he liked.

As he descended from the pentagon, the doors to the room whisked open and Kaavin entered. Tall, slender and elegant, she stopped and inclined her head as well.

"Accompany me," said Thul.

He walked out into the corridor, Kaavin at his side. Like any good Thallonian second-in-command, she would remain silent until he demanded something of her.

"Report," the governor told her.

Kaavin glanced at him, all polish and efficiency. "Everything proceeds according to plan, my lord. No one appears to suspect our role in the massacre of the Melacronai colony."

He nodded. "Good."

Naturally, he thought, the Melacron had only seen

what Thul wanted them to see—a Cordracite warship bearing down on a defenseless research outpost. That was what their sensors had picked up, what their now-deceased master scientist had screamed into her communications system before she was obliterated by the vessel's energy fire.

Of course, if the Melacron hadn't been so ill-disposed toward the Cordracites to begin with, they might have been more skeptical of the circumstances surrounding the attack. They might have looked beyond their loathing, beyond their species-hatred, and analyzed the colony's sensor data with more sophisticated instruments.

If the Melacron had done that, they would surely have been in for a surprise—for they would have discovered that the aggressor vessel's ion trail was different from the kind left by Cordracite warships. They would have seen, then, that it wasn't a Cordracite vessel that attacked and destroyed Lir Kirnis and her esteemed colleagues after all, but another kind of ship entirely, its appearance altered to make it seem like a Cordracite vessel.

The Melacron didn't have the wherewithal to disguise a spacegoing vehicle. Neither did the Cordracites or any other species in the sector. The Thallonians, on the other hand, had perfected magnetic-pulse imaging technology years earlier.

Granted, it was seldom used. But people only saw things where they thought to look for them. And what would the Thallonian Empire have to gain by exacerbating hostilities in the Kellasian sector?

Nothing. Nothing at all.

So instead of insisting on the truth, the Melacron shouted and screamed and raged at the top of their lungs, accusing the hated Cordracites of destroying a colony full of innocents. And the Cordracites, who of course knew they hadn't done anything wrong, believed that the Melacron had simulated a massacre to set off a war.

And in both cases, Thul's purposes were served.

The governor had always prided himself on his poise, his equilibrium. But as he and Kaavin approached a lift, he had to fight the urge to whoop with glee. It was going to work, he reflected, and work perfectly. The fools were going to destroy each other.

All it would take was one more outrageous, intolerable affront to tip the scales in favor of war, and Thul was about to see to it that that one final affront would take place.

"Bridge," he said, as he and his second-in-command entered the lift compartment. A moment later, the doors whispered closed behind them and the compartment began its journey through the ship.

"When this is over," the governor told Kaavin with a surge of generosity, "you will be amply rewarded."

She looked at him, no doubt wondering in what shape the reward would come. After all, Thul's second knew nothing about his ambitions—only that he wanted to spur a war in this sector. And being a loyal subject, she hadn't questioned that ambition.

"I am honored," Kaavin told him.

You don't know *how* honored, the governor thought.

Then the lift doors opened and his ship's bridge was revealed to him. At the sight of their lord, his officers leaned back in their seats and thrust their chins out.

Thul smiled at them as he emerged from the lift compartment. They were Thallonians all. There was no mixture of inferior aliens here, such as could be seen on Picard's Federation vessel. They were warriors, professionals. And whether they admitted it to themselves or not, they hungered as he did for something more than what their blood-rights had granted them.

Soon, the governor reflected, these steadfast souls would become the lords of his new empire. They would serve him as he presently served Tae Cwan and they would reap the benefits accorded such service.

Thul eased himself into his center seat and turned to his helmsman, a stocky fellow with a dueling scar down the side of his face. "Set course for the fleetyard on Cordra Three."

He recited the coordinates from memory. He had been looking forward to this for a long time.

"Aye, lord," replied the helmsman, and entered the course. The governor settled back to mull over the final stage of his plan.

His own vessel was now equipped with the same magnetic-pulse technology as the one that had destroyed the Melacronai outpost. Like the scientists at the outpost, the Cordracites at the fleetyard would never know it was a Thallonian ship that had attacked them.

As he watched the stars streak by at impulse speed on his forward monitor, Thul tried to picture the destruction of the fleetyard in all its brutal, explosive glory. It was difficult for him to do it justice.

But the results . . . those were easier for him to imagine. The war would get under way instantly, of course. And the first victory—thanks to his crippling of the Cordracites' shipbuilding capabilities—would be claimed by the slightly weaker Melacron.

What's more, he told himself, there would be several hundred fewer Cordracites for the Melacron to kill. And it would no doubt spur the victims' kinsmen to violence unmatched in the history of the sector.

The governor smiled and thought of his son . . . his loyal, efficient, infinitely clever son. What Thallonian in his right mind would have imagined that Mendan Abbis could prove so useful to Thul's cause? Who, indeed, but the governor himself?

Once he understood his father's scheme, once he embraced it, the boy had risen to the challenge. He had executed each and every step of the plan flawlessly, knowing whom to contact for a particular assignment and how to make the most of their talents.

That alone would have been enough, Thul reflected. No—it would have been more than enough. But in addition, Mendan Abbis had demonstrated a flair for the dramatic.

The assassination of the Melacronai G'aha, the bomb that slew the Cordracite commuters, the poisoning of the reservoir on Cordra III . . . all these things were accomplished with a sense of theater and spectacle that would have been a credit to the most skillful Thallonian courtier.

Thul sighed. He had not done right by the boy as a child; he knew that. He recalled showing up for a visit at his humble home every so often, handing Mendan's mother a small pouch full of latinum and regarding the fruit of their reckless union with patrician distaste.

Whose fault had it been, then, that Abbis had grown up with a chip on his shoulder—with a sense of inferiority and a need to prove himself at every opportunity? Whose fault but that of his father?

But that was over, the governor promised himself. He'd given the boy a chance and Mendan Abbis, bastard, had seized it better than any privileged Thallonian whelp ever could have.

Thul himself had been snubbed by his Emperor because he wasn't high-born enough to marry Mella Cwan. The governor would never make that mistake when he sat on a throne. His Empire would be based on merit, on skill and talent, not on accidents of birth.

As for Mendan Abbis . . . he would get what his father had promised him: a seat on Thul's right hand, the time-honored place of the Emperor's rightful heir. And why not?

The boy had earned it.

The commander and his Vulcan companion stumbled into the heart of the dance hall, clad in the filthy, smelly garb of their guards, which they had liberally sprinkled with alcoholic beverages.

Crusher hoped no one noticed how poorly Tuvok's clothes fit—an unfortunate but unavoidable problem given the differences between the ensign's spare physique and that of Old Scowly's lookalike. With luck, any potential observer would be more interested in Grace, who walked between the Starfleet officers with her arms linked through theirs.

There was a Pandrilite on the stage and the loud music that accompanied her gyrations thundered in the commander's bones, more primal than the subtle, sultry sound of the flute to which Grace had danced. The place was significantly more crowded as well, though Crusher wouldn't have believed such a thing was possible.

He laughed and pretended to fall in his drunkenness, then called something to one of the other dancing girls. But that was only what would have been expected of him. And Grace held her head high, saying without words that she had two customers who wanted her favors tonight, and wasn't she just glorious enough to deserve it.

Thus they walked unnoticed and unchallenged to the private quarters where more intimate business was transacted, and Grace closed the door. Inside were a few beds covered with rank-smelling linens, and a couple of candles that represented a pathetic attempt at ambiance.

Grace's feral face shone in the yellow light. "No one suspected anything," she told the commander.

He nodded. "Excellent."

"Indeed," Tuvok added.

Grace went to the room's only window and opened it with an effort. The soft sounds and hard, pungent smells of the night wafted to them on cool, moist drafts of air.

"If you have access to this room and this window," asked Crusher, "why haven't you run away before now?" He found he was a little suspicious at how easy their progress had been to this point.

The slave girl gestured to her shackles. "I have these on all the time, except when I dance. And this," she said, pointing to a tiny box that flashed red and blue and was suspended from the shackles, "will not permit me to leave the building."

The commander decided that he believed her. Wordlessly, he drew the energy weapon formerly owned by Mendan Abbis. Understanding his intent, Grace held out her hands and stood still.

Crusher's objective was to destroy the control box without hurting Grace—not as easy as it sounded with an unfamiliar weapon in his hand. His eyes met hers and she nodded trustingly, clenching her jaw.

The human took a breath to steady himself. Then he placed the weapon's nose within six centimeters of the box and pressed the trigger. The weapon spit out a dark blue stream of energy.

Grace gritted her teeth against the heat. Sparks flew haphazardly. But after a few seconds, there was a satisfying crack and the box clattered to the floor in two pieces. Grace laughed wildly from her belly.

"Free!" she whispered, and savagely kicked at the box, sending it scuttling along the floor.

"We will only remain that way if we make haste," Tuvok warned them, and this time Crusher wasn't inclined to argue with him.

They helped Grace out the window first—though with her catlike agility, she didn't need much assistance. The Vulcan went next and the commander brought up the rear.

As Crusher poked his head out, he saw that his companions were standing in a narrow alleyway alongside the dance hall. Clambering through the window opening and swinging down, he landed in something that squished and smelled awful. Fortunately, the darkness prevented him from analyzing the substance too carefully.

"We must return to our ship," Tuvok told Grace.

"Where is it?" she asked.

"In the foothills west of town," said the commander. "Don't worry, we know the way."

The Orion snarled softly beneath her breath. It was a sound Crusher had never heard before.

"What is it?" he asked.

"We are on the easternmost side of the city," she pointed out. "By the time we reach your vessel, they will have found Mendan Abbis and his friend and realized that I am gone."

"And they will overtake us," the Vulcan concluded.

Grace nodded—and even that small gesture was alluring. "Can you not purchase passage on a—?"

"No," Tuvok said emphatically.

Crusher shrugged, apologizing for his friend and agreeing with him in the same gesture. "I'm afraid it's not an option."

"Very well," the Orion told them. "Follow me." And she started off down the length of the alley.

"We came from the other direction," the commander told her, plodding through the muck to catch up.

"I am aware of that," Grace replied. "However, if you take the direct way back, we will almost certainly be caught. I know a more winding route that may get us there safely."

Crusher looked back at Tuvok. The ensign looked concerned about the change in plans, but he came along.

Grace turned out to know the streets rather well for someone who had to that point in her life been prevented from leaving the dance hall. What's more, she seemed to have an instinct for when to duck into the shadows and when to slip boldly out into the moonlight.

The commander asked her about it.

"I have many hours," she whispered back. "I talk with the men who come to me. They tell me much, not thinking that I am truly listening to them. They even show me maps—pointing out their businesses, their homes, where they like to eat." Her voice dripped contempt.

And Crusher didn't blame her one iota. It couldn't have been an easy life she had led.

Later, when they were sitting in the lee of a building waiting for a band of drunken revelers to make their way across the street, he asked her another question. "How long have you been on Debennius Six, Grace?"

The slave girl turned to look up at him. Her face was cloaked in deep shadow, but her bright green eyes caught the light of a streetlamp and glittered like distant stars.

Crusher had heard all the rumors about Orion "animal women," how no man could resist them, how they were all heat and allure and violent sexuality. He knew now that the rumors were true. Like a witch out of Terran folklore, Grace had already cast a spell on him.

"My mother was known for breeding fine female stock," she said. The words hurt the commander as if they were weapons. "I was bought as a child, and I have lived most of my life here on the Last Stop to Nowhere."

"It's not *your* last stop," Crusher assured the Orion. "You're free now, Grace, and we're going to take you to a place where you'll be safe. I promise you that."

"Commander . . ." said Tuvok.

Crusher returned his glance. "Yes?"

"It is unwise to make promises you may not be able to keep," the Vulcan advised him solemnly.

The human was about to respond when Grace said, "Your friend is correct, Commander Crusher. We may not even live long enough to get back to your ship. But you are right about one thing . . . I am free now."

Crusher found that his mouth was dry all of a sudden, and decided not to say anything more.

Chapter Sixteen

EVEN AFTER TWO GLASSES OF WINE, Picard found he couldn't sleep. His mind was filled with violent, haunting images: flashes of red and blue, of exploding ships, of murdered people—Melacron, Cordracites, Benniari—all of them floating bloodily in the void.

Had Culunnh been wrong about third-party intervention, after all? Was this simply the logical if tragic progression of relations between two firmly entrenched adversaries?

If only he had heard something from Crusher and Tuvok, he might have had an answer. However, they had yet to report in. In fact, the captain was beginning to wonder if something had happened to them.

Finally, he decided that enough was enough. He

crossed the room to the communications cube that sat on an endtable and tapped it. It lit up instantly, filling the place with a gentle blue radiance.

"This is Culunnh," came the Benniari's reedy reply.

"Sorry to disturb you at this hour," said Picard.

"Ah, Captain Picard," said the First Minister, and his voice grew warm and sad at the same time. "It would not be possible for you to disturb me. How may I assist you?" he asked. "Or," and Culunnh sounded more hopeful suddenly, "do you have news to impart?"

Picard sighed before replying. "No news, First Minister, save that I feel I must return to my ship. I appreciate your hospitality, but I have to question if there's anything more I can accomplish here."

"I see." The Benniari's voice was soft . . . resigned.

"I think the wisest course of action," said the captain, "may be for me to brief Starfleet Command on what has taken place here . . . and to advise them to prepare for the worst."

Culunnh made a whistling noise. "I cannot help agreeing with you," he replied, "though I wish it were not so. The Melacronai and Cordracite delegations have alerted me that they will depart in the morning, sooner than I expected. And most of the other diplomats will leave as well, as soon as they realize the Melacron and the Cordracites are gone."

"I am sorry to hear that," Picard said sincerely.

"There will be a formal breaking of fast in the morning for whoever has remained," the Benniari continued. "But at this point, I think there will be so few left that I may be able to host that meal in my quarters."

The captain sighed. "I hope it fills the council chamber," he told the First Minister, though he hadn't the least expectation that his wish would come true.

"Shall I see you off?" asked Culunnh.

"No," said Picard, "that won't be necessary. I've bothered you enough tonight as it is. We will be in touch, however, I assure you." He paused. "I only regret we were unable to be of more help."

"You staved off an armed conflict for several days," the First Minister told him. "As you yourself pointed out, that was an accomplishment. Travel safely, Captain Picard."

"Thank you, First Minister. It has been a genuine honor to work with you." Then something else occurred to him. "Say good-bye to Governor Thul for me, will you? Tell him I enjoyed working with him as well."

"I will do that," Culunnh promised.

Unfortunately, there wasn't much more either of them could say. "Good night," the captain added.

"Good night," came the reply.

With that, the cube went dark. Frowning, Picard tapped his communicator badge. "Picard to Ben Zoma," he said.

A pause. Then, "Ben Zoma here. What can I do for you, Captain?"

"A change of plans. I won't be staying the night here after all," Picard informed him.

"Nothing more for you to accomplish?" asked the first officer.

"Nothing," the captain agreed. "Alert the transporter room, will you? I'm ready when they are."

"Aye, sir. Ben Zoma out."

Picard had time to look around his quarters one last time and wish he were leaving Debennius II a happier man. Then there was a shimmer in the air and he found himself back in the *Stargazer*'s lone transporter room.

As Crusher watched, Grace slunk out of the shadows and took off, leading the way again.

He and his Vulcan companion followed her through a labyrinth of dark alleys, backstreets and, once, even into a sewer tunnel. Then, as if by magic, they were outside the city limits, on a lonely, unpaved road that wound its way through the hill country.

The commander was thoroughly delighted to leave town. The dirt felt good underneath his boots and the air smelled cleaner. He glanced now and then at Grace, both of them doing their best to keep up with the rapid pace Tuvok was setting for them, and his heart lifted.

They had done what Captain Picard had asked of them. They had identified the elusive third party responsible for the attacks of terrorism in the Cordra and Melacron systems.

Now that the quarry had a name, he could be tracked down and stopped. And they had accomplished this while doing something else exceedingly worthwhile—freeing a woman from a life not fit for a—

"There they are!" came a deep-throated cry.

Crusher turned in time to see blue energy blasts light up the night, striking and pulverizing the stones at their feet. As one, he and Tuvok dove for cover behind some larger rocks.

The commander had imagined that Grace would do the same, lithe and athletic as she was. He thought she would be the least of his troubles. But she continued to stand there in the line of fire, her body taut, her head thrown back in a defiant howl.

"No!" she snarled. "You will not take me back!" Bending, she took hold of a stone and lifted it over her head, ready to hurl it at her attackers in a useless but valiant gesture.

Crusher clenched his jaw and went back out after the slave girl. But before he could get to her, there was a hideous flash of blue light and she crumpled to the ground.

"Grace!" the commander cried out.

She was writhing on the ground, moaning in agony. And what he could see of her abdomen didn't look good.

Anger coursing through him, Crusher raised his weapon and fired. He heard himself shouting something—he didn't know what. But he kept shouting and firing and shouting and firing . . . until Tuvok put his hand on the commander's arm and told him there was no one left to fire at.

Crusher took a deep, shuddering breath and lowered his weapon. Then he went to Grace, dropped down at her side and slipped his hands underneath her, so he could pick her up.

"Hang on," he urged her, even as his eyes told him that her wound would be fatal. "We'll take you to our ship and—"

"Liar," she said, wincing at the pain in her blackened, bloody belly. "I am dying. We Orions know such things. I—" Before she could say any more, she went rigid with a sudden surge of torment.

"Grace . . ." he hissed.

A slender green hand covered with blood reached up to grasp the commander's filthy shirt. The Orion's expression was a defiant one, even now. She bared her teeth as she spoke.

"I . . . die . . . free. . . ." she moaned, her eyes blazing with an inner fire. "Not a slave . . . *free*."

Then, with a pitiful expiration of breath, Grace's hard-muscled body went limp in his arms.

Crusher gazed helplessly at the Orion, his vision blurring. Damn it, he thought miserably. They had been so close to escaping, all of them. Why did she have to make a stand all by herself? Why couldn't she have gone for cover the way he and Tuvok did?

He knew the answer, though, didn't he? All her life, Grace had been trained to act on instinct—and that was what she had done this time as well. But this time, her instincts had led her astray.

Gently, the commander released the Orion and shut her bright green eyes. Then he stood and turned to the

Vulcan, who had been checking on the bastards who had murdered her.

"There were only four of them," Tuvok reported. "Barrh must have split up his henchmen into small groups to improve his chances of finding us."

Crusher gazed at Grace. "We met her, what . . . a couple of hours ago? And yet I feel as if I've lost one of my best friends."

"Commander," said the Vulcan, his voice unusually soft, "do not allow Grace's sacrifice to be wasted. We must hurry before we are again apprehended by Barrh's men."

Crusher blinked to clear his vision. "I hear you," he said.

They would find their captain, he vowed, and tell him of Thul's treachery. War would be averted, and millions would be saved.

And who would ever know how big a part an Orion slave girl had played in it? Who would ever understand how brave she had been?

Only he. And Tuvok.

And what had she gotten for her trouble? Just a small taste of freedom, the commander reflected. But for her, maybe that had been enough.

"Come on," he told the Vulcan.

As Tuvok had advised, Jack Crusher would make sure his friend hadn't died in vain.

The sight of his transporter room was unexpectedly comforting to Picard. However, it didn't make up for the discomforting outcome he had brought back with him.

He had hoped to report another diplomatic success to Starfleet Command; it would have been a nice prelude to a few days of rest and relaxation at Starbase Three with Admiral Ammerman and his family. But it was not to be. The captain bore a message of war, not peace, and the future looked grim for this small sector of space.

Picard nodded his thanks to the ensign who had transported him up. Then he crossed the room, meaning to head for his quarters.

"Cadwallader to Captain Picard," came a summons, stopping the captain in his tracks.

The comm officer's voice, upbeat at the worst of times, was now positively bubbly. Wondering simultaneously what she was doing at her post at this late hour and what had caused her excitement, he replied, "Picard here. What's going on, Ensign?"

"A message for you, sir," said Cadwallader. "It's from Commander Crusher. Ears only, it seems."

The captain's heartbeat sped up. "I'll take it in my ready room."

"Aye, sir," said the comm officer.

A minute later, he emerged from a turbolift compartment onto his bridge. His officers—Ben Zoma in the center seat, the Asmund twins at helm and navigation, and Cadwallader at communications—all turned to him with expressions of relief on their faces.

What's more, Picard understood why. They had been worried about their friend Jack. A message meant that he was still alive.

Without a word, he made his way across the bridge

and headed for his ready room. As the doors slid apart for him, he called back to his comm officer. "Patch it through, Cadwallader."

"Acknowledged, sir," she told him.

Circumnavigating his desk, the captain sat down and eagerly faced his monitor. Then he tapped in the command that would play the message for him. As it was a simple audio transmission, the Starfleet insignia remained on the screen throughout.

"This is Commander Crusher," said the second officer's voice. He sounded pleased and weary at the same time. "Sir, we're en route to your position in our Benniari craft. It seems First Minister Culunnh's hunch was right—there *is* a third party behind these attacks. They were instigated by a Thallonian governor . . . a man named Gerrid Thul."

Picard felt a cold like that of the vacuum of space settle in his stomach. "Thul?" he muttered, bewildered.

The Thallonian had seemed so concerned about the situation, so determined to avert a war. However, Crusher didn't sound as though he harbored any doubts—and Tuvok, a Vulcan, would have argued with his conclusion if he had. If they said Thul was responsible for the attacks, they must have discovered proof that it was so.

Thul, the captain repeated inwardly.

He listened as Crusher went into the details of the governor's plot and his motivation. Each word Picard heard served to infuriate him a little more. By the time he heard the last one, his face was crimson with rage and indignation and his hands had clenched into fists.

Thul was fortunate he wasn't on the *Stargazer,* the captain told himself. He was fortunate indeed.

"Cadwallader," Picard barked, getting up from his chair and heading for the exit, "locate Thallonian Governor Gerrid Thul on Debennius Two."

As he strode out onto the bridge, still filled with righteous ire, the ensign was manipulating her controls. She spoke softly into her headset for a moment, listened, then turned to the captain.

"You're not going to like this, sir," she told him. "The Benniari report that Governor Thul left Debennius Two an hour and a half ago."

Picard swore under his breath.

"What's going on?" Ben Zoma wanted to know.

"Our quarry has been here all the time," the captain informed him, "right under our noses. It seems our good friend and ally Governor Thul was behind the attacks."

The first officer's eyes widened. "Thul . . . ?"

"Yes. And now he's disappeared. We have to catch him before he makes the situation worse than it already is."

Ben Zoma thought for a moment. "Sir," he said, "a Thallonian ship leaves a distinctive ion trail . . ."

"Which we can follow," Picard noted crisply. "Quite right, Number One." He turned to Gerda Asmund, his statuesque, blond navigator. "Find that trail for me, Lieutenant."

"Aye, sir," said Asmund.

The captain regarded Idun Asmund, Gerda's twin. "When we find it," he told her, "pursue at full impulse." *At least until we leave the planet's gravity well,* he reflected.

"Full impulse," the helm officer repeated.

Finally, Picard addressed Cadwallader. "Send the following message to Commander Crusher and Ensign Tuvok," he instructed. "Message received, quarry has departed. We are following the trail, bearing—" He raised an eyebrow as he regarded his navigator.

Gerda Asmund frowned for a moment as she analyzed the sensor data. At last, she looked up. "Bearing three two four mark nine," the lieutenant said with the utmost confidence.

The captain nodded, grateful for the quality of his bridge personnel. It was hard for him to imagine having a more efficient officer in charge of his navigation console.

"Bearing three two four mark nine," he repeated for Cadwallader's benefit. "Make your best speed to intercept. Picard out."

He watched Idun Asmund out of the corner of his eye as she set a course in accordance with the Thallonian's escape route. Like her sister, she was as proficient as they came.

"Course set," the helm officer announced when she was finished.

"Thank you," the captain told them, "one and all."

He took his center seat and trained his eyes on the viewscreen, where the field of stars wheeled by as

Idun Asmund brought the *Stargazer* about. Ben Zoma came over to stand at his side.

"That old fox Thul has led us on a merry chase," the first officer noted without any of his characteristic good humor.

Picard nodded. "Yes," he agreed, "that he has. But the hounds are finally on the right trail."

He imagined the Thallonian's vessel centered on his screen, in his phaser sights. Now, the captain added silently, it's just a matter of how fast the old fox can run.

Chapter Seventeen

JACK CRUSHER FINISHED LISTENING to Picard's return message through his Benniari headset. Then he turned to Tuvok, who was seated beside him. "They want us to rendezvous with them," he said.

"Our Benniari vessel cannot match the speed of a Constellation-class starship," the Vulcan observed.

The commander shrugged. "I know. I guess we'll just have to do our best."

Tuvok nodded and tapped in their new heading. The ship came about smoothly under the Vulcan's direction.

Crusher leaned back and unfolded his long legs, which were starting to cramp. There was nothing to do now, he reflected, but activate the warp drive when they escaped the gravity well of Debennius VI—and hope they were in time to be of some help to their captain.

"Commander?" said Tuvok.

Crusher looked at him. "Hmm?"

"I have been spending a great deal of effort reviewing this mission . . ."

The human smiled wanly. "Me too."

"And I have come to two conclusions," the ensign announced. "First, that I was insubordinate to a superior officer. And second, that I was incorrect in my assessment of his methods."

Crusher realized his mouth was agape. He closed it. "You're kidding, right?" And then, before Tuvok could correct him, he added, "Don't say it. Vulcans never kid."

"That is true," Tuvok remarked.

"But how can you say that about my methods?" the human asked. "All I did was manage to get us captured by Barrh's men. As you yourself said, I put us in unnecessary danger."

"Nonetheless," the Vulcan insisted, "we obtained the requisite information and survived to report back to our captain. If we are in time, and it is my sincere hope that we are, we will have averted a catastrophe from which the Kellasian sector might never have recovered."

"But that was all your doing," Crusher insisted. "If you hadn't read the Indarrhi's mind and discovered what Thul was doing, we would still be on square one—or worse."

Tuvok arched an eyebrow. "I would not have had

the opportunity to read the Indarrhi's mind, as you put it, if you had not led us to Mendan Abbis. Had we proceeded as I wished, we might still be in The Den drinking what passes there for alcoholic beverages."

The commander couldn't challenge the Vulcan's statement. After all, Tuvok was right.

"Your methods were . . . unorthodox," the ensign allowed. "However, our mission was an unqualified success—and as Surak himself once said, it is illogical to argue with success."

Crusher shrugged. "Surak . . . ?"

"The visionary leader who introduced the philosophy of logic to Vulcan. He was nothing if not practical."

Then something else occurred to the human. "What about Grace?" he asked. "I didn't do her any favors, did I?"

"You took calculated risks," Tuvok conceded. "But you did not force her to take them with you. You simply made the opportunity available to her. I believe she would thank you for that, if she were able to."

Crusher's throat constricted. "Maybe." He peered at his companion. "Anyway, thanks for saying so."

"No thanks are required," the ensign assured him dispassionately. "I am merely stating the obvious."

The commander sighed. "Well, maybe I needed to hear the obvious as stated by a Vulcan."

Tuvok considered the possibility. "Perhaps you did," he said.

In the dark brown depths of the Vulcan's normally

implacable gaze, Crusher could have sworn he saw a flicker of warmth. It was gratifying to know that he had helped put it there.

"So," the human said as they streaked toward their rendezvous with the *Stargazer,* "tell me about your kids."

Thul considered his viewscreen, where the Cordracite fleetyard sprawled across several kilometers of orbital space. He wondered if he had ever seen a more lovely sight.

There they were . . . a hundred or more Cordracite vessels, from the powerful Predator Class warships with their sharp and unattractive angles to the quicker, more delicate-looking Racer Class reconnaissance vessels. They hung in space as if they didn't have a care in the world.

The governor savored the moment. He scanned each vessel in turn, deriving pleasure from its vulnerability, delighting in the knowledge that it wouldn't be there much longer.

Finally, he turned his attention to the cavernous drydock facility, where various ships were in the process of being repaired or upgraded or simply maintained. His intelligence reports had told him there were more than two hundred Cordracites manning the station.

And none of them had registered the Thallonian's presence. After all, Thul's ship was outside their rather primitive sensor reach. His intelligence reports had enlightened him in that area as well.

"Activate the magnetic-pulse envelope," he said. "Then move into their sensor range. Full impulse."

"Full impulse, my lord," his helmsman confirmed.

On the viewscreen, the fleetyard gradually loomed larger. The governor smiled. He was enjoying this immensely.

To this point, it was his agents alone who had planted the seeds of chaos in which his empire would take root. Finally, the Thallonian had an opportunity to plant some seeds of his own.

There was something exciting about that, something that appealed to the aggressor in Thul. It was the same instinct that had raised him from his modest origins to the leadership of a large and important colony.

"My lord governor, we have entered the Cordracites' sensor range," his navigator announced crisply.

Thul nodded. Any moment now, he told himself.

Nakso, his comely communications officer, turned to him. "My lord, the Cordracites are hailing us."

Ah, there it was . . . the first challenge. The governor sat up straighter in his chair. "Put it through," he instructed Nakso, "but on an audio channel only, as we discussed."

"Complying, lord," the communications officer responded.

A moment later, the rasping voice of a Cordracite filled Thul's bridge. "Fleetyard Commander Yov to approaching Melacronai vessel. State the nature of your business in our space."

The governor glanced at Nakso again. In accordance with their plan, she made no attempt to respond. After all, they didn't want to puncture the illusion that they were Melacron.

"Maintain speed," said Thul.

The Cordracite commander spoke again. "Our ships are armed and ready to defend themselves, Melacronai vessel. If you come any closer, we will assume hostile intent and fire."

The governor chuckled. "Please do," he whispered.

He knew that the Cordracite was bluffing. Had any of those ships been as "armed and ready" as he pretended, at least some of them would have been deployed already—and of course, they hadn't been.

Thul had caught them totally unaware. It was an exhilarating feeling, one that raised his senses to a fever pitch. And of course, the best part was yet to come.

"Repeat," snapped the Cordracite, and this time there was a hint of urgency evident in his voice, "if you come any closer, we will fire."

The governor could almost smell the terror floating rank and musky off the Cordracites at the drydock facility. "Maintain speed," he said again. He turned to Ubbard, his burly weapons officer. "Range?"

"Momentarily, my lord," came the reply.

Thul eyed the fleetyard. There was still no response, no movement among the ships, though he was sure the Cordracites were scrambling to organize a defense. Unfortunately for them, they would be too late.

"Range," his weapons officer reported.

The governor smiled, anticipating the taste of victory already. "Target weapons," he said.

"Targeting," responded his weapons officer, working at his control panel. He looked up. "Ready, my lord."

Now, Thul thought.

He was about to give Ubbard the order to fire when his navigator spoke up again. "Governor . . . a vessel is approaching."

A vessel? Thul wondered. He turned to Nakso. "Put it on the screen," he told her.

A moment later, their view of the vulnerable Cordracite fleetyard gave way to the image of a single ship. What's more, the governor recognized it—recognized it all too well, in fact.

It was the *Stargazer.*

Cursing under his breath, Thul whirled to face his helmsman. Fortunately, he had taken great care to arm his vessel to the teeth. "Bring us about and prepare for engagement."

The helmsman nodded, already implementing the order with admirable efficiency. "As you wish, my lord."

The governor turned to the forward viewscreen again. Picard would find himself at a considerable disadvantage, he reflected. He hadn't learned very much about the armaments of the *Stargazer,* but what he *had* learned told him the captain didn't stand a chance.

"My lord," said Thul's communications officer, "the Federation vessel is hailing us."

The Thallonian smiled grimly. "Answer their hail and establish a communications link, Nakso."

"As you wish, my lord," came the officer's reply.

Before Thul could draw another breath, he found himself face to face with the image of Jean-Luc Picard on his viewscreen. The human didn't look at all pleased with the situation.

"Captain Picard," the governor said in an affable tone. "What a surprise. I had not expected to see you again so soon. Tell me . . . did you finish the rest of that delicious wine?"

Picard came forward until his face seemed gigantic on the screen, the muscles working in his jaw. "I know what you're up to, Thul," he told the Thallonian in a voice that cracked like a whip. "In fact, I have been apprised of your entire scheme."

The governor felt the blood drain from his face.

"I know about the hired assassins," said the human, "about your grandiose plan to build an empire of your own, about the treason you intended with regard to your Emperor."

Thul absorbed the information. It unsettled him, he had to admit, to know that his intentions had been laid bare. After all, he hadn't been apprised of any security leak.

However, he reminded himself, he still had the upper hand.

"And you are here . . . why?" asked Thul, allowing a note of disdain to color his voice. "Not in an attempt to stop me, I hope."

"That is *precisely* why I am here," Picard confirmed, his resolve evident in his eyes. "The game is over, Governor. Stand down and surrender, or I warn you, I will have no compunction about destroying your vessel."

The Thallonian lifted his chin. "Forgive my ignorance," he said with studied calm, "but I thought your hands were tied. Did you not tell me it was the Benniari alone you were ordered to look out for?"

The human frowned. "Under the circumstances," he answered, "I don't think the Cordracites will object if I save their fleetyard and their base crew from obliteration. Do you?"

Thul chuckled drily. "I see your prime directive is subject to your convenient interpretation of the circumstances."

"No," said Picard. "It's subject to reason alone—and reason dictates that only a fool would stand by while you do to this fleetyard what you did to that Melacronai research colony."

The Thallonian shook his hairless head. The human had been thorough, hadn't he? "I will miss your mind, Captain, and that's not something I find myself saying very often. It's a shame you and I came down on opposite sides of this conflict. In another life, another set of circumstances, we might have been allies . . . even friends."

The captain shook his head as well—but more firmly. "No, Governor. You and I could not have been friends in any life. You see, I don't tolerate the company of *murderers.*"

Thul was stunned by the boldness of Picard's

invective—not to mention the ringing sincerity behind it. For just an instant, hot shame coursed through him . . . but it rapidly became anger.

"All right," he told the captain, doing his best to keep his voice free of emotion. "Have it your way." Then he glanced at his weapons officer again. "Target the *Stargazer*, Ubbard. Weapons to full intensity."

"Aye, sir," came the obedient reply.

The governor turned to Picard, wishing to see the human's face as he gave the order. "All stations . . . fire!"

Abruptly, the *Stargazer* was buffeted by twin blasts of fiery blue energy. Her shields absorbed the brunt of the impact, but Thul knew that they couldn't do that indefinitely.

"Fire again!" he snarled.

But this time, the Federation vessel was on the move, veering to the Thallonian's right. As a result, Thul's azure bursts missed their target and vanished into the vastness of space.

The governor smiled thinly. "All right, then," he said. "I like a game as well as the next fellow."

But he was confident that it wouldn't go on for long.

"Red alert!" Picard ordered, leaning forward in his center seat. "Lieutenant Asmund, evasive maneuvers!"

They wheeled as the red glow of the alert lights filled the bridge. A blue burst of energy glowed for an instant on the viewscreen, but the *Stargazer* managed to avoid the impact this time.

"Shields down twenty-four percent," said Vigo, his face grim as he bent his massive frame over a control panel.

He barely got the words out before another volley struck the ship, sending it lurching dizzily to starboard. It was only the armrests on the captain's chair that kept him in his seat.

"Fire phasers!" he bellowed.

Twin shafts of red fury sped toward the Thallonian vessel. As Picard watched, they slammed savagely into the enemy's shields.

"Direct hit," said Vigo.

But in the same heartbeat, another barrage from the Thallonian sent the *Stargazer* staggering to port. One of the aft consoles blew up, spewing sparks and billows of thick, black smoke across the bridge.

"Report," Picard demanded.

"Shields down fifty-eight percent," the Pandrilite told him, hanging onto his console for all he was worth. He glowered at his monitor, his face bathed in its ruddy glow. "But we barely made a dent in their deflectors, sir. We can't match their firepower."

The captain nodded as Idun Asmund wove her way through an elaborate maneuver, eluding another series of devastating energy discharges.

"Hard to port, Lieutenant Asmund," the captain said. "Mr. Vigo, prepare to fire photon torpedoes on my command."

The *Stargazer* dove to the left under the skillful hands of her helm officer. A moment later, the blue blaze of a Thallonian energy blast passed harmlessly beside them.

The ship was still in the roll as Picard shot a glance at Vigo and cried out, "Now!"

A rapid volley of photon torpedoes struck Thul's vessel dead on, detonating when it hit the Thallonian's deflectors. Picard didn't need his weapons officer's report to know he had made the right choice. He could see how quickly the enemy withdrew in the wake of his assault.

"We made some headway that time," Vigo reported. He grinned at his monitor. "Their shields are down thirty-eight percent . . . and we seem to have taken out one of their weapon ports."

The captain decided to press his advantage. Given the disparity in their weapons systems, Thul wouldn't be expecting it.

"Bear down on them," Picard told Idun Asmund. "Mr. Vigo, ready phasers and torpedoes. Full spread."

"Aye, sir," said the helm officer.

"Aye, sir," said the Pandrilite.

The governor's ship was still looping about in an almost casual manner, her flank very much exposed. The captain's eyes narrowed eagerly as she loomed on his screen.

"Fire!" he barked.

Suddenly, the *Stargazer* hammered her adversary with all the might at her disposal. The Thallonian seemed to recoil from the barrage, ruby-red phaser beams ripping hungrily at her shields, photon torpedoes exploding around her to spectacular effect.

If Picard was going to win this battle, he told himself, he would do it now or not at all. "Fire!" he barked.

Again, Vigo unleashed a hail of phasers and torpedoes, tearing apart the enemy's defenses with overwhelming efficiency. The Thallonian tried to escape, but to no avail. No matter how Thul's ship tried to elude her, Idun clung to it like a predator worrying her prey.

One more volley, the captain thought, and it would all be over. One more volley and the enemy vessel would be crippled.

"Fire again!" he told his weapons officer.

But no sooner had the words left his mouth than the Thallonian turned the tables. Instead of trying to shake his pursuer, he did the last thing Picard had anticipated . . . he came about and fired back.

All the captain saw was a blue-white burst of brilliance on his viewscreen. Then he was catapulted out of his chair like an ancient cannonball. The next thing he knew, he was pulling himself up off the deck, a distinct taste of blood in his mouth.

He looked about—and didn't like what he saw. The *Stargazer*'s bridge had been transformed into a scene out of hell. Control consoles blazed and smoke gathered in dark clouds under the low ceiling. All around

Picard, his officers were struggling to get to their feet, trying to shake off the bludgeoning effects of the Thallonian's counterattack.

"Casualties on decks six, seven, ten and eleven," Ben Zoma bellowed, waving smoke away so he could see one of the aft consoles.

"We've lost weapons," Vigo announced sharply, wiping some blood from his forehead with the back of his hand. "Shields as well."

"Propulsion and helm control are offline," Idun observed grimly.

"So is navigation," Gerda added.

The captain turned to the forward viewscreen. Through the thick, acrid smoke, he could make out Thul's ship. She seemed to be hanging in space, her portals dark.

"What about the Thallonian?" he inquired as he made his way back to his center seat.

"Looks like he's in bad shape too," Ben Zoma reported, checking his sensor readings. "No shields, no weapons, no propulsion . . ." He turned to Picard. "That killer's in the same boat we are."

The captain grunted at the irony—not that he wasn't grateful for it. "Picard to engineering."

"Aye, sir?" came Simenon's response.

"How does it look down there?" he asked the Gnalish.

"Like we've been turned inside out," came the answer. "I've got half my people working on restoring propulsion and the other half on the EPS system . . . unless, of course, you've got a better idea."

"No," Picard sighed. "Can you tell me how long it will be before the shields are restored?"

"A couple of hours?" the engineer ventured.

"Make it thirty minutes," the captain told him. He could hear Simenon hiss a curse. "Picard out."

Next, he turned to Cadwallader. Her strawberry-blond hair was in disarray, but outside of that she looked all right.

"Hail the Thallonian," he told her.

She nodded. "Aye, sir."

A moment later, the ruddy face of Gerrid Thul graced the viewscreen, replacing the sight of his crippled ship. Picard took the opportunity to survey the enemy's bridge. There was damage there, though the Federation vessel had suffered worse.

"Ready to surrender, Captain?" asked the governor. He was grinning like a damned jackal.

Picard feigned surprise. "That's odd," he retorted. "I was about to ask the same thing of you."

Thul glanced at his bridge and shrugged. "A small setback, I assure you. In the long run, it won't help you a bit."

"We will see," said the captain, "won't we?"

The governor's smile faded. A moment later, he severed contact. Once more, the image of his damaged ship filled the viewscreen.

Picard turned to Ben Zoma again. "We know so little about Thallonian technology," he said ruefully. "If only I had some idea of how quickly they can effect repairs . . ."

His first officer grunted. "I know how long it's going to take *us*." He looked at the viewscreen less than optimistically. "Of the two of us, sir, I would put my money on the Thallonians."

It wasn't what the captain had wanted to hear.

Chapter Eighteen

THUL SAT BACK IN HIS CHAIR and tried to control his anger. "You're certain?" he asked his sensor officer.

"Quite certain, my lord," said the Thallonian. "They are just as helpless as we are."

The governor eyed the *Stargazer,* which was hanging in the void like a crippled bird. Without shields, she was utterly defenseless. One good energy barrage would destroy her.

But the Thallonian vessel couldn't muster an energy barrage. With its weapons systems offline, it couldn't muster a single shot.

"Make the weapons systems operational!" he demanded of Ubbard.

"Yes, my lord," said the weapons officer, placating him as best he could. "As soon as possible, my lord."

The governor scowled. He didn't want obeisance. For the love of the Twelve, he wanted *results*.

"Governor," said his sensor officer, "another ship has entered the vicinity of the fleetyard."

Thul looked at him, trying to absorb the unexpected information. "A . . . Cordracite ship?" he wondered.

That could prove disastrous, the governor reflected. To think he had had the entire fleetyard at his mercy not so long ago . . . and now he was worrying about a single vessel!

"No, my lord," said the sensor officer, scrutinizing his monitors. "It appears to be a Durikkan vessel. But its commander identifies himself as Mendan Abbis . . . a Thallonian."

Thul's brow creased. Mendan . . . ?

What was the boy doing there? Certainly, he had known of the governor's plan to attack the fleetyard, since Thul had held nothing back from him. However, they had made no plans to rendezvous here.

The governor stroked his chin. "Answer the vessel's hail, Nakso. And establish a visual link."

"Yes, my lord," came the woman's response.

Abruptly, the image on the viewscreen changed. Thul found he was no longer looking at the crippled *Stargazer*, but rather the familiar visage of his bastard son.

"Why are you here?" the governor asked, intensely

aware of the questions Mendan's presence would raise among his command staff.

"Why?" the boy echoed, smiling a thin smile. "I've been informed that you lied to me." His voice was strangely cold, strangely distant.

"What?" Thul couldn't believe what he had heard. "Lied . . . ?" He glanced at the faces of his bridge officers, who looked stunned. After all, they had never seen their lord receive such an affront.

Mendan's eyes narrowed. "I encountered some Starfleet officers on Debennius Six," he said. "They knew everything . . . and I mean *everything* . . . though I still have no idea how."

The governor felt the scrutiny of Kaavin, Ubbard and the others. His face flushed. "This is neither the time nor the place for this discussion," he told his son.

"I beg to differ," Mendan replied. "These Starfleet people . . . they said you had no intention of making me heir to your new empire, Father." He leaned forward in his seat. "They told me that once you had gotten what you wanted, you were going to kill me—that you wanted a son of noble lineage, not some poor, stupid bastard."

The boy fairly spat out the word, making Thul feel as though a knife had been twisted into his gut. And now his officers were exchanging wide-eyed glances, putting the pieces together for themselves.

But then, they would have found out his intentions eventually, the governor told himself. If it came a little sooner, what difference did it make? None at all, Thul reflected.

More importantly, Mendan's vessel was well-armed for its size, and the governor's ship was an easy target at the moment. If the boy acted out of anger and resentment, without thinking . . .

Thul shook his head. "No, Mendan," he said, hoping his sincerity would come through in his voice, "it's not true. I don't know what these Starfleeters told you, but they are the liars—not I."

He searched his son's face, to see if his protest had had any effect. But the hardness in Mendan didn't seem to have gone away.

The governor swallowed away a dryness in his throat. "I swear on my life," he said. "I could never betray my own offspring."

Still the boy remained silent, inscrutable.

"You have earned your place at my side," Thul assured him. "More than earned it. You know I will not live forever. Who better to guide my empire after I am gone than the only son of my flesh?"

Mendan continued to stare at him—and for the space of a heartbeat, the governor was certain that his bastard would destroy him after all. Then, finally, the boy nodded.

"I believe you," he told his father in a more animated voice. "In fact, I never doubted you for a moment."

Thul's eyes narrowed. "Then why . . . ?"

"Why did I tell you all this?" asked Mendan. He smiled, and for just a moment, the governor thought he saw the child he had shunned and neglected shining through the eyes of the adult. "Because I wanted to hear the truth from your own mouth, Father."

The governor was relieved, to say the least. "And now you've heard it," he told his son. "The truth entire."

"I thank you," said Mendan. "But there's another reason I wanted to tell you about the Starfleet officers, Father. You see, I need to make amends—and I wanted you to understand why."

Thul tilted his head. "Amends . . . ?"

The bastard frowned. "These Starfleet people—they were able to surprise me, to get themselves free and . . ." He paused. "And kill my friend Wyl. Then they escaped and warned this starship." He jerked a thumb over his shoulder to indicate the *Stargazer.*

The governor grunted. He was beginning to understand why Picard had tracked him there.

"You would have arrived here unopposed if it weren't for me," said Mendan. "You would have been watching this shipyard burn by now. As it is, the Starfleet beasts were able to stop you." His mouth twisted with what was clearly a thirst for revenge. "But now they're helpless, unable to defend themselves. This is my chance to even the score."

"Abbis's ship is coming about," Kaavin announced. "It is approaching the Federation vessel." She looked at the governor, clearly uneasy with this turn of events.

He's going to attack it, Thul realized numbly.

"My lord," said Kaavin, "it is inadvisable for our . . . ally to fire on the enemy ship, even in its crippled state. He will need to let his shields lapse in order to power an effective disruptor burst, and the Federation vessel may still have some tactical capability of which we are unaware."

They hadn't severed contact with Mendan, so he had heard Kaavin's warning. But it didn't seem to faze him—far from it. The reckless grin that was so sickeningly familiar to the governor spread across the youth's face.

"I'll take my chances," he chuckled.

"No!" Thul was out of his seat and striding in the direction of the screen, as if his son were standing there on the bridge and could be stopped by physical means. "Please," he counseled, "there is no need for haste, Mendan. At least take some time to probe the enemy before you fire on her."

The younger man turned his attention to his control panel. "I'm targeting her now," he announced.

"Mendan!" Thul barked, a drop of cold sweat making its way down the length of his spine. "I know your worth. I know your courage. You do not have to demonstrate it anymore . . . not to *me*."

His son's laughter had an unnerving strain of bitterness in it. "Perhaps not to you, Father. But I allowed those Starfleet officers to slip through my fingers and Wyl is dead as a result. That leaves me with a need to prove something to *myself*."

"Damn your stubbornness!" the governor roared. He had a bad feeling about this. "Listen to me, Mendan! You have *time!*"

But his son wasn't heeding his warning. He was

working feverishly at his control console, determined to gather all the power his tiny vessel could bring to bear.

Suddenly, Mendan looked up, his eyes alight with anticipation. "I hope you enjoy this, Father. I know *I* will."

Picard eyed the Durikkan vessel that had appeared scant minutes earlier and established contact with the Thallonian. "Anything yet?" he asked.

"No, sir," Cadwallader said. "However they've protected their communication, I can't seem to break through."

The captain scowled, wary of the newcomer. "And the Durikkan still won't answer our hails?"

"That's correct," the communications officer responded.

Picard swore beneath his breath. "Keep trying," he told Cadwallader. Angrily, he thumbed a control. "Engineering, this is the captain. We may need those shields in a matter of moments."

"I wish I could give them to you," the Gnalish answered, his voice drenched with frustration. "Unfortunately, sir, we're not even close."

"Then what about weapons?" asked the captain. "Would a single port be too much to ask?"

"I'll see what I can do," Simenon promised drily.

"Sir," said Ben Zoma, who was sitting at one of the peripheral stations, "the Durikkan is coming about."

Picard regarded the viewscreen again. As his first officer had warned him, the newcomer was indeed turning away from the Thallonian vessel . . . and pointing its bow at the *Stargazer*.

"Open a channel," the captain told Cadwallader, not knowing what other option to exercise.

"Aye, sir," she answered. "Channel open."

"Durikkan vessel," Picard snapped, "this is Captain Jean-Luc Picard of the Federation starship *Stargazer*."

The smaller vessel began to close in.

"State your purpose here," the captain demanded.

Cadwallader shook her head. "Still no response, sir."

"Captain," said Gerda Asmund, duranium in her voice, "the Durikkan is dropping her shields and directing all power to her weapons."

Picard bit his lip. The *Stargazer* had no protection. One good barrage would split her end to end like a walnut in a nutcracker.

"Mr. Simenon," he said in a chill voice, "if I don't get a functional weapons port very, very soon, all of this will be academic."

"We can't work any faster, Captain," the engineer replied, his voice high and strained.

"You'll have to," Picard told him.

But even as he uttered the words, he already suspected that it was too late. Modestly equipped, the Durikkan would have been no threat under normal conditions. Given the situation, however, the *Stargazer* was little more than the proverbial sitting duck.

Inexorably, the enemy approached.

Picard realized that his hands were clenched into fists and relaxed them by force of will. This was a hell of a way to go down, he told himself, a hell of a way to perish. It was one thing to succumb in the heat of battle against a superior adversary, defending a fleet of innocents from destruction. But to bow to this little ship, a vessel a fraction the size and sophistication of the *Stargazer* . . . ?

He didn't even know who was at the controls. An ally of Thul? A rogue? A mercenary? He would never find out, would he?

And it irritated him.

"Captain!" Gerda Asmund's athletic body was taut as she turned suddenly in her seat, her eyes ablaze with excitement.

"What is it?" he asked.

"There's a vessel approaching!" she told him. "A Benniari vessel!"

Picard knew instantly what it meant. "Jack," he breathed. "And Tuvok." They had followed the ion trail, albeit more slowly than the *Stargazer*—but the important thing was that they were *there*.

"Sir," said Ben Zoma, "the Benniari vessel is powering up *her* weapons!" The first officer paused. "She's firing, Captain!"

Picard studied the viewscreen, where the Durikkan was so close it seemed it would ram itself down their throats at any moment. But before it could send a volley at the *Stargazer,* the Benniari ship sliced into the picture and unleashed an energy barrage of its own.

Caught by surprise, the Durikkan had no time to put her shields up. She had no time to do anything but take the full impact of the other vessel's assault. For a moment, the Durikkan heeled under the force of it and glowed with an eerie blue fire.

Then her warp engine tore itself into atomic particles in a savage fit of white-hot splendor.

Thul stood there in front of his center seat, refusing to believe the evidence of his eyes, denying what he had witnessed with every shred of strength in his body. Mendan, he thought. My son . . .

My son is *dead.*

Feverish with rage, robbed of his ability to reason, he staggered over to his weapons officer. "Fire!" he bellowed at the top of his lungs. "Destroy the *Stargazer!* Destroy Picard!"

Ubbard looked up at him helplessly. "My lord, our weapons are still offline. We are incapable of firing."

"No!" cried Thul, slamming his fist down on the weapons console. "You will fire, do you hear me? You will annihilate Picard and his crew!"

Ubbard held his hands up, palms exposed. "My lord, I—"

Before the governor knew what was happening, a blast of blue energy struck the officer and he went flying backward out of his seat. When he landed, there was a smoking hole where his chest had been.

And Thul's pistol was in his hand, still hot from use.

He rounded on the officer who sat at the next console. "You!" he thundered, pointing his hand weapon in the Thallonian's face. "Fire the weapons! Do it now, damn you!"

The officer gaped at the pistol, stricken with fear. He moved his mouth, but nothing came out. Worst of all, he didn't move a muscle to comply with his governor's command.

Abruptly, he too was driven out of his seat by a dark blue beam. And like his comrade before him, his chest had become a blackened ruin.

Thul whirled and saw the wide-eyed expressions of the others. They were backing off from their consoles, hands held in front of them, begging for their lives. But not a single one of them offered to blow the *Stargazer* out of space for him.

What kind of bridge officers were they? he wondered wildly. Why could none of them carry out a simple command?

He would have to punish them as he had punished the first two. He would have to hammer them with one crushing energy beam after another until they remembered who was in command of this vessel.

Maybe then he would get some—

"Thul!" said a voice, taut with urgency.

It wasn't Thallonian, but there was something familiar about it nonetheless. The governor turned to find out who had had the gall to call his name and saw Picard standing in front of him.

Picard! he seethed.

But before he could aim his disruptor pistol, before he could do anything at all, he felt something smash him in the face. As he stumbled backward, it occurred to him that his weapon had slipped from his fingers.

Then his head struck something and consciousness flickered. When his senses stabilized again, he saw that he was slumped on the deck at the base of a control console, the taste of blood strong in his mouth.

Thul spat it out, grabbed the edge of the console and pulled himself up. He had to fight back, he told himself. He had to regain his ship and get his revenge on the bloody, interfering human.

Suddenly, the object of his hatred loomed in front of him again, his eyes hard and determined. "Don't move," said Picard, the governor's pistol clenched firmly in his right hand.

He wasn't alone, either. Four of his security people had beamed over with him and were pointing their weapons at Thul's surviving officers.

A howl of pain and fury erupted from the Thallonian's throat. "My son!" he grated at Picard, his fingers opening and closing as if of their own volition. "You murdered my son!"

"He attacked my ship," the human told him, his tone flat and expressionless, his eyes colder than Thul had ever seen them. "My people had no choice but to fire back at him."

"You lie!" the governor shrieked, and flung himself at Picard.

But the human was too quick for him. He sidestepped Thul's lunge and let him crash to the deck. Once again, the Thallonian found a console to latch onto and dragged himself to his feet.

"You think you've won," he told Picard. "You think you've heard the last of me. But you haven't."

The human didn't try to silence Thul. He just frowned and let the governor go on.

"Remember this day," Thul raged at him, wiping bloody spittle from his mouth as he eyed each Starfleet officer in turn. "Remember my promise, damn you. One day, I will have my revenge on you, Picard—you and your entire Federation!"

He was still shrieking, still cursing the captain and everything he stood for, as the human officers wrestled him away.

Chapter Nineteen

PICARD AND BEN ZOMA were sitting in their customary seats on the podium when Cabrid Culunnh took his place at the lectern.

For days, the captain had been trying to convince the intrasector congress to maintain order, to observe decorum. Yet now, when every delegate and observer in the place made a clamor that shivered the Council Chamber to its foundation, Picard was far from displeased.

In fact, he was quite happy about it. After all, the delegates weren't bickering or threatening or accusing each other, as they had in the past. They were unanimously cheering the Benniari First Minister, who had cajoled and prodded and warned them into postponing a war.

By making them wait, by keeping the sparks of hatred from becoming a conflagration, he had bought time for his Federation allies. As it turned out, it was all the time they had needed.

The captain would not have wagered on this outcome when he last left the Council Chamber. And yet, here it was—a phoenix peace, risen from the ashes of acrimony and discord and suspicion.

"My fellow Kellasians," Culunnh said in a soft, breathy voice, barely audible over the roar of accolades, "please . . . if I may . . . I would like to say a few words to you."

Little by little, the applause died down. Finally, it was quiet enough for the First Minister to be heard. He chirped lightheartedly, his medallion gleaming in the filtered sunlight.

"You are much too kind," he told the assembly, "but I am an old man and I will take my recognition where I can get it."

Again, the congress broke out into a tumult of praise for Culunnh. And again, he had to wait until it faded before he could speak.

"We were duped," he said, "all of us in equal measure. We were set upon each other like ravening animals, pawns of a stone-hearted power seeker . . . a Thallonian who will find it a lot more difficult to seek power in the imperial prison he now calls his home."

Though the First Minister hadn't mentioned Thul by name, everyone knew whom he meant. The reference was met with a wave of hoots and catcalls and other assorted sounds of derision.

"What's more, he came close to accomplishing his objective," Culunnh went on. "Perilously close. He almost had the war of devastation that he sought." He turned to Picard. "Fortunately for us, he underestimated our friends on the Federation starship *Stargazer.*"

By then, every being in the congress had heard the story. At once, they rose to their feet or whatever analogous appendages they stood on and raised a thunder that exceeded what had come before. It was a staggering spectacle, a stunning tribute.

Picard turned red in the face. Despite his embarrassment, the First Minister beckoned for the captain to take the lectern.

"Gilaad," the captain told his first officer, "I don't know if it is such a good idea for me to go up there. They're liable to tear me limb from limb."

"Don't worry, sir," Ben Zoma chuckled in his ear. "I'll bring your remains back to the ship."

Picard turned to him. "How thoughtful of you."

"I try to please," said the first officer. "Besides, I've always wanted to be *Captain* Ben Zoma."

Picard grunted. "I suspected as much."

Taking a deep breath, he stood and pulled down on the front of his tunic. Then he confronted the members of the Kellasian Congress with all the dignity and humility he could muster, and he tried not to think about how much his executive officer was enjoying his discomfort.

Gradually, as the captain stood there, the applause gave way to a respectful silence. Picard cleared his throat.

"I accept your gratitude," he said, "on behalf of all those under my command who helped to stop Gerrid Thul and stymie his grand ambition. Prominent among them were Commander Jack Crusher, my second officer, and Ensign Tuvok, on loan to us from the starship *Wyoming*."

Again, cheers erupted from hundreds of alien throats. And again, they died down in time.

"However," the captain continued, "I am told—and I must take my colleagues' word for it, because I was not there—there was another who played a critical role in this effort . . . someone who had nothing to do with the Federation or the Melacron or the Cordracites, yet contributed nothing less than her life to seeing peace restored to them."

He paused, noting the intrigue expressed in the faces of his audience, and recalled what Crusher and Tuvok had told him of this person. "Her name," he said with due regard, "was Grace . . ."

Bin Nedrach was thirsty.

After all, the sun was hot on Melacron II. And as good as its rays felt on one's naked skin, they had a tendency to dry one out.

Fortunately, there was no shortage of beverages on Melacron II—especially for a man with latinum. And thanks to his recent labors, Bin Nedrach possessed a great deal of latinum.

Suddenly, he felt a band of cool shadow cross his chest. "Ah," he said, "you're just in time. I was getting thirsty."

It was no secret that Sulkoh Island had the most attractive female attendants on the planet, if not in the entire Melacron system. In the last couple of days, Bin Nedrach had discovered that they were alert as well. Whenever he even thought of needing a drink or a warm-oil rubdown, they were there at his side.

It was almost as if they were mindreaders, like that Indarrhi who had dogged Mendan Abbis's tracks. He shuddered at the memory. From now on, he vowed, he would steer clear of mindreaders.

"I'll have another Sulkoh Sunset," he said.

"I beg to differ with you," a decidedly masculine, decidedly *un*-Melacronai voice responded.

In a heartbeat, Bin Nedrach was on his feet, assessing his situation, deciding which of the many unarmed combat maneuvers that he had mastered would allow him to escape his predicament. Unfortunately, none of them seemed to fit the bill.

"Go ahead," said a human Starfleet officer, one of four who stood with their hand weapons trained on the assassin. "Try to get away. This phaser may only be set for stun, but it's got a kick like a Missouri mule."

"If I were you," said the only Vulcan in the group— the one who had roused Bin Nedrach in the first place—"I would surrender. My colleague's assessment is as accurate as it is colorful."

"Don't badger him, Tuvok," said the human. "He's a grown assassin. Let him make up his own mind."

"Very well," the Vulcan replied with an air of resignation. "You *are* the ranking officer here."

Bin Nedrach glanced about. To his back was the

pool, to his left the featureless, white wall of the indoor recreation center. Neither direction was an option. That left the areas directly in front and to the right of him, both of which were blocked off by the Starfleet people.

The Melacron knew what would happen to him if he were put on trial. The G'aha of Laws and Enforcements had been an exceedingly popular figure—and Bin Nedrach had cut the fellow down while he was inspecting an Inseeing scarf. Without question, he would receive the maximum penalty.

Call me evil, he had mused at the time. And they would.

Anything was better than a lifetime spent in a Melacronai penal colony, the Melacron told himself. Avoiding such a fate was worth any risk, any effort, any amount of pain.

"Well?" asked the human, the muscles working in his temples. "What's it going to be?"

Taking a deep breath, Bin Nedrach lashed out with his bare foot and knocked the weapon out of the officer's hand. Then the Melacron pushed past him and tried to make a break for it.

He didn't make it.

Picard was sitting at the desk in his ready room, going over one of a great many repair reports filed by Phigus Simenon, when he heard a chime. Looking up from his work, he said, "Come."

A moment later, the doors to the room slid aside with a hiss, revealing Jack Crusher and Ensign Tuvok.

They entered one after the other and crossed the room.

"You asked to see us, sir?" said the commander, when both he and the Vulcan were standing before the captain.

"Indeed," said Picard. He sat back in his chair and smiled. "I believe congratulations are in order. Your good work saved the lives of everyone at the fleet-yard, not to mention the millions who likely would have perished if the Cordracites and the Melacron had gone to war. What's more, you did an admirable job working with local law enforcement agencies to apprehend the assassins we were able to identify."

Tuvok inclined his head ever so slightly. "Thank you, Captain."

"But it was all in a day's work," Crusher said dutifully. He glanced at the ensign, his expression suddenly becoming sterner and more severe. "Figuratively speaking, of course."

Tuvok glanced back, perhaps just a touch less deadpan than when Picard had seen him last. "Of course."

Clearly, thought the captain, the two men had developed something more than a working relationship. It pleased him to see it. But then, it was the rare sentient being who couldn't get along with Jack Crusher.

Picard was also glad to see how much more comfortable the Vulcan looked on the *Stargazer.* Tuvok was a fine officer. It would be very much to Starfleet's advantage if he were to stay on this time.

"Apparently," he told the ensign, "undercover work agrees with you. I'm sure Captain Broadnax will be glad to hear that."

The Vulcan frowned. "Actually, sir, I believe I am more effective serving on a vessel than off it. However, if I am again required to go undercover, I am certain this experience will serve me well."

The captain nodded, still smiling. "No doubt."

Tuvok cast a sidelong look at Crusher—the kind of look that might be meant to dissuade someone from revealing something. If that was what it was, it seemed to work. The commander took a deep breath, but ultimately kept his mouth shut.

"That will be all," Picard told them. "You're dismissed, gentlemen."

Crusher nodded. "Thank you, sir."

And with that, the two of them turned and departed, leaving the captain curious as to what their conversation might be once they were by themselves in the nearest turbolift.

Tuvok waited until the lift doors closed in front of him. Then he turned to Jack Crusher.

"I am grateful," he said, "that you refrained from describing to the captain our misadventure in The House of Comfort."

The commander shrugged. "It didn't seem necessary."

"Though," the Vulcan went on, "it no doubt would have made for a very humorous story, by human standards."

"A *very* humorous story," Crusher agreed. He glanced at Tuvok. "Are you going to tell your wife about it?"

The Vulcan sighed. "I vowed to share everything with T'pel when she and I were linked in marriage. I cannot make an exception . . . as dearly as I would like to."

The human grunted. "Me either."

Tuvok nodded approvingly. As it turned out, he and Crusher had much in common after all.

For a moment, they stood there in companionable silence. Finally, the commander broke it.

"You know," he said, "you took quite a chance when we were Abbis's prisoners back on Debennius Six."

The Vulcan cocked an eyebrow. "Explain."

"That story you told about the treachery Thul intended and how we had discovered proof of it . . . Abbis could have had his Indarrhi pal read my emotions to see if you were telling the truth. And even if he didn't, he could have chosen to discount your claims about Thul and simply told his father that Starfleet was onto them."

"Thereby endangering not only our mission, but the *Stargazer* as well," the Vulcan finished. "I can see where an individual of your species might reach that conclusion."

"Let's not bring species into this," Crusher told him.

"However," Tuvok went on, undaunted, "what you fail to consider is that we, our mission and indeed this entire *sector* were already very much at risk. It was only by applying native ingenuity that we were able to remove ourselves from Abbis's grasp and eventually turn failure into success."

The commander frowned and wagged a finger at him. "Uh-uh. You don't get off that easily. You still had no idea how Abbis would react."

"On the contrary," said the Vulcan, "I had a very good idea. Remember, I had previously experienced mental contact with the Indarrhi—a link which permitted me to search his mind even as he was searching mine. As a result, I had come to know Mendan Abbis through his associate's impressions of him, and therefore could predict with reasonable certainty how our captor would react to my ploy."

Crusher sighed and shook his head. "I should know better by now than to argue with a Vulcan."

Tuvok shot a look at him. "For once," he commented, "I find myself agreeing with you."

The commander smiled. "I won't tell anyone if you won't."

The Vulcan maintained his composure, despite an inexplicable impulse to smile. "It is a deal," he said.

Jack Crusher basked in the grins of his beautiful bride and his impish baby son. "And since our rendezvous with the *Wyoming* was so close to Earth," he continued, "I saw my chance and booked some time on subspace."

"You couldn't have been the only one," said Beverly.

"That's true," the commander agreed. "But rank has its privileges." He shrugged. "Actually, I didn't take any more time than anyone else with family in the sector—I just went first."

His wife chuckled and shook her head. "You're always thinking of others, aren't you?"

"Right now," Crusher told her, "I'm thinking about you. And about Wes. And about how much I miss the two of you."

Beverly sighed. "Any prospect of shore leave?"

"None right now," he said. "But you never know. Just keep hoping." He paused. "Honey, there's something I want to tell you about."

She must have sensed something in his voice, because her eyes narrowed. "Is something wrong, Jack?"

"No," the commander said, "nothing like that."

Then he brought her up to date about his mission on Debennius VI. He started with the explosive diplomatic situation the *Stargazer* had sailed into and proceeded through the beginning of his adventures with Tuvok.

"Sounds dangerous," Beverly said, clearly none too thrilled about the idea but resigned not to say too much about it.

"Maybe a little," Crusher conceded. "But the worst part . . ."

She looked at him. "Yes?"

"Was at a place called The House of Comfort." And he went on to tell his wife all about it.

The commander wasn't sure what reaction he

expected—but it wasn't the one he got. When he had finished with his description of what happened in the bathhouse, Beverly broke into peals of laughter—so much so that little Wesley gaped at her, startled.

"Jack," she exclaimed when she was able to catch her breath, "that's the funniest thing I've ever heard!"

"It is?" he blurted. "I mean . . . of course it is. Absolutely. That's why I . . . er, wanted to share it with you, because it's so funny. And you're not . . . upset or anything, right?"

His wife looked at him askance. "You mean . . . am I angry that my husband was willing to go to any length in that place to get the information he needed?" She thought about it for a moment. "Yes, I guess I *am* a little angry. But you were doing your duty, Jack."

"That's right," Crusher confirmed.

"And for a very worthy cause."

"Right again," he told her.

"And if our positions were reversed and I had to do what you did, you would understand too . . . wouldn't you?"

The commander was about to agree again when he realized just what he would be agreeing to. Suddenly, he didn't know what to say.

Again, Beverly broke into laughter—and this time, Wesley laughed along with her. "Honestly, Jack, you must be the most predictable man in all of Starfleet. Don't you know when I'm kidding you?"

Crusher blushed. "Um . . . sometimes?"

"But what happened after that?" his wife asked.

She stifled a snicker. "After you and Tuvok got out of the bath, I mean."

He told her the rest—about the fight in the dance hall and their ensuing imprisonment at the hands of Mendan Abbis. About Grace, whose violent end saddened her. About his warning to the captain, and about his timely arrival with Tuvok at the Cordracite fleetyard.

Beverly smiled. "Then the good guys won?"

The commander nodded. "This time."

"And what about Thul?" she asked.

He shrugged. "As I understand it, the Thallonians are pretty intolerant when it comes to treachery. No doubt, Thul will be placed in prison for a long time. Maybe the rest of his life."

Beverly sighed. "Wherever he is, I hope he never gets a chance to carry out that revenge he was ranting about."

Crusher shook his head. "Don't worry, honey. I think we can be pretty sure we've heard the last of Gerrid Thul."

Epilogue

IN HIS NIGHTMARE, he was once again standing on the bridge of his ship, watching the hideous, blinding flash of his son's vessel as it reduced itself to sub-atomic particles on his viewscreen.

"Thul!" someone said.

He looked about at the faces of his officers. They stared back at him, uncertainty etched in their every feature.

"Thul!" someone said again, louder this time.

But the summons hadn't come from anyone on his bridge. He turned to his viewscreen. There was no one there either.

"Thul!" someone growled.

With a shock, the governor bolted upright—and saw that he wasn't on his ship after all. He was on the hard, uncomfortable pallet that had served him as a bed for the last several months, ever since he became an inmate of the Reggana City Imperial Prison.

Rubbing sleep from his eyes, willing his heart to slow down, Thul swung his legs over the side of the pallet and stared through the translucent energy barrier that separated him from the corridor beyond. There was a guard standing there . . . and someone else. Someone wearing a dark, hooded robe.

Someone whose bearing was vaguely familiar.

"A visitor," the guard spat.

A feminine hand emerged from the robe and deposited something in the guard's big hand. Quickly, he stuffed it into a pocket of his tunic, but not before Thul saw the distinctive glint of latinum. Then, with a glance at the prisoner, the guard walked away.

Thul was alone with his guest. "Who are you?" he asked as he approached the energy barrier—though he had a feeling he knew the answer.

"It is I," the hooded one said in a soft whisper. Pulling back her hood, she revealed herself as Mella Cwan.

The prisoner had forgotten how plain the emperor's sister was, how flatly unappealing. Nonetheless, he managed to put all that aside and smile his most fervent smile.

"My lady," he said breathlessly.

Mella Cwan smiled back at him, affection and sadness illuminating her eyes. "Lord Governor . . . how it grieves me to see you like this."

No more than it grieves me, Thul thought bitterly.

But what he said was, "Please, my lady . . . I am no longer a governor; that exalted position has been stripped from me. I am once again General Thul. It is the penalty for ambition."

Her brow knotted over the bridge of her nose. "And a long penalty it is," she replied. "A lifetime . . ."

"Is very long," he agreed. "But the worst part of my imprisonment is not its length in years, but the knowledge that I will never share any of them with you—as I surely would have if my plan had borne fruit." He heaved a heavy sigh. "If only your brother had not been so stubborn when I came to him in his throne chamber . . ."

"He *is* stubborn," Mella Cwan agreed. "But he is also the emperor. No one can oppose his wishes."

That wasn't what Thul wanted to hear. "True, you can't oppose them," he began, "but surely, there is a way for you—*us*—to have our hearts' desire short of actual defiance."

The emperor's sister tilted her head, a hint of wariness in her eyes. "What do you mean?"

Careful, he thought. You won't get another chance like this one. "Why," he said, "only that not every flower flourishes in sunlight. Some live in shadows, and smell that much more sweetly for it."

Her dark eyes widened as understanding dawned. "You speak of an illicit affair? Between you and me?"

Thul smiled sadly. "Only in the absence of the marriage I would have preferred. But if that is denied to us, must we give up everything? Do we not deserve some small measure of happiness?"

Mella Cwan drew a shuddering breath as she considered it. "You ask much, General."

"I *dare* much," the prisoner said, coming within a hair's breadth of the energy barrier to prove it.

"If we were ever exposed . . ." she said, her voice trailing off into the grimmer realms of imagination.

He held up a hand. "Don't think about that," he insisted. "Think about us, my dear. Think about our being together at last."

The Emperor's sister frowned. "You're right," she told him. "I cannot live in fear. I must think about my happiness."

"Exactly," Thul replied.

"I must think about the two of us."

"Yes," he said encouragingly.

Mella Cwan's expression became resolute. "I must think of a way to free you," she decided.

He nodded. "I would never have asked it of you, my lady . . . but clearly, it is the only way."

She bit her lip in a very unimperial way. "It will take time. I have never done anything like this before."

"I could make suggestions," Thul offered. "I know people who can arrange almost anything for latinum."

The emperor's sister smiled. "Latinum will not be a problem." She reached a hand lovingly toward his face, almost touching the energy barrier herself. "As long as I know that when you get out, you'll be mine."

"I'll be yours," he told her. It wasn't the first promise he had ever broken, nor would it be the last.

A sound came from the far end of the corridor. It was the guard, no doubt, telling them that he didn't dare give them any more time—not even for all the latinum he could carry.

Mella Cwan pulled her hood up. "Have courage," she said.

Thul smiled a thin smile. He thought again of his bastard son, whose death at the hands of the Federation cried out to him for vengeance. "I will," he assured the emperor's sister. "For is courage not the first virtue?"

And I am nothing, he thought, if not a virtuous man.

OUR FIRST SERIAL NOVEL!

Presenting one chapter per month . . .

The very beginning of the Starfleet
Adventure . . .

STAR TREK
STARFLEET: YEAR ONE

A Novel in Twelve Parts

by
Michael Jan Friedman

Chapter One

Commander Bryce Shumar felt the labored rise of his narrow, dimly lit turbolift compartment, and sighed.

The damned thing hadn't been running as smoothly as he would have liked for several months already. The cranky, all-too-familiar whine of the component that drove the compartment only underlined what the commander already knew—that the system was on its last legs.

Under normal circumstances, new turbolift parts would have appeared at the base in a matter of weeks—maybe less. But lift parts weren't exactly a tactical priority, so Shumar and his people were forced to make do with what they had.

After a few moments, the component cycled down and the commander's ascent was complete. Then the doors parted with a loud hiss and revealed a noisy, bustling operations center—Ops for short. It was packed with one sleek, black console after another—all of them manned, and all of them enclosed in a transparent dome that featured a breathtaking view of the stars.

The first day Shumar had set foot there, the place had impressed the hell out of him—almost enough to make him forget the value of what he had lost. But that was four long years ago. Now, he had learned to take it all for granted.

The big, convex viewer located in the center of the facility echoed the curve of the sprawling security console below it. Fixing his gaze on the screen, Shumar saw two ships making their way through the void on proximate parallel courses.

One was a splendid, splay-winged Rigelian transport vessel, its full-bellied hull the deep blue color of a mountain lake. The other was a black, needle-sharp Cochrane, capable of speeds as high as warp one point six, according to some reports.

It was hardly an unusual pairing, given the Cochrane's tactical advantages and the dangerous times in which they lived. Vessels carrying important cargo were almost always given escorts. Still, thought Shumar, it wouldn't hurt to make sure the ships were what they appeared to be.

"Run a scan," he told his redhaired security officer.

Morgan Kelly shot a glance at him over her shoulder. "Might I remind the commander," she said, "no Romulan has used subterfuge to approach an Earth base since the war began? Not even once?"

"Consider me reminded," Shumar told her, "and run the scan anyway."

"Way ahead of you," said Kelly, only half-suppressing a smile. She pointed to a monitor on her left, where the vessels' energy signatures were displayed. "According to our equipment, everything checks out. Those two are exactly what they're cracked up to be—a transport and its keeper."

Shumar frowned. "Tell them I'll meet them downstairs."

"Aye, sir," said the security officer. "And I'll be sure to tell them also what a lovely mood you're in."

The commander looked at her. "What kind of mood would *you* be in if you'd just learned your vessel had been destroyed?"

Kelly grunted. "Begging the commander's pardon, but it was nearly a month ago that you got that news."

Shumar's frown deepened. Had it really been that long since he learned what happened to the *John Burke?* "Time flies," he remarked drily, "when you're having fun."

Then he made his way back to the turbolift.

Though not a human himself, Alonis Cobaryn had seen his share of Earth bases floating in the void.

The one he saw on his primary monitor now was typical of the breed. It possessed a dark, boxlike body, four ribbed cargo globes that vaguely resembled the legs of a very slow quadruped on his homeworld, and a transparent bubble that served as the facility's brain.

There was also nothing unusual about the procedure he had been instructed to follow in his approach. And now that he was within a few kilometers of the base, Cobaryn was expected to begin that procedure.

But first, he pulled a toggle to switch one of his secondary monitors over to a communications function. After all, he always liked to see in whose hands he was placing his molecular integrity.

The monitor screen fizzed over with static for a moment, then showed him the Earth base's security officer—a woman with high cheekbones, green eyes and red hair pulled back into a somewhat unruly knot. What's more, she filled out her gold and black jumpsuit rather well.

All in all, Cobaryn mused, a rather attractive-looking individual. *For a human, that is.*

It took her about a second to take note of the visual link and look back at him. "If you were planning on cutting your engines," the woman told him, "this would be as good a time as any."

Cobaryn's mouth pulled up at the corners—as close as he could come to a human smile. "I could not agree more," he said. Tapping the requisite sequence into the touch pad of his helm-control console, he looked up again. "I have cut my engines."

"Acknowledged," said the security officer, checking her monitors with admirable efficiency to make sure all was as it should be.

Next, Cobaryn applied his braking thrusters until he had reduced his vessel's momentum to zero and assumed a position within half a kilometer of the base. The facility loomed larger than ever on his primary monitor, a dark blot on the stars.

"That'll be fine," the redhaired woman told him.

"I am pleased that you think so," he responded.

The officer's green eyes narrowed a bit, but she wasn't averse to the banter. At least, that was how it seemed to Cobaryn.

"I suppose you'd like to beam over now," she said.

"If it is not too much trouble."

"And if it is?" the woman asked playfully.

Cobaryn shrugged. "Then I would be deprived of the opportunity to thank you for your assistance in person."

She chuckled. "You Rigelians don't lack confidence, do you?"

"I cannot speak for others," he remarked thoughtfully, "but as for myself . . . I do indeed believe that confidence is a virtue."

The officer considered him a moment longer. "Too bad your pal in the Cochrane doesn't have the same attitude."

Cobaryn tilted his head. "And why is that?" he inquired, at a loss as to the human's meaning.

A coy smile blossomed on the officer's face. "No offense, Captain, but the Cochrane jockey's a lot better-looking." Then she went on, almost in the same breath, "Get ready to beam over."

Cobaryn sat back in his chair, deflated by the woman's remark—if only for a moment. Then he recalled that humans often said the opposite of what they meant. Perhaps that was the case here.

"Ready," he replied.

"Good," said the security officer, embracing a lever in each hand. "Then here goes."

Commander Shumar stood in one of his base's smallest, darkest rooms and watched a faint shimmer of light appear like a will-o'-the-wisp over a raised transporter disc.

Gradually, the shimmer grew along its vertical axis. Then a ghostly image appeared in the same space—a vague impression of a muscular humanoid dressed in loose-fitting black togs.

The transport captain, Shumar remarked inwardly. Obviously, he had been nicer to Kelly than the pilot of the Cochrane, or the security officer would have beamed the other man over first.

The base commander watched the shaft of illumination dim as the figure flickered, solidified, flickered again and solidified a bit more. Finally, after about forty-five seconds, the process was complete and the vertical blaze of light died altogether.

A moment later, a host of blue emergency globes activated themselves in a continuous line along the bulkheads. By their glare, Shumar could make out his guest's silvery features and ruby-red eyes, which gleamed beneath a flared brow ridge reminiscent of a triceratops' bony collar.

He was a Rigelian, the commander noted. More specifically, a denizen of Rigel IV, not to be confused with any of the other four inhabited planets in the Rigel star system. And he was smiling awkwardly.

Of course, smiling was a peculiarly Terran activity. It wasn't uncommon for aliens to look a little clumsy at it—which is why so few of them even made the attempt.

"Welcome to Earth Base Fourteen," said the human.

"Thank you," the Rigelian replied with what seemed like studied politeness. He stepped down from the disc and extended a three-fingered hand. "Alonis Cobaryn at your service, Commander."

Shumar gripped the transport captain's offering. It felt much like a human appendage except for some variations in metacarpal structure and a complete lack of hair.

"You shake hands," the base commander observed.

"I do," Cobaryn confirmed.

Shumar studied him. "Most nonhumans don't, you know."

The Rigelian's ungainly smile widened, stretching an elaborate maze of tiny ridges that ran from his temples down to his jaw. "I have dealt with your people for a number of years now," he explained. "Sometimes I imagine I know as much about them as any human."

Shumar grunted. "I wish I could say the same about Rigelians. You're the first one I've seen in person in four years on this base."

"I am not surprised," said Cobaryn, his tone vaguely apologetic. "My people typically prefer the company of other Rigelians. In that I relish the opportunity to explore the intricacies of other cultures, I am considered something of a black sheep on my homeworld."

Suddenly, realization dawned. "Wait a minute," said the human. "Cobaryn . . .? Aren't you the fellow who charted Sector Two-seven-five?"

The alien lowered his hairless silver head ever so slightly. "I see that my reputation has preceded me."

Shumar found himself smiling. "I used your charts to navigate the Galendus Cluster on my way to—"

Before he could finish his sentence, the emergency illumination around them dimmed and another glimmer of light appeared over the transporter disc. Like the one before it, it lengthened little by little and gave rise to something clearly man-shaped.

This one was human, the base commander noted—the pilot of the *Cochrane*, no doubt. Shumar watched the shape flicker and take on substance by turns. In time, the new arrival became solid, the shaft of light fizzled out and the emergency globes activated themselves again.

This time, they played on a tall, athletic-looking specimen with a lean face, close-cropped blond hair and slate-blue eyes. His garb was civilian, like that of most escort pilots these days—a brown leather jacket over a rumpled, gray jumpsuit.

"Welcome to the base," said the commander. "My name's Shumar."

The other man looked at him for a second, but he didn't say a thing in return. Then he got down from the platform, walked past his fellow human and left the transporter room by its only set of sliding doors.

As the titanium panels slid closed again, shutting out the marginally brighter light of the corridor outside, Shumar turned to Cobaryn. "What's the matter with your friend?" he asked, as puzzled as he was annoyed.

The Rigelian smiled without much enthusiasm. "Captain Dane is not very communicative. The one time we spoke, he described himself as a loner." He regarded the doors with his ruby-red orbs. "Frankly, given his attitude, I am surprised he takes part in the war effort at all."

"The *one* time?" Shumar echoed. He didn't get it. "But he was your escort, wasn't he?"

"He was," Cobaryn confirmed in a neutral tone. "Still, as I noted, he was not a very loquacious one. He appeared to be troubled by something, though I cannot imagine what it might have been."

Shumar frowned. "It wouldn't hurt him to say a few words when he sets foot on someone else's base. I mean, I'm not exactly thrilled about my lot in life either right now, but I keep it to myself."

The Rigelian's eyes narrowed. "You would rather be somewhere else?"

"On a research vessel," Shumar told him unhesitatingly, "conducting planetary surveys. That's what I did before the war. Unfortunately, I'll have to get hold of a new ship if I want to pick up where I left off."

"The old one was commandeered, then?" asked Cobaryn.

Shumar nodded. "Four years ago, when I was given command of this place. Then, a little more than a month ago, it was blown to bits by the Romulans out near Gamma Llongo."

The Rigelian sighed. "You and I have much in common, then."

The commander looked at him askance. "Don't tell me they pressed *you* into service. You're not even human."

"Perhaps not," said Cobaryn. "But it is difficult to pursue a career as an explorer and stellar cartographer when the entire quadrant has become a war zone." His eyes crinkled at the corners. "Besides, it is foolish to pretend the Romulans are a threat to Earth alone."

"A number of species have done just that," Shumar noted, airing one of his pet peeves.

The Rigelian nodded wistfully. "Including my own, I hesitate to admit. However, I cannot change my people's minds. All I can do is lend my own humble efforts to the cause and hope for the best."

The commander found the sentiment hard to argue with. "Come on," he said. "I'll arrange for some dinner. I'll bet you're dying for some fresh muttle pods after all those rations."

Cobaryn chuckled softly. "Indeed I am. And then, after dinner . . ."

Shumar glanced at him. "Yes?"

The Rigelian shrugged. "Perhaps you could introduce me to your security officer? The one with the splendid red hair?"

The request took the commander by surprise. "You mean Kelly?"

"Kelly," Cobaryn repeated, rolling the name a little awkwardly over his tongue. "A pleasing name. I would be most grateful."

The commander considered it. As far as he knew, his security officer wasn't attracted to nonhumans. But then, the Rigelian had asked for an introduction, not a weekend in Tahoe.

"If you like," Shumar suggested, "I can ask the lieutenant if she'd like to dine with us."

"Even better," said Cobaryn.

The Rigelian looked like a kid in a candy shop, thought the commander. He wasn't the least bit self-conscious about expressing his yen for Kelly—even to a man he had only just met.

Shumar found it hard not to like someone like that.

As Connor Dane entered the rec lounge at Earth Base Fourteen, he didn't even consider parking himself at one of the small black tables the base's crew seemed so fond of. Instead, he made his way straight to the bar.

The bartender was tall, thin and dour-faced, but he seemed to perk up a little at the sight of the newcomer. Of course, he probably didn't see too many new faces in his line of work.

"Get you something?" he asked.

Dane nodded. "Tequila, neat. And a beer to chase it with."

"We've got a *dozen* beers," said the bartender.

The Cochrane jockey slid himself onto a stool. "Your choice."

The bartender smiled as if his customer had made a joke. "You sure you wouldn't want to hear our list?" he asked.

"Life's too short," said Dane. "Just close your eyes and reach into the freezer. I promise I won't send it back, whatever it is."

The bartender's brow knit. "You're not kidding, are you?"

"I'm not kidding," the captain assured him.

The bartender shrugged. "Whatever you say."

A moment later, he produced a shot glass full of pale gold liquor. And a moment after that, he plunked a bottle of amber beer down beside it, a wisp of frosty vapor trailing from its open mouth.

"There you go," he said. He leaned back against the shelf behind him and folded his arms across his chest. "I guess you'd be the Cochrane jock who checked in a couple of minutes ago."

Dane didn't answer, hoping the man would get the message. As luck would have it, he didn't.

"You know," said the bartender, "my brother flew one of those needlenoses back before the war." He looked at the ceiling as if he were trying to remember something. "Must have been ten, eleven—"

"Listen, pal," Dane snapped, his voice taut and preemptive.

It got the bartender's attention. "What?"

"I know a lot of people come to places like this for some conversation," the captain told him. "Maybe your commander does that, or that foxy redheaded number behind the security console. But I'm not looking for anything like that. All I want is to kick back a little and pretend I'm somewhere besides a hunk of titanium in the middle of—"

Suddenly, a high-pitched ringing sound filled the place. Scowling at the interruption, Dane turned to the emergency monitor above the bar—one of hundreds located all around the base.

A moment later, the screen came alive, showing him the swarthy, dark-browed visage of the man in charge of the place. What was the commander's name again? he asked himself. Shumac? No . . . Shu*mar*. He didn't often pay attention to things like that, but this time the name seemed to have stuck.

"Attention," said the base commander, the muscles working in his temples. "All hands to battle stations. Our long-range scanners have detected a Romulan attack force at a distance of twenty-six million kilometers."

The Cochrane jockey bit his lip. At full impulse, the Romulans would arrive in something under eleven minutes. That didn't leave him much time.

As the lounge's contingent of uniformed officers bolted for the door, Dane raised his glass of tequila and downed it at a gulp. Then he took a long swig of his beer and wiped his mouth with the back of his hand.

The bartender looked at him as if he'd grown another head. "Didn't you hear what the commander said?" he asked.

The captain nodded. "I heard." Ignoring the man's concern, he held his beer up to the light, admiring its consistency. Then he raised the bottle's mouth to his lips and took another long pull at its contents.

"But . . ." the bartender sputtered, "if you heard, what the devil are you still *doing* here?"

Dane smiled grimly at him. "The Romulans may rip this base in half, pal. They may even kill me. But I'll be damned if they're going to keep me from enjoying a refreshing beverage."

Finally, he finished off his beer and placed the bottle on the bar. Then he got up from his stool, pulled down on the front of his jacket and headed back to the base's only transporter room.

His message to his staff delivered, Commander Shumar turned from the two-way viewscreen set into the Ops center's comm console and eyed the officer seated beside him.

"Have you got the *Nimitz* yet?" he asked.

Ibanez, who had been Shumar's communications officer for the last two and a half years, looked more perturbed than the commander had ever seen him. "Not yet," the man replied, making adjustments to his control settings.

"What's wrong?" Shumar asked.

"They're just not responding," Ibanez told him.

The commander cursed under his breath. "How can that be? They're supposed to be listening twenty-four hours a day."

The comm officer shook his head from side to side. "I don't know what the trouble is, sir."

Shumar glared at the console's main screen, where he could see Ibanez's hail running over and over again on all Earth Command frequencies. Then he gazed at the stars that blazed above him. Why in blazes didn't the *Nimitz* answer? he wondered.

According to the last intelligence Shumar had received from Command, the Christopher-class vessel was within ninety million kilometers of Base Fourteen. At that distance, one might expect a communications delay of several seconds, but no more. And yet, Ibanez had been trying to raise the *Nimitz* for nearly a minute without success.

Without the warship's clout, the commander reflected, they wouldn't be able to withstand a Romulan attack for very long. No Earth base could. Clearly, they had a problem on their hands.

Of course, there was still a chance the *Nimitz* would respond. Shumar fervently hoped that that would be the case.

"Keep trying them," he told Ibanez.

"Aye, sir," came the reply.

Crossing the room, the commander passed by the engineering and life support consoles on his way to the security station. When he reached Kelly, he saw her look up at him. She seemed to sense his concern.

"What's the matter?" the redhead asked.

Shumar suppressed a curse. "We're having trouble raising the *Nimitz.*"

Kelly's eyes widened. "Tell me you're kidding."

"I'm not the kidding type," he reminded her.

She swallowed. "That's right. You're not."

The commander leaned a little closer to her. "This could be a mess, Kelly. I'm going to need your help."

She took a breath, then let it out. It seemed to steady her. "I'm with you," the security officer assured him.

That settled, Shumar took a look at the monitors on Kelly's console. The Romulan warships, represented by four red blips on the long-range scanner screen, were bearing down on them. They had less than ten minutes to go before visual contact.

The commander turned his attention to the transporter monitor, where he could see that someone was being beamed off the station. "That Cochrane pilot had better be good," he said.

Kelly tapped a fingernail on the transporter screen. "That's not the Cochrane pilot. That's Cobaryn."

Shumar looked at her. "What . . . ?"

The woman shrugged. "The Rigelian showed up in the transporter room and the Cochrane jock didn't. Who was I to argue?"

The commander's teeth ground together. True, Cobaryn had a valuable cargo to protect—medicines and foodstuffs that might be of help to some other Earth base—and technically, this wasn't his fight.

But the Rigelian had seemed so engaging—so *human* in many respects. And by human standards, it seemed like a slimy thing to abandon a base at the first sign of trouble.

"Transport complete," said Kelly, reading the results off the pertinent screen. "Cobaryn is out of here."

Shumar forced himself to wish the Rigelian luck. "What about the Cochrane pilot? He's got to be around the base—"

His officer held her hand up. "Hang on a second, Commander. I think our friend has finally arrived." Her fingers flying over her controls, she opened a channel to the transporter room. "This is security. Nothing like taking your sweet time, Captain."

"Better late than never," came the casual response.

Obviously, Shumar observed, Dane wasn't easily flustered. But then, that might be a good thing. After all, the Cochrane might be all the help they would get.

"Get on the platform," said Kelly.

"I'm on it," Dane answered.

The security officer took that as a signal to manipulate her controls. Pulling back slowly on a series of levers, she tracked the dematerialization and emission processes on her transporter screen. Then she glanced meaningfully at the commander.

"He's on his way," said Kelly.

Shumar nodded soberly. "I sincerely hope the man's a better pilot than he is a human being."

The first thing Connor Dane noticed as he materialized in his cockpit was the flashing proximity alarm on his control panel.

He swore volubly, thinking that the base's scanners had been off a few light years and that the Romulans had arrived earlier than expected. But as he checked his external scan monitor, the captain realized it wasn't the Romulans who had set off the alarm.

It was the Rigelian transport.

Craning his neck to look out of his cockpit's transparent hood, Dane confirmed the scan reading. For some reason, that idiot Cobaryn hadn't taken off yet. He was still floating in space beside the Cochrane.

Shaking his head, Dane punched a stud in his panel and activated his vessel's communications function. "Cobaryn," he said, "this is Dane. You've got to move your blasted ship!"

He expected to hear a response taut with urgency. However, the Rigelian didn't sound the least bit distressed.

"I assure you," said Cobaryn, "I *intend* to move it."

The human didn't yet understand. "For Earthsakes, when?"

"When the enemy arrives," the transport captain replied calmly.

"But it'll be too late by then," Dane argued, fighting the feeling that he was swimming upstream against a serious flood of reality.

"Too late to escape," Cobaryn allowed. "But not too late to take part in the battle."

The human didn't get it. Maybe the tequila had affected him more than he'd imagined. "You've got no weapons," he reminded the Rigelian. "How are you planning to slug it out in a space battle?"

"I would be perfectly happy to discuss tactics with you," Cobaryn told him reasonably, "but I think the time for discussion is past. It appears the Romulans have arrived."

Spurred by the remark, Dane checked his scan monitor. Sure enough, there were four Romulan warships nearing visual range.

Bringing his engines online, he raised his shields and powered up his weapons batteries. Then he put the question of the transport captain aside and braced himself for combat.

Shumar eyed the Romulan vessels, each one a sleek, silver cylinder with a cigar-shaped plasma nacelle on either side of it and a blue-green winged predator painted on its underbelly.

No question about it, the base commander mused grimly. The enemy had a flair for the dramatic.

"Shields up," he said. "Stand by, all weapons stations."

Kelly leaned forward and pulled down on a series of toggles.

"Shields up," she confirmed. She checked a couple of readouts. "Weapons stations standing by, awaiting your orders."

Shumar's stomach had never felt so tight. But then, in the past, Romulan assault forces had been deflected from the base by the *Nimitz* or some other Terran vessel. In four years as commander, he had never had to mount a lone defense against an enemy attack.

Until *now*.

"Fifty kilometers," said Kelly. "Forty. Thirty. Twenty . . ." Suddenly, she looked up at the transparent dome and pointed at a swarm of tiny silver dots. "There they are!"

Continued
Next Month . . .

Look for STAR TREK Fiction from Pocket Books

Star Trek®: The Original Series

Star Trek: The Next Generation®

Star Trek: Deep Space Nine®

Star Trek®: Voyager™

Flashback • Diane Carey
Pathways • Jeri Taylor
Mosaic • Jeri Taylor

#1 *Caretaker* • L. A. Graf
#2 *The Escape* • Dean W. Smith & Kristine K. Rusch
#3 *Ragnarok* • Nathan Archer
#4 *Violations* • Susan Wright
#5 *Incident at Arbuk* • John Gregory Betancourt
#6 *The Murdered Sun* • Christie Golden
#7 *Ghost of a Chance* • Mark A. Garland & Charles G. McGraw
#8 *Cybersong* • S. N. Lewitt
#9 *Invasion #4: The Final Fury* • Dafydd ab Hugh
#10 *Bless the Beasts* • Karen Haber
#11 *The Garden* • Melissa Scott
#12 *Chrysalis* • David Niall Wilson
#13 *The Black Shore* • Greg Cox
#14 *Marooned* • Christie Golden
#15 *Echoes* • Dean W. Smith & Kristine K. Rusch
#16 *Seven of Nine* • Christie Golden
#17 *Death of a Neutron Star* • Eric Kotani
#18 *Battle Lines* • Dave Galanter & Greg Brodeur

Star Trek®: New Frontier

#1 *House of Cards* • Peter David
#2 *Into the Void* • Peter David
#3 *The Two-Front War* • Peter David
#4 *End Game* • Peter David
#5 *Martyr* • Peter David
#6 *Fire on High* • Peter David

Star Trek®: Day of Honor

Book One: *Ancient Blood* • Diane Carey
Book Two: *Armageddon Sky* • L. A. Graf
Book Three: *Her Klingon Soul* • Michael Jan Friedman
Book Four: *Treaty's Law* • Dean W. Smith & Kristine K. Rusch
The Television Episode • Michael Jan Friedman

Star Trek®: The Captain's Table

Book One: *War Dragons* • L. A. Graf
Book Two: *Dujonian's Hoard* • Michael Jan Friedman
Book Three: *The Mist* • Dean W. Smith & Kristine K. Rusch
Book Four: *Fire Ship* • Diane Carey
Book Five: *Once Burned* • Peter David
Book Six: *Where Sea Meets Sky* • Jerry Oltion

Star Trek®: The Dominion War

Book 1: *Behind Enemy Lines* • John Vornholt
Book 2: *Call to Arms . . .* • Diane Carey
Book 3: *Tunnel Through the Stars* • John Vornholt
Book 4: *. . . Sacrifice of Angels* • Diane Carey

Star Trek®: My Brother's Keeper

Book One: *Republic* • Michael Jan Friedman
Book Two: *Constitution* • Michael Jan Friedman
Book Three: *Enterprise* • Michael Jan Friedman

1252.01